VERITAS

KELLY ST. CLARE

Edited by Melissa Scott and Robin Schroffel
Cover illustration and design by Amalia Chitulescu Digital Art

VERITAS

Exosia
Kentro
Maltu
Pleo
Selkie's Cove
Syraness
Portum
Febribus
Charybdis
Neos
Zol
Caspian Sea

Dynami Sea

Medusa's Lair

N

W

E

S

Exosian Realm

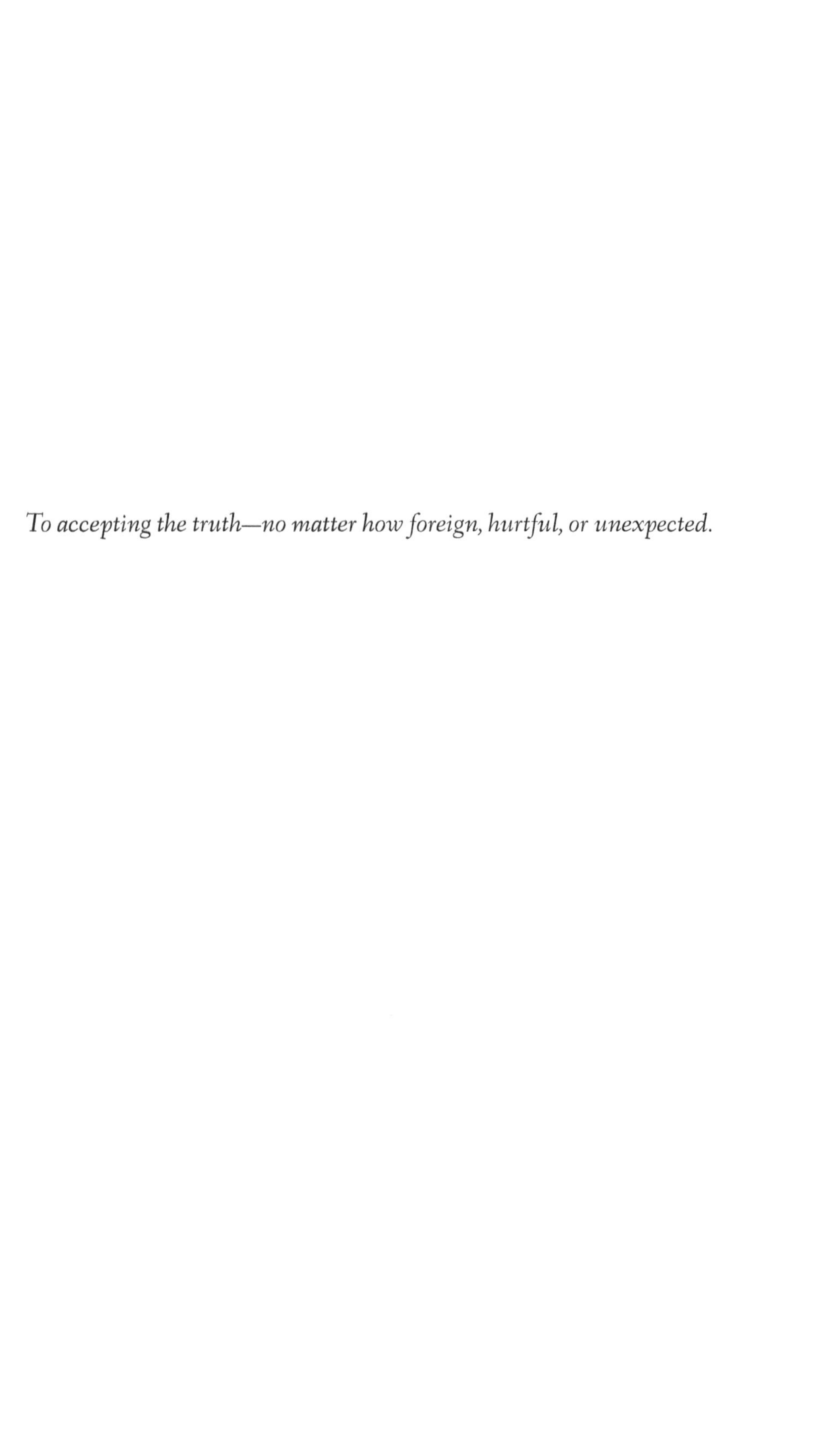

To accepting the truth—no matter how foreign, hurtful, or unexpected.

ONE

"Just keep her away from grog," Ebba-Viva Fairisles hollered, hanging over the port bulwark. "And if she ain't drinkin', keep her away from wood. She chews it sumpin' fierce."

The queen of the wind sprites had switched one bad habit for another when the *purgium* cured her of alcoholism.

Sally, or Queen Saliha as she was actually called, waved from the middle of her minions. Or flipped Ebba off. That was very possible.

Stubby rested a hand on her arm. "They'll be takin' care o' her, lass. And ye know she can hold her own."

After her mother had died, Sal decided to take a holiday. That holiday turned into an alcohol-fueled bender. But now, she was finally listening to the call of duty to her people. The sprites would go back to their kingdom by Charybdis, the great whirlpool.

"Aye, don't worry over her, little nymph," Plank said. "She has fierce sharp teeth." He rubbed his forearm where the queen had bitten him just that morning.

Ebba sniffed and dashed a stained sleeve over her eyes.

She cast another look at her tiny flying friend, now a speck in the distance, and then glanced behind at her six fathers, Jagger, and Prince Caspian.

"Why are ye all loungin' about?" she snapped. "We've got sails to furl and . . . and . . . lots o' other stuff. Get to it."

Edging closer, Peg-leg patted her shoulder. "Aye, lass. We'll get to work." He hobbled away with the signature *tap-tap-tap* of his wooden peg.

Her lower lip trembled.

Barrels adjusted his cravat and reached forward to squeeze her hand. "I'll see to the sheets with Plank."

"Good," she replied hoarsely. "They ain't tight enough."

Considering the sails weren't raised, that was a given. Stubby and Plank glanced at the bare mast but, very wisely, didn't voice their thoughts.

Locks disappeared after her other fathers, shooting a small smile her way.

Grubby stepped forward. He twisted his Monmouth cap in white-knuckled hands. The cap had frayed along the edges from the regular abuse and probably wouldn't last until they were back in the Caspian Sea.

If they got back. That was a real concern—especially as the only immortal being in their company had just flown away.

Grubby inched closer, and Ebba blinked furiously to keep her tears at bay. The youngest of her fathers, just forty-six, quit his cap-twisting and wrapped both arms around her. He rested his head atop hers.

"It's okay to be sad about yer friend leavin'," he said. "I was sad to leave my selkie kin behind."

Ebba swallowed several times, panic rising in her throat as she began to lose the battle to not cry. She whispered, "But ye can talk to them when ye're in the water."

"Not now we be in the Dynami Sea," he said, rubbing her back. "Too far away. Or maybe it be because the water here is full o' magic creatures."

Or maybe the taint had spread through the sea in the Exosian Realm, and Grubby's kin no longer possessed their will. Though Grubby's octopi still traveled between Zol and *Felicity* to bring messages, so Ebba's home seas couldn't be completely taken over.

She buried her face in Grubby's chest, using his stained tunic to wipe away the few tears that had escaped her iron grip.

He pulled back. "Ye'll see her again."

Grubby made for the bow, and Ebba turned to face the sea, her face wet. Jagger and Caspian still lingered, and out of the whole crew, they were the people she *least* wanted to see her cry.

"Someone will need to. . . ." She trailed off.

Sod it, Ebba couldn't think of a single thing to order them about with.

A large warm hand rested between her shoulder blades. She took a shaking breath, knowing that if she lifted a hand to dry her tears, the game would be up.

. . . Though maybe she'd already failed at that.

Caspian stood close, just behind her. "Mistress Pirate, it's okay to cry."

Ebba sighed. "Caspian, ye ain't supposed to say someone be cryin' if they're tryin' to hide it."

He paused, and she could practically hear the rum in his skull sloshing about as he pondered that comment.

"That's a pirate truth, I gather?" the prince said.

Well, he was less a prince and more of a king shoved out of his kingdom by the most powerful evil force of all time. The pillars of six ruled and resided on *his* throne, enslaving *his* people, but Ebba wasn't about to point that out. Everyone knew not to point out such things. Apart from him, obviously.

"Aye, pirate truths are the only truths worth knowin'," she answered flippantly.

His teeth clicked as he snapped his mouth shut.

Granted, pirates pretended not to see the truth an awful lot. But that was the essence of a pirate truth—only seeing the truths needed for survival. Of course, Ebba now believed *some* truth might be a necessary evil. The question was: How much truth was enough? And how much was too much?

Those answers were as yet unclear, and she wanted to make an informed choice about this whole truth business.

Caspian's hand still rested on her back. Warm. "What do you need me to do?" he asked.

Ebba quickly dried her face. "Nothin'. Just go and see if the ship be ready."

He dropped his hand but hovered for several more seconds. Enough to make her feel bad because she'd once badgered the prince not to shut her out. After losing his left arm, he sank into himself for a good, long time.

"You're sure?" he murmured in a low voice that made her shiver.

Ebba would be lying—to herself, which she was trying not to do anymore—if she didn't confess that their recent conversation about deeper regard had made the prince even more caring and bright-eyed than usual. Ever since she'd told him she wanted to explore the waters between them, Caspian stood closer and touched her in small ways—like the hand-on-her-upper-back thing.

Ebba didn't mind it.

She often found those small touches exciting. But not right this moment.

Not with Jagger standing there.

His silver eyes scorched into the back of her skull as he most likely judged her. If he wasn't there, Ebba might have leaned back against the prince and talked of how sad she was that the only other female on *Felicity* had left. She might have spoken about how people leaving her never felt right. Her fathers leaving tore her apart inside, but even when friends left, their absence played constantly in the back of her skull. She *might* have said all that if the flaxen-haired pirate wasn't lingering—likely for nefarious reasons—to eavesdrop on their conversation.

After the Medusa run-in, Ebba decided to trust Jagger, but he'd always put her on edge, and that hadn't changed; that puzzle remained unsolved.

"I be sure," she replied.

Caspian moved away, leaving her back cold.

Ebba shivered again. The Dynami Sea was a far cry from the cerulean tropical sea they'd left—black water, frigid air, dark skies, and a constant rolling swell that would only be experienced during the start of a storm back home. This sea was every bit as dreary as Plank had recited in his tales of old magic. She couldn't wait to be back in the Caspian Sea, safely anchored at their sacred haven at Zol. But for that to happen, Zol had to *be* a safe haven. So first, they needed to form the root of magic by finding the remaining two parts. And somehow defeat the six pillars to save everyone in the realm.

No problem.

She shook her head. Luck had to be a big part of winning because Davy Jones knew there was no planning of any sort happening on their end. All their crew knew was that Ebba, Caspian, and Jagger were the three watchers—mortals who brought balance to the presence of immortalkind in the realm by regulating the root of magic. And that Jagger was an immune—resistant to magical influence. As for Ebba's and Caspian's role? Nothing. No notion.

"I'm goin' to climb to the crow's nest," Jagger said.

Ebba wrenched her thoughts back to the present. She whirled from the bulwark as Jagger strode past her.

"What did ye say?" she called.

The oversized pirate didn't stop but glanced over his shoulder. "I'm goin' to climb the shrouds."

Ebba dashed a sleeve over her face and scowled at him. "Nay. That be my job."

She ran across the deck after him and grabbed his arm. He slowly turned, and Ebba tipped her head back, and then back some more. *Definitely* oversized for a pirate.

"Ye seem content to be gazin' out at the water and orderin' others about, so I'll be takin' it upon myself to do the job," he said.

He didn't even bother to sneer anymore. Not like before when he was part of *Malice*'s crew. Now, he looked at her without expression, as though he couldn't be bothered with the effort to arrange his facial features into disdain. Only very occasionally could she glean his true thoughts. Was the impassive mask a step up or a step down?

He pulled free of her grip and continued striding toward the rigging.

"Nay," Ebba said, walking quickly to catch up.

His hip bumped hers. *On purpose.* She bumped him right back.

They lunged for the rigging at the same time.

"Aye," he told her.

"*Nay*," she hissed, flinging an arm out to whack his thieving hands away from the ropes.

Her fingers touched his bare skin, and she hurriedly wiped them off against her slops. His scraggly flaxen hair swung forward as he watched her, jaw clenched.

Jagger had a natural resistance to magic; however, he'd sailed aboard *Malice* for two years. In time, he'd throw off any remaining taint, but having been victim to the taint herself, Ebba wasn't about to risk catching it again. His eyes weren't flooded black. That meant he wasn't contagious. But none of the crew was taking any chances. She'd keep wiping her hands, just in case.

His eyes bore into hers. "Ye only want to go to the crow's nest because I said I'm goin'. Or is that it, Viva? If ye want to spend time with me in close quarters, ye just have to say the word."

What word? Her mind stuttered. How did they get on to this subject? She narrowed her eyes, realizing Jagger was attempting to unsettle her.

Heat crept up her neck, and Ebba leaned in, opening her mouth.

Peg-leg's wooden peg tapped in rapid staccato, interrupting her thoughts. Ebba blinked. Sink her, when had she and Jagger drawn so close?

She leaned back slightly, but Jagger crowded her so they

remained nose-to-nose. A twinge of alarm coursed through her as his mouth drew within a finger-width of hers—not quite touching.

"Ye're still a spoilt princess," Jagger declared.

Ebba *was* a princess. Not that being tribal royalty meant a whole bunch to her. She objected to the first part. "I ain't so spoilt." *Anymore.*

It was mostly true.

"Aye, yer fathers cater to yer moods."

Her moods were Peg-leg's fault. He taught her that. And anyway, there were some perks to having six fathers that she wasn't willing to part with.

Jagger was a bloody pain in her hull.

Heat crept from her neck into her jaw. The moods she could blame on Peg-leg. Her temper was all Locks.

"Has anyone ever told ye that ye're an annoyin' shite?" she shot at him, fists clenching.

"One coin for the swear jar, my dear," Barrels sang, ambling over with the rest of her fathers.

Ebba waved a hand, not breaking the stare-off with Jagger. She hated paying the coin jar. Which was Barrels' fault. He was tight with his coin and had instilled such principles in her. "I only said it because it be true. And . . . I was upset about Sal leavin'."

Locks clucked sympathetically. "Aye, true enough. We'll let her off this once, lads."

"Only 'cause yer heart be hurtin'," Plank agreed.

Jagger whispered low. "See? Spoilt."

The heat flooded her face. Ebba shoved him away and whirled for the rigging.

He was back beside her in a flash.

"Get off my riggin'," she hissed at him.

"That be enough o' that, children," Stubby said, joining them from the helm.

Jagger stilled and drew himself tall as he turned.

Stubby lifted his gray brows. "That's right. Ye're actin' like a child, too, Jagger."

"Ha!" Ebba shot him a triumphant look through her thick black lashes. Then frowned. "Hey."

She wasn't acting like a child. *Much.*

Surprisingly, Jagger didn't seem angered by her father's comment. A small smile curved his lips, and Ebba studied him with no small amount of suspicion.

What was he playing at?

"Now, ye both need to. . . ." Stubby's voice took on a droning quality.

Babies with shark's teeth, he was settling into a lecture.

Ebba stopped listening and let her gaze drift out over the ship's side again. She sighed. The sprites were completely gone from sight, as though they'd never been here. Deep down, a part of her had held hope Sally would change her mind and come back.

Jagger dug his elbow into her gut.

"Ouch," she exclaimed, more from shock than actual pain. "Why'd ye do that, ye flaxen bastard?"

"Ebba-Viva Fairisles," Stubby said in a quelling tone. "Mind yer tongue. Are ye even listenin' to a word I be sayin'?"

Her spine snapped straight, and her face dropped. "He dug his elbow in my gut."

"How old are ye, Ebba-Viva?" her father demanded.

"Eighteen and a bit," she muttered.

Stubby shifted his firm gaze to Jagger.

"Twenty," the pirate supplied without prompt. His eyes slid to her, and he added, "And a bit."

"Ye had a birthday?" She turned to him, cutting off her father. "When?"

Jagger folded his arms, glancing away. "A week ago. Not long after yers."

They'd missed it. Not that she should feel bad when he'd kept it a secret like he did everything. "Well, Stubby be right. Ye should act yer age. Ye're in yer twenties and should know better than me."

"Ye *both* need to act yer age," Stubby boomed.

Where was this coming from? She never had to act her age. Ebba cast a woeful look at her father, and Stubby's expression faltered. She watched as Plank grabbed the back of Grubby's belt to stop him approaching.

"Ebba's sad," Grubby whined.

Plank grunted, visibly digging his heels in. "She ain't sad, matey. We be tellin' her off. This be disc'pline."

Stubby's tone had softened when he spoke again. "What I was *sayin'* is that we need the three o' ye to focus and find out where we be headed next."

She was still attuned to Jagger's buzzing presence next to her and snuck a look up at the crow's nest. There was no way Jagger was reaching the shrouds before her. He'd become too comfortable in her territory and it had to stop.

Ebba prepared to jump onto the bulwark. "I'll just—"

"Nay, ye won't. Neither o' ye will," Stubby snarled.

She scanned the faces of her fathers, searching for the weak link. Grubby was restrained. Barrels, avoiding her eyes. Yet one of them held a particular softness for the heights of the nest.

Her eyes sought out Peg-leg.

He wasn't avoiding her, and he stared for a long beat before saying, "I know why ye want to go up there, lass."

Ebba's eyes began to burn again. His comment stole her voice for a scant second, long enough that she couldn't come up with a quip in return. His assumption was correct. There were few places aboard a ship to have a good cry. Below deck echoed. There was the tip of the bowsprit, but Ebba wasn't sure she wanted to perch over the black Dynami Sea as she tended to do in the safer waters of the Caspian. According to Grubby, there were a whole heap of things under the surface that gave him the willies. Then there was the crow's nest.

Sally had left, and Ebba wanted to leak a tear or two in private.

"I'll go up again," Peg-leg announced.

He would?

Her father used to be a rigger until the depraved captain of *Eternal* had ordered his leg amputated in petty revenge. Minus a leg, carrying a past filled with horrific abuse, and with the taint still in him driving his thoughts to black places, her father only recently regained the confidence to climb the shrouds.

He'd gone up once, and Ebba knew the more he climbed to the nest, the more he'd heal.

Mouth drying, she rushed to say, "That be a great idea, Peg-leg."

"What's going on?" Caspian said, exiting the bilge door.

"I'm goin' to climb the shrouds," Peg-leg told him. "Locks, did ye get a chance to make me that foot?"

Locks nodded. "Aye, it be below deck. I'll grab it."

The ship carpenter disappeared into the hold, and everyone's gaze dropped to Peg-leg's fake leg.

"Thought a wider surface would be makin' it easier to climb," he said defensively.

Caspian's breath hitched in his throat. "A missing limb doesn't change a thing, Sir Pirate?"

Peg-leg winked at him. "Nay, lad. A missin' limb doesn't stop ye from a thing."

Locks returned and knelt to fit the end of Peg-leg's peg into a deep groove on an otherwise flat strip of wood about the length of a foot.

Stubby clapped the cook on the back. "Up ye get then, matey. We'll ready the ship and figure out where to go."

Testing his new foot a few times, Peg-leg then ambled to the rigging. Ebba scowled at Jagger, waiting until he released the ropes before doing so herself.

The oversized pirate walked to the mast, and she trailed after him toward Caspian.

She stood on the prince's right, patting her belt. "Hold on, I put the *scio* down somewhere."

"You tied it to Pillage again, my dear," Barrels reminded her.

Oh, aye. She'd initially wanted to see if the *scio* helped her talk to the ship cat. But when his meows continued to just be meows—stupid cat—Ebba had decided to re-test the feline as a hiding place. She'd used the *scio* so he wouldn't gouge holes in the deck again—using the *dynami* last time hadn't been such a great idea.

Blast. Pillage could be anywhere. Whenever she didn't want to find him, he was around. As soon as she did, he tucked himself into some obscure corner of the hold. The ship cat did it on purpose, she was certain.

"Where be the *dynami*? I'll use that instead," she said. They could use any three parts of the root to find the way to the next piece.

Barrels blew out a breath. "I'll go find the *scio*." No one answered, and he exhaled loudly again, leaving through the bilge door.

"Anyone have the *dynami*?" she called across deck.

"Here, have the *purgium*. I'll go search for Pillage as well," Caspian replied.

From the starboard bulwark, Plank called, "Aye." He reached under the sash holding his pistols to his chest. He drew out the *dynami*. "Here ye go."

Caspian handed her the *purgium* as Plank tossed her the *dynami*. Flustered, Ebba dropped the healing tube to catch the *dynami* but managed to miss that too.

Both parts rolled across the deck, and everyone immediately started after them—though the tubes were too big to be lost out the scuppers.

The bilge door crashed open.

Ebba jumped and whirled about, clutching her chest.

"She stole my bloody cat," Barrels shouted.

Plank asked, "What?"

"That *sprite* stole Pillage. I found the *scio* on my desk with a note saying the queen has 'borrowed Pillage to act as her noble steed.'"

No one on the ship really liked Pillage aside from Barrels, but Ebba pushed down her bubbling laughter. "That be terrible."

Plank snorted. "Ye need to put a mite more effort into that, little nymph."

"That be terrible!" she cried.

Plank nodded. "Better."

Caspian threw her an amused look, the corners of his lips quirking, and she flashed a grin back.

"Laugh if you will, but I consider this a gross misdemeanor after the hospitality we afforded her," Barrels snapped, some of his peppered hair escaping the leather tie he used to hold the strands back.

Fancy words. Ebba took them to mean her father was greatly peeved.

"She was *your* pet, Ebba-Viva Fairisles," he continued. "I expect you to put things to rights."

They were in the Dynami, so she felt pretty safe agreeing to do so. "Sure thing. Wait, has Sal been able to write this whole time?"

"I wrote the note for her," Jagger told them, drawing everything to a screeching halt. "She dictated usin' the *scio*."

"You *knew*?" Barrels screeched, rounding on the pirate.

Jagger shrugged a shoulder. "Aye."

Ebba snickered, taking a large step away from him.

"Oopsie," Grubby exclaimed from directly behind her. "Look what ye dropped."

She peered over her shoulder to where he stood across deck. Ebba whipped fully around as Grubby bent down, his fingers stretching to the *purgium* and the *dynami*.

"No matter," he said happily.

"Nay, Grubby," Ebba choked out. "Don't touch them."

Too late.

White light exploded.

TWO

Ebba came awake, grimacing at the aches riddling her body. Her eyelids were sore. Was that a thing?

Someone squeezed her hand tight. "You're okay, Ebba."

She looked through bleary eyes at Caspian. He'd called her Ebba, not Mistress Pirate.

"What happened?" Her other fathers were down here. Everyone but Locks and Peg-leg.

The prince was pale, his eyes red-rimmed as though he hadn't slept a wink. "You don't remember Grubby touching two parts at once?"

Gasping, she sat bolt upright in her hammock. "Grubby!"

Ebba remembered the flash of white light. The force of the explosion had thrown her clean across the deck. But that was the least of her concerns.

Grubby was tainted and he'd touched the *purgium*. They'd been warned months ago that none of her fathers could ever touch the healing tube. The *purgium* would heal their taint, and there was no telling if they'd survive the sacrifice demanded by the part. When Caspian touched the healing tube while tainted, he lost an entire arm. He'd been wounded and infected with the taint, but her fathers had been influenced by a weaker taint for a lot longer.

Was her father gone? She couldn't bear it if her father was gone. Darkness wavered at the corners of her mind, ready to descend, and Ebba dragged in a stuttering breath. "Grubby?"

Caspian hurried to reassure her. "Yes, Ebba. Grubby is okay."

"He be safe, lass," Stubby said from where he leaned against a hammock post.

The words penetrated whatever fog had surrounded her and she clawed the rest of the way back to the surface by herself, shaking her head to be rid of the all-consuming terror.

"Grubby's okay," she repeated thickly, looking at the prince and returning the gripping pressure of his hand like he was the only tether in a storm.

"He's . . . breathing."

"I need to see him." Ebba let go of the prince and tried to stand.

Plank stopped her with a hand on her shoulder. "Hold on, little nymph. Ye had a nasty knock to the head."

She relaxed back down. "I did?" Reaching around, Ebba palpated her skull, wincing when she found the tender spot. "How long was I out?"

"Three days," Barrels told her.

Three days? But her head wasn't even that sore. "Really? Ye didn't give me anythin' to help me sleep?"

"Not a thing," her eldest father replied.

She stood, this time evading Peg-leg's attempt to keep her in the hammock. If Ebba had slept for three days; so had Grubby. He *wasn't* fine.

Her fathers parted for her, and she dropped next to Grubby's hammock, trying to control the burning ball in her throat.

His chest rose and fell in steady rhythm. "Why isn't he awake?" she asked, placing her hands either side of his pale face.

All of the crew were tanned from the sun. Ebba's tribal skin was extra dark, but none of them were pale. No pirate would be, so why was Grubby's face drained of all color? He looked. . . .

Ebba's heart galloped in her chest. She couldn't even think the word without panic grasping her tight.

"No idea, lass," Locks answered, kneeling beside her. He settled his fingers on Grubby's wrist. "The blast threw him clear into the ocean. Took us a while to get out there and bring him in, and by then, he'd drank a fair amount o' water. His heart was still goin', though." He sat back, lips pressed tight.

A vision of Grubby face down in the water flashed before her eyes, and Ebba released a shaking breath. "He be a selkie. He can breathe underwater."

Silence reigned.

"Well, yes." Barrels broke it. "Though recalling that took us a day . . . or two."

Ebba swallowed hard, not shifting her eyes from Grubby's face. "What did the *purgium* take from him in exchange for healin' the taint?"

Plank rested a hand on her shoulder. "No notion. We hope it'll just make him sleep a few days. But there ain't no way o' tellin' until he wakes."

Barrels spoke quietly. "We don't want to risk touching him with the *purgium* again. We have no idea what a double-healing would do. The *purgium* demanded this sacrifice, after all."

"Aye, we can't touch him a second time," she said, knowing in her gut that wasn't the way.

Ebba hung her head. She'd dropped the *purgium* and didn't pick it up straightaway. Even knowing it was dangerous to leave such things lying about with Grubby onboard. With *any* of her fathers onboard.

"We'll have to wait out whatever it is," Stubby said, a tremble in his voice. He sucked in a breath. "Keep him warm and watered."

Lifting her head, Ebba studied the boatswain. Out of all of them, he looked the worst. His blue eyes were dull, his gray curls limp and disheveled.

Stubby caught her studying him and averted his gaze to the wooden floor.

For the first time, Ebba noticed the rolling of the ship. "We're movin'."

"Aye," said Stubby with a bite. "I told them we shouldn't shift until ye were both awake and well." His chest heaved, and he clenched his jaw so tight Ebba swore she could hear his back teeth grinding.

Stubby was acting . . . strangely. Her eyes strayed to Plank, who had a knowing gleam in his eyes.

Barrels cleared his throat. "We understand you felt strongly about remaining anchored until everyone was better, but that is not the way this ship runs. It's a voting system. Medusa told us the pillars would be on their way. Remaining anchored by her lair put everyone in danger, including Grubby and Ebba."

Stubby cursed and, whirling, stalked to the ladder. He climbed to the top, slamming the bilge door shut behind him.

Why was he taking Grubby's injuries to heart?

Ebba returned her stare to her pale, unconscious father. "There must be sumpin' we can do to help him."

"Come now, little nymph," Plank said, helping her stand. "Grubby will be okay—"

Turning shining eyes on him, she asked, "How do ye know?"

"Because he's breathin' when he might not've been. There be a reason for that."

That shouldn't make sense, but it did. Her entire life had been based on believing things without a reason. And though Ebba now knew there was a place for truth, maybe there was also a place for believing in things because of hope.

She sat on Peg-leg's hammock, directly opposite Grubby. She'd stick by his side until he woke.

He *would* wake.

"So where are we headed?" she asked in a bid to distract herself from worry. "Ye used me to find the way to the next part while I was out o' it, I'm s'posin'?"

Caspian cast her a confused glance. "How did you guess that?"

She lifted a shoulder. "Makes sense."

"Well, yes," he admitted, a wrinkle between his brows. "We did."

"Jagger and Caspian tried to find the direction without you. We wondered if finding the direction might depend more on Jagger—seeing as he's the immune," said Barrels.

A small part of her felt a hollow pang at the thought she might not be needed—or may not be one of the three watchers. In the brief time she, Jagger, and Caspian had known about their greater role in saving the realm, part of her had grown used to thinking there might be a reason she was on this quest. That there might be an explanation for this madness thrust upon them. She'd been chosen somehow or possessed something special. Her reaction to Barrels' words surprised her. From the outset, she'd longed for the return of how things used to be, so the presence of any disappointment, no matter how tiny, was almost shocking.

"The theory was disproved," Barrels continued. "Finding the way depends on the three of you. We thought you wouldn't mind if we pressed on, considering everything. . . ."

"Nay, I don't mind." She was just surprised Jagger had ventured below deck. There was little else the pirate feared after his stint with *Malice*.

"Northwest," Plank answered before she could ask her next question. "Jagger be up in the crow's nest, keepin' a lookout."

Her father froze as she narrowed her eyes.

Jagger thought he could slip into the nest while she was injured, did he? Ebba wouldn't be budging from Grubby's side, but there would be hell to pay when she ventured to the main deck.

"What lies northwest?" she asked, trying to draw up a visual of the only Dynami Sea map in their possession.

"Not a thing." Caspian shook his head. "At least, not on

our map."

Ebba nodded, gripping her trembling hands together. Distracting herself wasn't working. Not one bit.

Grubby lying there so still made every horrible thing that had happened in recent months seem like a tiny scare. To think that her youngest father—any of her fathers—could have died struck a bone-deep, open-mouthed horror within her. The feeling was the worst experience of her life to date. Even more horrifying than having the taint—because she could handle anything as long as her fathers were whole.

She wanted to cling to her six fathers and never let go. For if she ever had to let them go, doom would work its swift misery. Her fear of being parted from them didn't make a lick of sense. From what Ebba could see, her reaction wasn't normal. But that didn't stop the terror from shaking her until her teeth rattled.

"Grubs nearly died because I dropped the parts and left them lyin' around," she said, hanging her head.

Locks sat beside her and wrapped an arm tight about her shoulders. "Nay, I'd be blamin' Plank. That was a shite throw."

"It was," Plank immediately agreed.

Ebba appreciated their attempt to make her feel better. She rubbed her temples, swinging gently in the hammock. "I just can't think about doin' anythin' until he opens his eyes."

"Aye, lass," Stubby choked out. "I know. But the ship must be sailed. And a pirate must be at their best if they mean to care for another."

Locks released her and guided Ebba down to lie in the hammock. "Ye sleep now, Ebba-Viva. Grubby will be right here. We know where we're headed. Ye just leave the rest to us."

She turned on her side and stared across at her unconscious father. Truthfully, if they'd asked her to help in some way, Ebba wasn't sure she could have.

Grubby had to wake up.

Ebba couldn't think of what she'd become if he didn't.

THREE

Someone shook her shoulder gently. "Ye need to eat, little nymph."

Ebba blinked up at Plank and turned her head to check on Grubby in the hammock opposite.

"Did he wake while I slept?" she rasped.

"Nay, but he be a scant bit better," Plank said cheerfully.

Too cheerfully.

She rubbed her eyes and gave Grubby another once-over. "He still looks the same." His breathing was an even, easy pace. His skin, chalk white. It was as though the *purgium* had placed him in a sleep he might never wake from.

She jolted at a rattled snore from Grubby's other side.

Ebba squinted across Grubby at where Stubby slept in a sitting position, head resting back against a post.

"Has Stubby left his side?" she asked.

"Nay. And I wouldn't think he'd be inclined to."

Plank tilted his head to the hold. Swinging up, Ebba followed him through the narrow passage to the kitchen shoved in the front corner.

She sat on a barrel and accepted a goblet of grog from him, waiting as he lifted a pot lid and sniffed.

"Sausage stew or sumpin' close," he muttered.

She took a plate of the stew from him, listening as he began humming his favorite daydreaming tune.

"Why is Stubby so upset about Grubby?" she asked after draining her drink.

Plank whisked away her empty goblet and filled it again, sipping from it before he answered. "He was upset about yer injury too. He held it together for a couple o' days but fell apart on the third. And he fell apart for the same reason Peg-leg hadn't climbed the riggin' in twenty years. For the same reason Barrels never returned to Exosia."

"It has to do with what happened to him while ye sailed under Cannon," she stated, having already come to that conclusion herself.

She'd never seen Stubby react to anything so strongly. Nothing except damage to the ship drew him to displays of high emotion. And what he'd displayed over Grubby's injury was far more than that.

Most of her fathers had relayed the stories of their pasts by now—aside from Grubby who probably didn't remember. Stubby and Plank were the last to tell theirs. They didn't *have* to; she was adamant about that despite the oath she'd forced from them on Pleo. She glanced at Plank, and the air between them grew heavy. He stared at her for a beat before slamming the pot lid back over the stew.

"Here," he said, extracting the *scio* from his belt. "Take this above deck and check the d'rection again, would ye?"

Ebba took the *scio,* tucking it in her belt as she watched her father closely.

Plank was fobbing her off.

"Be sure to wash yer dishes afore ye go up." He hurried to the sleeping quarters.

"But I was goin' to stay by Grubby again," she hollered after him.

"I'll watch him until ye're back. Go get some fresh air. That ain't a request."

Ebba sighed, shoving the sausage stew into her gob. Judging by

Plank's startled exit a moment ago, he wasn't planning on telling the story of his past anytime soon. She assumed his memories were particularly painful. He'd had a wife once, and Ebba guessed his story had something to do with her fate.

Finishing the last of her stew, she shoved her plate in the sink beneath a pot. Peg-leg would do it. Nothing could break his spirit since the successful testing of his rigging foot, and there were definite perks.

Hurrying down the passage, she reached for the ladder and began to climb. The sooner she got fresh air, the sooner she could go back down to stand vigil over Grubby.

"Did ye clean yer dishes?" Plank called low from the sleeping quarters.

Ebba pretended not to hear as she pushed open the bilge door.

An icy breeze hit her face, and she shivered, hugging her arms around her body.

"Seen anythin' yet?" she yelled to Locks at the bow.

"Nay, lass. Just black water," he called back. Spray sprinkled over him as a wave broke across their mermaid figurehead.

She caught sight of Caspian and Barrels huddled over their map of the Dynami Sea. Starting toward them, Ebba wrenched to a halt as a wavering strand of flaxen hair caught her eye from high above.

"Motherfisher," she said through gritted teeth.

He *was* in her nest. Maybe while she was unable to help, his presence there was . . . permissible. But not anymore.

Ebba ran to the rigging and swung up, climbing in a simmering fury that wasn't entirely due to Jagger. The thin ropes cut into her palms and the arches of her bare feet. The burn of her arms was dwarfed by her mounting anger. She'd told Jagger once, she'd told him twice. *She* was queen of the crow's nest. A smile graced her ruby lips as she recalled how she'd forced him out last time. Jagger had a penchant for secrets and grew highly uncomfortable when asked directly about them.

Unfortunately for her, he'd heard her approach and made sure to stand well back as she swung into the crow's nest. Last time she managed to knee him in the gut. Canny bugger learned fast.

"Get out o' my nest, Jagger," she said mildly.

He leaned back against the opposite side of the barrel, sleek frame on display. Couldn't he stand straight? Ebba had to wonder; always leaning this way or that way, showing off his body.

"Nay," he said, smirking.

Challenge accepted. Ebba drew in a massive breath.

"What's changed between ye and the landlubber?" Jagger cut in. "He be touchin' ye a whole heap more. And ye're lettin' him."

The wind was stolen from her.

"What?" she wheezed.

"He hovers. He talks to ye as though he has a right. Sumpin' has changed."

She stared at him, trying to remember the questions she'd prepared to hurl at his head. "Uhm."

"One kiss with him and ye're in love, is that it? Do ye even know what love and passion feel like, Viva?"

He stepped closer. The nest wasn't that big. Even with Ebba pressed against the opposite side of the barrel, his body ended up flush with hers.

Jagger was using her own ploy against her.

"More than one kiss. And get back to the other side," she said, refusing to budge in her own territory.

The pirate did the opposite.

. . . Maybe that was the trick to him.

"Come closer," she tried.

He obliged, bringing his lips as near to hers as they could be without touching—just like the other day during their rigging fight.

"I didn't mean that," she rushed to say, placing a hand on his chest. She shoved. To no effect.

A drawling smile crossed his face. He continued to hover his mouth above hers, and Ebba's mind slowly blanked. The areas closest to Jagger—her mouth, her chest, the fronts of her thighs—all of them began to tingle, overtaking her every thought. What would happen if those areas made contact with him? What would that feel like?

She sucked in a breath, and her gaze flew to meet his silver eyes. It was the second time he'd stood this close. The second time his mouth had nearly connected with hers. Why was he nearly kissing her but not?

What was his game?

His eyes darkened to the unpolished gray of her pistols. Heated. Jagger's gaze tunneled into her, breath fast, his lips slightly parted. He didn't close the space.

He didn't move away.

She might have decided to trust his intentions, but this scenario had nothing to do with his loyalty to the crew and ship. This was . . . this was. . . .

Ebba felt for the edge of the crow's nest.

The slight movement startled him. He reeled back as she awkwardly lifted a leg over the side of the nest and then the other. This was *not* the ideal way to get out of a wooden barrel, and both of them knew it.

"Leavin' so soon?" he asked, voice strained.

He folded his arms, but she wasn't fooled. He was just as unsettled as she; his chest was rising too quickly.

She didn't answer, sliding awkwardly over the lip of the nest.

Ebba began climbing down, her mind whirling. Jagger was a law unto his own; she'd known it from their first meeting. She wasn't sure what had just happened. Or rather, if what had happened meant what she thought it did. He'd brought up the kiss with Caspian several times. Did he actually want to kiss her? Or was he messing with the prince?

Or was he just trying to get her out of the nest by making her uncomfortable?

What she did know was that if their lips had touched—no matter the reason—she would have regretted it. Sorely. She might not be totally in the know about the ins and outs of deeper regard, but as one person knew another, Ebba understood Caspian would be hurt if she kissed the pirate. Yes, she'd never promised the prince to return his regard, but Ebba knew she'd feel guilty for touching Jagger in an intimate way. It just didn't feel honest.

And wouldn't happen. Kissing Jagger had never entered her head before.

Halfway down to the deck, Ebba glanced up as Jagger shouted.

The pirate leaned over and met her eyes.

"King o' the crow's nest," he hollered. "*King*. Don't ye be forgettin' it."

She'd drown the bastard one day. In mud.

Ebba scampered down the rope as quickly as she could. When close to the deck, she swung around the edge of the rigging onto the ship, landing with a thud.

She stomped over to Caspian and Barrels.

"Everything okay?" the prince asked her.

"Aye," she said, arms crossed. *Nay*. "*Some* people think because they be an immune, they can throw their weight about."

Belatedly, she wiped her hands off where she'd touched Jagger. Her eyes rounded. Seaweed-loving gummy sharks, she couldn't *kiss* Jagger. He was tainted.

Ebba had forgotten all about that.

She released a shaking breath as Caspian took her hand and tugged her down to sit by his side.

Barrels stared at their hands but remained silent.

Honestly, the hand-holding in front of her fathers made Ebba feel strange. They weren't aware of what had transpired between her and Caspian, and she knew they wouldn't like it because they were *a little* overprotective.

She slipped her hand from the prince's, ignoring the veiled look he threw her. Caspian turned to peer up at the crow's nest. When he looked back down at the map, a slight wrinkle had appeared between his brows.

"What're ye lookin' at?" she asked her father.

Barrels glanced between them, opening his mouth. Ebba stared at him pointedly, daring him to ask what the problem was.

Her father wasn't a stupid man.

"Uh, we're adjusting the map to include what we've come across so far," Barrels said, pointing at the map. "We added Medusa's Lair here, and the Daedalion, and took off two of the islands we should have encountered but didn't."

"We won't be headin' back there, though," Ebba said, shifting to have a better look.

Her eldest father lifted a shoulder. "We can't know that."

True enough.

The map consisted of two halves. On the left was the Caspian Sea, with the islands she'd grown up visiting exactly as they should be. On the right was the Dynami Sea where they currently sailed, a place no pirate usually dared to enter for fear of never coming out.

A handful of small islands dotted the map over the Dynami, mostly to the west where the Caspian met this sea. The waters they currently sailed were notoriously rough and almost their own pirate superstition—at least in her mind. But Ebba had to wonder if the superstitions about this sea had carried over from times of old magic. The thunderbird had called this sea *immortal* waters, saying that marine immortals greatly preferred the isolation and rugged sea floor of the Dynami.

Luckily, the marine immortals had kept to themselves so far. The only immortals they'd encountered were the thunderbird, already marked at the south-western corner of the sea, Medusa at her lair to the south-east, and the Daedalion.

"Does the map show anythin' about where we're headed?" she asked, tapping her bottom lip.

"Not a thing." He gestured to the empty space to the north.

Caspian tore his eyes from her face to look at the map. "Aside from the thunderbird, the map hasn't been totally accurate anyway."

A loud thud sounded behind them. Ebba glanced back and caught sight of Jagger and Peg-leg speaking at the base of the rigging.

With his wooden foot attached, Peg-leg set off up the shrouds to take the younger pirate's place.

She sniffed and turned her back on Jagger.

"We should check the direction again," Locks said, joining them from the bow.

His emerald eye blazed as he passed her the *dynami*.

She ran her fingers over the rounded end of the tarnished silver tube. Each of the parts was a slightly different shape, though all—aside from *veritas*—were the same length. The *purgium* had two flat ends. The *scio* one pointy end.

The *scio*. . . .

Her jaw dropped, and she sucked in her gut to peer at her belt.

"Sink me," she whispered.

The *scio* was on her, and she held the *dynami*.

Caspian cast a cursory glance her way. "What is—?"

He stared at her hand and then her belt.

"I'm holdin' two o' the parts," she whispered. "And they ain't blastin' me."

Locks scowled at her, red tinging his cheeks. "That was careless."

After what had happened to Grubby, she agreed. "I didn't think o' it. Plank just passed me the *scio* in the hold." Ebba ripped her eyes from the two tubes. "Why can I hold two all o' a sudden? They've always reacted bad-like."

Barrels tapped one finger against the corner of his mouth. "Do you think you can hold any two of the parts now?"

She shrugged. "I dunno. Ain't likely to try, am I? Bloody hurts when the things fling ye to Davy's."

"You should try with the *purgium* too," Caspian urged, lifting his gaze to hers.

"Ye want me to be hurt?" she asked in confusion.

He reached out and squeezed her hand. "Never."

Locks and Barrels stared at their hands, and Ebba slid free again, trying to ignore the hurt in the prince's amber eyes as she did.

"The landlubber be right," Jagger called from where he leaned

—*again*—against the mast. "We need to know as much as we can about the root o' magic. Ye should test the theory."

Perhaps.

The parts had to fit together, after all. But why *she* should be the one to risk being catapulted into the sea from a magical explosion was a mystery. Locks and Barrels were both nodding, too, and she groaned dramatically. "Fine. But if I get hurt, ye're all my slaves for a week."

"Servants, my dear," Barrels corrected.

"Same thing," she shot back.

He and Caspian shared an amused look.

She stood and tossed the *dynami* back to Locks. "Place it on the ground there, Caspian, and everyone get back smart-like."

Ebba winced, recalling the last time she'd picked up two parts and been blasted to Davy's. She'd had bruises for weeks.

The others formed a ring around her, and she waved them farther back. These tubes packed a punch. "Don't let me drown."

Gripping the *scio*, she took several quick breaths and edged closer to the *purgium* the prince had placed on the deck between them. Closing one eye, Ebba extended her little finger to the tarnished silver tube, slowly, slowly, *carefully*.

She made contact and screamed, yanking her hand back.

Nothing happened.

Ebba stared at the *purgium* and touched it a second time, this time for longer. "Aye, I can be touchin' these two as well."

"Ye gave me a flamin' fright, screamin' like that," Locks scolded her.

"I was expectin' pain," she explained. "It was a reflex scream."

"Ye should try with *veritas*," Jagger said, holding the sword out. He was never far from the weapon and hadn't been since Caspian had loaned it to him. The prince had a theory that the truth sword showed Jagger which thoughts were real and which were caused by the taint. Since Jagger was yet to give the sword back, Ebba guessed he still needed the extra help.

She eyed the sword. "I ain't touchin' that for a ship filled with gold coins."

"If you've had a particular result with a different part, I believe we can safely assume the same would happen with the *veritas*," Barrels said.

"Aye," Ebba said, jerking a thumb at her father. "What he said. It'll be okay with the lot o' them."

Caspian moved to stand by her side. "Let's check the direction, then."

She glanced up and took his only hand in hers, smiling as his face softened. She hoped he knew that her discomfort with holding hands in public wasn't a personal dig. Ebba didn't just have one father or two parents. She had *six*. The thought of them watching her and Caspian kind of sucked the enjoyment out of touching him. Though maybe on Exosia, when two people courted, more touching was expected.

Jagger rested a hand on her shoulder and white light exploded from their trio.

Warmth surged through her, and she closed her eyes for the briefest moment, reveling in the pleasant sensation. Opening her eyes, she braced for the sight of the bronze aura shooting off her skin. The rich hue blazed out like usual, encompassing her, as though it originated from deep within. Jagger was a brilliant silver that made his flaxen strands appear nearly white while Caspian was bathed in molten gold.

She smiled at them, and both men smiled back in a wordless exchange of how right the connection felt. They knew almost nothing about the phenomenon, but they had that.

The three of them kept up their shining hold, and Ebba studied the beam shooting out of the white glow surrounding them.

The direction was clear.

And yet . . . not.

Ebba stepped away, almost loathe to break the link. "That can't be pointin' back northeast. It pointed northwest afore."

They all stared in the opposite direction.

"We should've checked more often," Jagger said. "We've sailed past the island."

Locks swore under his breath. "Let's bring the ship about, then. From now on, we're checkin' every few hours."

"Aye," she chorused with the others.

Ebba hoped the dramatic change in direction wasn't something to do with her and Caspian. They didn't know what their role was in this quest. Not really. What if they were doing something wrong?

Shaking her head, she made for the sheets with Locks, but Barrels stopped her with a tap on the shoulder.

"My dear, we've missed our lessons the last few days. I thought we could make up for it today with a triple reading and writing session."

Ebba schooled her features into an eager mask. "Okay!"

Barrels grinned, and she forced her mouth to do the same.

A triple lesson? Dread filled her.

Ebba wanted to read and write. But the daily lessons were a bit much. And to have to make up for a string of days while she was unconscious seemed cruel. Still, while several years ago, she would've ranted and raved, now she had a reason to learn. Ebba was willing to quash her reluctance and get on with learning. Then one day, she'd be able to read her fathers' memories in the scrapbook they'd gifted her.

Barrels turned for the helm, and Ebba let her fake grin slip away. Shoulders sagging, she trailed after her eldest father, ignoring Jagger's snort.

FOUR

"How is he?" Ebba asked, tiptoeing through the line of hammocks to peer down at Grubby.

"More color in his cheeks," Stubby answered gruffly. "Might be wishful thinkin'."

He appeared about the same to Ebba, but she'd endured a reading lesson for the last three hours, so maybe she'd missed the change.

She set her eyes on Stubby. His bloodshot eyes were fixed on Grubby. Great bags hung underneath. He hunched against the post behind him, sunk in on himself, expression vacant.

"All the letters be swirlin' about my head," Ebba told him as she sat on the hammock on Grubby's other side.

Stubby's lip twitched. "Aye, lass. I remember the same thing myself. But it'll all make sense in the end, and ye'll be better off for it."

No doubt she would. But she'd like to reap the benefits sooner rather than later.

"When did ye learn to read, Stubs?" she asked, her jaw cracking as she yawned. "I thought ye were always a pirate like yer father afore ye and his father afore him."

Stubby blinked and glanced up from Grubby, peering across to Ebba who swung gently in a hammock on the other side.

"I was. Well, born on land like most, but as soon as I had my sea legs, my father took me away to sail on his ship. My mother had already started to teach me to read—per my father's request. And my father carried on the lessons after that."

That struck her as strange, which was strange in itself, considering she'd grown up with fathers who'd always encouraged her to learn whatever she wished. "What was yer father like?"

The blood drained from Stubby's face. He leaned back, sagging against the post behind him and breaking off eye contact.

"Sorry, Stubs. Ye don't have to say if ye don't wish."

He dragged a hand over his face and shook his head. "Nay, I'm sure ye've wondered about my behavior these last days. I should explain. I just don't rightly know where to start."

A lot of her fathers had said that in the last few months. She supposed it made sense. If their past was one big knot they couldn't understand, it must be difficult to find the rope end and untangle the knot enough to explain the matter to someone else. How could Stubby make sense of his father to her if he couldn't explain it to himself?

"How about yer mother?" Ebba asked. She already knew a bit about Joan. The subject was safe territory.

He smiled. "My mother. The sweetest woman that ever did live. Made the nicest toffee apples in the entire Caspian Sea."

"I've never had a toffee apple."

Peg-leg had made toffee fish one time. It ended up chum in the sea. After that, he hadn't ventured toward toffee in his recipes.

"And ye should've. I should've taken ye to see my mother before she died. She would've loved—" He cut off and cleared his throat, staring hard at Grubby before starting again. "She would've loved ye, lass. Just *loved* ye."

Ebba felt sad for not knowing her. "When did she pass?"

"Ye were but ten years old."

She wanted to ask why he hadn't gone back, but watching her fathers cry broke her heart, and the urge to avoid that overwhelmed her curiosity. She asked instead, "Did ye see yer mother often when ye sailed with yer father?"

"My father took his ship and crew back to Febribus so we could see her every two months. I only recall it because all o' the other pirate ships thought him strange for bein' so attached."

"Sounds like his ship was a bit strange, like us."

"I like to think we be o' the same make. I've strived to make it so. The same honesty and morals, the same loyalty in the crew, the same met'culous care o' the ship."

Right. So there was a reason Stubby went extra overboard caring for *Felicity*.

The rest of Ebba's fathers hadn't started out as pirates. Grubby, Plank, and Peg-leg were teens who'd wanted to change their fortunes, and Locks and Barrels were full-grown. All of them knew how to sail and care for the ship, but the extra know-how, the *soul* of their ship, came from family pirate lore. Things that Stubby's father handed down to him that he'd received from *his* father.

"We're right lucky to have ye, Stubby," she said, realizing just how true that was. Much of what she'd learned about ship navigation and the like, she'd learned from him.

He reached across Grubby to take her hand. "I ain't sure ye would've said that if ye'd met me twenty years ago, lass."

"I ain't even twenty so I wouldn't have said anythin', would I? I wasn't born."

Stubby snorted softly. "Nay, I be guessin' not." He took a huge breath. "Okay, I'm just goin' to come out with it."

Ebba waited.

And waited some more. "Are ye goin' to start?"

Stubby took another breath. "Aye, aye." He paused and repeated, "Aye."

Poor sod. "It be sumpin' to do with Grubs, I gather," Ebba prompted.

Stubby squeezed his eyes shut. "I remember as if it were only a minute ago though I was only twelve at the time." He cleared his throat once more when his voice shook. "We were steal-tradin' with Kentro, but on the way back to Febribus to trade our plunder for riches, we were set upon by a smaller ship."

Ebba had only seen one ship attack in her life—the night Caspian came into their lives.

"Those days, it wasn't so rare as it is now. Our cannons were always ready. As were our guns. I even recall my father crackin' a smile at the smaller ship. His exact words on the other ship were, 'like a cat scratching a dog.'"

Considering cats were bastards, Ebba thought Stubby's father's words could be labelled under 'tempting fate.'

"It was Mutinous," her father said flatly. "And ye know he only lost one fight in his life."

"Against King Montcroix," she whispered, bending closer. "So yer crew lost the battle?"

Stubby pressed his lips together and dipped his head.

Ebba watched as her father's face screwed up in pain, his eyes showing his hurt even four decades after the battle.

His voice was hoarse when he began again. "The fight went on for hours. Back-and-forth cannon fire. Both ships were damaged, along with many an injury to both crews. But Mutinous never did take no for an answer. He boarded us at dawn. The first rays of sunlight were just comin' across the water, and I remember lookin' out and thinkin' the water had turned to blood, so much red had been spilled that night."

Stubby shifted, his Adam's apple bobbing. "He came aboard, what remained of his crew behind him. I was standin' behind my father at the bow. The rest o' our crew were mostly dead. Mutinous didn't say a word; he just strode up to my father and shot him square through the chest. I don't think a string of seconds have ever gone by so slow in all my years, lass," he said, eyes shadowed. "I was still processin' the sound o' the pistol firing as my father toppled backward from the force o' the shot. He staggered back, and I was so shocked I couldn't move. He . . . he tripped over my foot." Stubby tried again in a firmer tone. "He tripped over my foot and fell over the bulwark into the blood sea."

Her father's words came tumbling out after that. "My legs unlocked, and I ran to the side, forgettin' Cannon's pistol was trained on me. I ran to find my father, and there he was—the man who'd loved me, taught me, who I'd always looked up to—just bobbin' in the water face down."

Ebba flinched violently as the memory of Grubby in the same state hit her between the eyes. She struggled to push her remembered terror away. "B-but he was shot through the chest, Stubs," she said quietly. "It wasn't ye trippin' him that killed him."

"And I hear what ye say, lass, I do. A part o' me sees that the water didn't drown him. The rest o' me wonders if maybe he might've lived if he landed on deck."

"I don't think Cannon would've given him the time or attention, m'hearty," she said.

"Perhaps not. But that's how the skull plays tricks, ain't it?"

"Aye," she whispered.

Stubby sighed. "Mutinous decided he had a use for me. My father's ship was larger than his. He took it, and I was forced—after a month in the holdin' cell—to be part o' his crew. Not a day went by in that first year that I didn't think of my father bobbin' in the red water, bright blood spreadin' across his back. I was bidin' my time. I was goin' to kill Mutinous and take back my father's ship. I was goin' to do my father proud. I was goin' to be a captain just like him with a loyal crew. I was goin' to do all that and take my revenge. For me. And for my mother."

A tear fell from his eye, dripping over his lips. He dashed it away. "I was goin' to do all that. The first year."

"What happened after that?" Ebba said, rounding Grubby to crouch next to her father.

"Then," he said with disgust, "then I began to forget. Or not forget, maybe. I began to see what had happened in a di'ferent way. My father had been at fault. He was weak. He'd lost the battle though he'd possessed a bigger ship. He'd failed to protect me. Cannon saved me. Slowly, month by month, the most hauntin' memory of my life was undone and put together again in an off-center and skewed way. By the end o' the second year, I held nothin' but hate for my father. And for a long, long time that's all I felt. All my loy'lty was for Mutinous. By the time I was fifteen, I was his first mate. Only three years later."

Ebba thought of Swindles and Riot by Pockmark's side—when he'd been alive—and shivered. She couldn't imagine Stubby in that spot, sneering and hurting and being cruel for no reason.

"Ye mostly know the rest. We were given the job to take ye and stole ye instead, abandonin' Mutinous to do so. Then started the hard part for us. We had to figure out why we'd done the things we'd done. We didn't know about the taint. We just knew sumpin' about Mutinous or the ship made us dark. We put it down to havin' sumpin' bad within us, thinkin' we'd only thought and done those things because the other crewmembers were doin' the same. I was ashamed, lass. So deeply ashamed o' myself. How I'd forgotten my father in the space of a year. I was too ashamed to return to my mother and tell her the truth. And that I was such a coward was nearly harder to bear than the rest. I couldn't bring myself to go and bring her closure, to let her know her son was alive. Or if she'd heard tell o' my misdeeds, to show her I was tryin' to sail the right course now."

Ebba didn't speak as she pushed back the burning lump in her throat and blinked back tears. She swallowed several times until she was certain she could trust her voice. "She knew, Stubby. Yer mother knew."

His head was bowed, face in his hands. "It's right sweet o' ye to say—"

"Nay, Stubs," she said aggressively. "She *knew*."

He raised his head to look at her.

She hugged him close. "I'm sure o' it. Because I have no doubt ye'll always do what's proper when in yer right mind. A mother would know such a thing too. If ye'd known then what ye know now, ye would've sailed straight to her and set the matter straight. But ye didn't. Ye were confused. Ye didn't realize ye'd been a victim. Stubs, none o' that stuff on the ship was yer fault. I've said it to the rest, and I'll say the same to ye. That evil was added to ye; it wasn't part o' ye before. It was put there."

Stubby's shoulders shook, and she stayed where she was, clinging to him, trying to anchor his very soul to the ship for fear he may choose to leave.

"Ye went through Davy Jones' Locker itself, m'hearty," Ebba whispered. "But ye came out the other side. And now ye have what ye promised yer father ye'd do. Ye have a loyal crew. They're honest and have morals—mostly. I think ye've done all right, aye?"

"Aye, lass. Mayhaps ye're right."

"I'm always right."

He chuckled and kissed the top of her head, and they swayed with the ship, Ebba's ear pressed against his chest to listen to his beating heart.

Her fathers meant so much to her, and Stubby had always been the hardest of their crew. She was glad he didn't have to carry his past burdens alone any longer.

"Stubs," she murmured, pulling back. "We could go see yer mother's house when we're back in the Caspian Sea."

He stilled. "Aye?"

"Ye could tell her house everythin' ye just told me. Maybe, if the thunderbird put her soul into a bird, she'll hear ye anyway."

". . . We'll do that, lass."

They resumed their swaying hug.

"Stubs?" She broke the silence again. "What was the name o' yer father's ship?"

He tightened his hold on her. "*Eternal.* Mutinous used my father's ship to reign terror over the Caspian Sea for the next twenty-odd years."

FIVE

"Let me get this straight," Stubby said. "First the magic beam said to go northwest, then it shifted northeast. And now it be pointin' southwest?"

Peg-leg screwed up his face and grunted. "Aye, that be about the size o' it."

Ebba turned in a full circle on the deck. Which unfortunately didn't provide any answers.

Caspian had a finger pressed to his lips. "Can it be that we're constantly sailing too far before checking the direction? That doesn't seem right."

"Either that or there is something wrong with the tubes," Barrels said, facing the prince. "We used the *dynami*, *purgium*, and *veritas* the first couple of times and have replaced the *veritas* with the *scio* since."

Caspian appeared to mull this over. "So let's test that—"

"Or is it me?" Ebba voiced her slight fear of being incompetent and unable to bear the burden. "Could it be that I'm doin' sumpin' wrong without knowin'?"

"That just be fear talkin', lass," Stubby said.

She agreed. Her crew's lives depended on her success. Ebba did her best to push her self-doubts aside. The point kept changing. So either they kept sailing past it . . .

. . . *or* . . . .

. . . Maybe they were looking at this wrong. Perhaps the magical *part* they were searching for was—

"It's moving," Grubby said lazily.

"That's what I was just thinkin'," Ebba said. She blinked and whipped to look at where her father stood by the bilge door. "Grubby!"

She raced to him but pulled up short. He stood with one hand in the pocket of his breeches. *Breeches.* Ebba hadn't known they'd had a pair on the ship. Only rich-lubbers wore them. He wore boots to the knee and a patterned doublet-vest. His scraggly hair had been washed and combed back with some kind of grease that kept the strands slicked in a suave style.

The entire crew stared in heavy silence as Grubby removed a monocle from a small pocket on his vest and held it to his eye, surveying them.

"Grubs?" she asked. "Is that a cravat ye're wearin'?"

"'Tis," he said, turning his monocle on her.

Ebba glanced behind. Locks shrugged. Barrels' mouth was ajar.

Peg-leg tapped forward. "Are ye . . . all right, matey?"

"Better than I've faired in some time, I assure you," Grubby answered.

"He's clean," Barrels whispered.

That about summed it up. Something was off.

"As I was saying," Grubby said with a sniff, "the only possible reason for our changing direction is that the part itself is mobile. Or a someone or something is in possession of the aforementioned part and is moving."

Shite. Whatever had happened to him, it wasn't good.

Ebba closed the distance and hugged her father awkwardly. "I'm glad ye're better, Grubs."

"Deplorable name," he sneered though he returned her embrace.

They'd worried about what sacrifice the *purgium* had demanded to cure Grubby of the taint. They hadn't considered the tube would also cure Grubby of his head injury from decades ago.

Her fathers exchanged a long look. The type they shared when they knew something she didn't. Ebba watched them carefully.

"So," Plank drew out. "What do ye propose-like?"

Grubby pinched the bridge of his nose. "You have no idea what it's been like to listen to you all prattle on all these years."

"Sheesh, Grubs. Tell us how ye really feel," Stubby said.

Seeing as her healed father looked like he might take Stubby up on the offer, Ebba jumped in, turning to the others. "What's the plan then—with the next part movin' somehow?"

A splash sounded behind her.

She whirled about. Grubby was gone. Only a pile of his fancy clothes remained.

"Where'd he go?" she demanded, racing to the side. Bubbles lingered on the surface where he'd disappeared into the water.

Locks groaned. "Can't say I'm sorry. He's like he used to be—afore Cannon bopped him over the head with the boom."

"Aye, I bloody hated him back then," Plank said. "Like a ruder version o' Barrels."

Barrels spluttered.

"Ye knew him like this twenty years ago?" she clarified, trying to keep up. "This be the real him?"

Peg-leg grimaced. "Aye, lass. I'm afraid so. We hoped he'd never heal and ye wouldn't find out he's a bastard."

At a choked laugh, she turned to look behind her.

"Stop laughin'," Ebba snapped at Jagger. "It ain't funny. The *purgium* changed him."

Jagger's grin only grew.

Caspian shook his head. "Grubby's smart? Really, really smart. I never would have guessed it."

"He be smart, all right," Locks said. "And he be knowin' it and fond o' tellin' everyone too."

She never would have guessed either. Like Locks, Ebba had to admit she wasn't sure about the change in her usually uncomplicated and joyful father.

"How do we fix him?" she hissed, feeling like a traitor for uttering the words.

Plank tapped a finger against his lips. "What I can't figure out is whether the payment for healin' him o' the taint was renderin' him unconscious for days or givin' his mind back."

Stubby said, "I could believe that. He's defin'tely traded down."

"Or did the *purgium* heal him o' both injuries and put him into the sleep as the payment for both?" Plank asked.

No one replied.

Water exploded behind them, and Ebba spun. With an outraged screech, she whirled right back as her very naked father reappeared on the deck.

Grubby clicked his fingers. "Clothing, mortals."

"Aye, someone give him sumpin' to wear," she echoed, nose wrinkled.

Stubby said, "I always thought ye were just a cocky bugger, but I'm wonderin' if that be part o' bein' a selkie."

"I *am* a selkie—"

"Nay, ye're only part. Ye can't shift into a seal. I ain't even sure ye're immortal. I've seen ye bleed just as surely as any mortal. And ye age like the rest o' us."

Ebba guessed only the leader of the selkies could fill in those blanks. Or maybe this . . . *healed* version of Grubby knew.

Grubby raised his voice. "The sooner I get to Kentro and fulfil my purpose, the better. You have no idea what it has been like to be in this buffoon's head. He has absolutely no sexual prowess. It's embarrassing."

Ebba had to give him that one. Grubby got all kinds of tongue-tied around women.

Peg-leg tapped her on the shoulder, and she turned around once more, relieved to find Mr. Grubby dressed.

He slicked his hair back.

. . . This would take some getting used to.

"Did you discover something overboard?" Caspian asked.

Grubby swept him a low bow. "King Caspian, a pleasure to formally make your acquaintance."

"Uh," the prince dipped his head. "Yes, you too . . . Grubby."

The selkie scowled. "Gustafio, Your Highness."

"I think I had that once," Peg-leg muttered, peering down his body. Her other fathers snickered quietly.

"Your findings . . . Gustafio?" Caspian tried again.

Mr. Grubby studied his nails, which were shaped and clean.

"I just spoke with my octopi slaves. They have not seen an object of similar shape and color to those we possess," he said.

Locks sucked in a breath. "What about Verity? Did they say anythin' about her? And the others."

"Yes, what about those we left at Zol?" Barrels asked, stepping closer.

Mr. Grubby shrugged. "They're alive."

"*Alive*," Locks replied, screwing his face up. "But how is she? What else did they say?"

"Didn't think to ask."

Her father's face reddened and slowly turned purple. Stubby and Plank each latched onto one of Locks' arms as he lunged at the selkie. A fair enough reaction when the octopi were their only means of communication with Zol and they had to wait weeks between messages.

Grubby brushed off a tiny speck on the cuff of his tunic. "After I threatened their young, they warned me that if we continue in this direction, we will soon come across Calypso."

"Calypso?" Jagger asked him.

Mr. Grubby returned to inspecting his nails.

She wasn't the only one who turned to Plank.

Plank released Locks, face paling. "We need to bring *Felicity* about and go around. Right now."

"Good luck with that," Mr. Grubby muttered.

"What's that s'posed to mean?" Stubby demanded.

The selkie shrugged again. "You have maybe one minute until you arrive there."

"Why didn't ye tell us that first?" Plank asked angrily. "Okay, short version. Calypso is kind o' like the siren—"

Ebba froze.

"—but she ain't set on revenge. She's just . . . lustful."

Lustful. Rotten innards of a whale. That's exactly what she *never* wanted to see—her fathers' butts. "All o' ye in the hold," she ordered. "Right now. In the hold. Tie yerself down. I'll take the helm and come get ye when we've passed by."

"Ye heard her, lads," Stubby said.

They made for the bilge door. Only Peg-leg turned back. "Will ye be okay?"

There wasn't time to think about that. Just like in Syraness, Ebba had to step up to protect her fathers because she was female, and that lent her resistance to some magical creatures. Who said women were bad luck on ships? To her thinking, it was the other way about.

"Aye, Peg-leg. Don't ye worry. I'll get us through."

"I have no doubt o' that." He shut the door, and Ebba stared about the empty deck. Or mostly empty.

"What are ye doin?" she asked Grubby.

He smiled at her. Mostly without sneering. "I will keep my mind around Calypso. Never mind me, mortal."

"Well, ye sure didn't keep yer mind around the siren."

"That was when the buffoon was in control."

Ebba placed her hands on her hips. "Grubby ain't a buffoon. We love him. And if ye want us to love ye, too, ye better talk about him right." The irony that she was scolding Grubby not to be nasty to himself wasn't lost on her.

Not waiting for an answer, she strode to the bow to look ahead.

A small outcrop of black rocks lay far off to the left. She ran back to the helm and spun the wheel to direct them farther away. On their current course, they would've missed the outcrop anyway, but Ebba wasn't willing to take any risks.

Grubby left her to stand at the bow, and Ebba set her thoughts to watching the rocky outcrop.

The outcrop wasn't anything unusual—aside from the fact it was out at deep sea. Even though they kept a person in the crow's nest to watch for such things, if their direction had been slightly different, *Felicity* might've run up against the dark rocks. As it was, even with the sun beating high above, only a weak shine penetrated the thick cloud plumes. The shine was just enough to lend the black rocks a subtle glow.

Or. . . .

Ebba squinted, hands tight on the wheel.

. . . Or was it the rocks themselves that glowed?

They couldn't be usual stones because they appeared almost soft. Like Ebba could lie down upon them and caulk as comfortably as she did in her hammock.

That couldn't be right.

Ebba peered ahead to check on Grubby at the bow. He was smoothing back his hair. Again.

"All clear ahead?" she called.

He waved a hand, which she chose to interpret as yes. Ebba let her gaze slide back to the glowing rocks. Just to check if they still glowed.

For some reason, that troubled her greatly.

She gasped. "Grubs, there be a person on the rocks."

Ebba shook her head again. Of course there was a person on the rocks. That was the whole point of her navigating *Felicity* while her fathers held tight in the hold. She held onto the wheel with one hand and grabbed the telescope from the small square trunk latched behind the wheel.

Extending it, she turned to peer at the woman.

Except. . . . Ebba adjusted the telescope.

Eight ridged abs drew her gaze as surely as a lighthouse beacon in the middle of the night. A wide chest tapered into material slung about Calypso's hips. The strip of material wasn't enough to contain the person's muscled thighs. Ebba ran her eyes all the way down the naked limbs and back up past the eight abs, past the bulging pecs and biceps, up to a square jaw and sculpted lips.

She gasped, a bolt of heat spearing the area between her hips as she took in Calypso's piercing green eyes . . . and their expression. . . .

A dare.

A challenge.

A promise.

Ebba licked her suddenly dry lips.

Calypso was a man.

SIX

Ebba pulled hard on the wheel, directing the ship toward the soft glowing bed, the most beautiful man she'd ever seen in her life beckoning her with a sultry smile.

"Where are you going, mortal?" someone asked her.

"Shh, I'm going to get the man," she answered in a whisper. If the person spoke too loudly, they'd scare him off. And Ebba wanted to touch the beautiful man.

"Excuse me? Oh, *oh*, Calypso is a man. My slaves didn't mention that tidbit. I'll have them punished. May I ask why you want to 'get the man'?"

Ebba couldn't shift her eyes from the specimen before her. Even his name, *Calypso*, made her want to faint in a gasping heap. Her knees were weak, her heart aflutter; her mind was filled with joyful white, and all because of him.

Because of Calypso. She loved him.

"Because I'm goin' to kiss his mouth," Ebba announced.

Grubby rested a hand on her shoulder, squeezing tight. "Nothing, and I mean *nothing* would make me prouder. I know we're not blood, but some of the buffoon's love for you has seeped into me.

Selkie don't tend to hang around for the child part. But I'm glad I accidentally have."

"I'm goin' to take off his clothes," she added.

"You are truly my daughter," he announced. "I can't wait to tell my kin about your prowess. Hop to it, young cub. I'll hold down the fort here."

Ebba let go of the wheel and walked to the bulwark. If her body's capabilities had reflected her heart and soul, she might've floated over.

Her lover came to greet her, and Ebba smiled shyly. She tucked a dread behind her ear, climbing up onto the bulwark. She'd never been so nervous nor so full of anticipation in her life. Yet somehow, inexplicably, Ebba knew Calypso felt the same. He would do anything for her. Go any distance. Fight off any foe.

"Ahoy," Ebba said quietly when he floated above the water directly in front of her.

He opened both arms. "I have waited an eon for you, lover."

She didn't know what an eon was, but if he'd waited, so had she.

"Jump, my dark queen."

As though lightly tugged by his warm, all-encompassing voice, her head tipped back. Bliss washed over her like a sweet breeze. She leaned out, smiling at him. And leaped into his strong arms.

She stared at the man, unwilling to blink for fear she'd miss one moment of seeing his face. Tentatively, Ebba reached a hand up to his jaw as, in a dream, they arrived at the rock bed, and he set her on her feet.

"Your name, lover?" he whispered in her ear.

She mouthed the answer, and he laughed at her fumbled attempt. Blushing, Ebba tried again. "Ebba-Viva Fairisles."

"You are an exotic beauty, my queen." He nodded, and she did feel like a queen. Which was odd because prior to meeting her soulmate, the title of princess had never sat right.

But everything was different now.

She ran her hands up his forearms, marveling at the strength contained within them. She gasped as Calypso wrenched her flush against him. He caught her chin, and her gaze flew to his as he studied her, pursing his lips. She did the same as he lowered his head.

So close.

The torment.

Ebba could live a thousand lives and never feel such torment.

Their lips touched, and Ebba groaned low in the back of her throat at the exquisite silky feel of his mouth, his body. She clutched at the sides of his abdomen, yanking him closer. But it wasn't enough. He was too tall or she was too short. But she was a rigger.

Ebba climbed up her lover's body, wrapping her legs around his torso. His hands cupped her upper thighs, holding her still.

She was exactly where she wanted to be.

Ebba set to kissing him. She pressed her lips against his, mouth moving, hands roaming. Bliss. Even when her lips began to feel raw, Ebba wouldn't have had it any other way.

Calypso pulled back, glancing away from her, and Ebba cried low at the loss of him.

"More," she demanded.

He dragged his gaze back to her and lowered her to stand on the bed. Tears hovered at the corners of her eyes until she understood he didn't want her to leave. His hands went to her black jerkin, and he didn't glance away as he undid the laces.

Heat crept up to her cheeks, down to her fingertips, filling her with burning want.

"Are you okay, lover?" he asked, pushing off her jerkin.

His hands went to her belt, and he pulled the leather free, pushing her slops down. Ebba kicked them away, legs bare beneath her tunic, which fell to mid-thigh. But enough was enough. Her hands went to the knot holding the material in place around his hips.

And she plucked it free.

The material fell away, and Ebba dropped her gaze, bashfulness long forgotten.

"Ye're beautiful," she said, glancing back up to his piercing green eyes.

He inched his hands toward the bottom hem of her tunic.

—A barrel careened into him.

Ebba screamed as Calypso was thrown into the ocean. He disappeared from view, and she fell to her knees on the soft bed to search for him in the water.

Hands were about her waist.

The wrong hands. Not his hands.

An iron grip held her, yanking her upward. She yelled her fury, legs kicking out as she tried to free herself from the person dragging her from the other half of her soul.

"Calypso!" she screamed.

Ugly men were forming a wall between her and her immortal lover. They were taking her from him. They were going to hurt him.

They'd only just found each other.

Her heart seized as she spotted her one and only hoisting himself back onto their soft bed.

"Don't harm him," she sobbed at the person behind her. "I'll do anythin'. Don't harm him."

"I did not sign up for this," the person pulling her off the rocks into a rowboat muttered.

Irritation spiked within her, and she twisted to glance into hideous silver eyes. "Aye, well, no one invited ye, ye lipless stingray."

The wall of ugly men was dispersing, and through their fragmented barrier, Ebba spotted her lover again.

"Calypso!" She stretched a hand in his direction.

Hideous silver eyes dumped her in the back of the boat, and Ebba scrambled to pitch herself over the side to swim back to the soft bed. Her efforts were thwarted by a russet-haired demon.

"Demon!" she shouted, kicking at the one-armed monstrosity.

The one behind her snorted.

The demon scowled at the other man and schooled his expression just as a manipulative demon might. "Ebba-Viva, it's me. Caspian."

"I don't know a Caspian," she said. "I only know Calypso. My lover."

The demon's gaze dropped to her bare legs, and Ebba scowled at him, yanking her tunic down to her knees. The demon startled and averted his eyes, a ruddy red filling his cheeks.

"Stay away from me," she warned him.

"Aye, demon," the one behind her said. "Stay away."

"You were the one with your hands all over her."

"Savin' her from danger."

"And enjoying it in the doing," the demon half-shouted, fist clenched.

"Aye, well, ye can't blame a pirate for that."

The boat rocked, and Ebba inched to the edge. The one behind her planted a boot on the bench, halting her second escape attempt.

"Hideous silver eyes," she hissed at him.

It was the demon's turn to laugh. "She doesn't like you either."

Hideous hummed low. "She only likes one man at the moment."

"Ha!" Ebba threw back her head. "My lover be no mere man. He be immortal. Perfection."

The two ugly people stared back at her in silence.

"I can't wait to replay this to ye later," Silver said. "The crow's nest is mine for good."

The demon's gaze was on her legs again, but sorrow filled his expression. "Look what he did to her legs."

Huh? Ebba glanced down and couldn't see anything the matter, just smooth dark-brown skin. She gripped the side of the vessel as the wall of ugly men clambered into the boat, surrounding her. Her heart leaped into her throat as she turned back only to find her lover was gone.

She launched to her feet, making everyone shout and reach for the boat's side.

"What did ye do to Calypso?" she shrieked, shoving the nearest one, a man with a wooden peg. "Where is my lover?"

"I hoped to never hear that word on my daughter's lips," he said, shuddering.

"Where is he?" she screamed so loudly her throat tore. Tears poured down her face as she glanced back at the empty bed. *Their* empty bed.

A man with peppered hair sighed. "Back to the ship. We'll see what is to be done once we're farther from his pull."

Ebba tried again to launch herself over the side into the water, and both the demon and hideous silver eyes joined efforts to stop her. She sobbed against their shoulders, sagging as exhaustion hit, sapping her energy. She didn't want to touch them, but her limbs were heavy with despair.

"Please take me back," she begged them. "I've got to go back. I have to."

A large hand stroked her back.

"Ye'll be just fine, Viva."

"Nay," she replied. Or tried to. The word was lost in the violent tremble of her voice.

She wouldn't be fine.

SEVEN

Ebba sat between the trunks that held her belongings, wrapped in a blanket, hammock overhead. She stared at her legs as her shocked mind attempted to deny the truth of what had happened. It wasn't working. Which meant that everything with Calypso had been real.

Her legs were a mess from where the rocks shredded her skin. Her feet were the worst. She hadn't even felt the deep scratches at the time. She'd thought they'd stood on a soft bed, not jagged stone. The rivulet cuts ran all the way from her ankles nearly to her hips.

Ebba flushed as she remembered Calypso had removed her clothes, leaving her only in her tunic.

Her hands began to shake. "It did happen."

She'd been. . . . He'd. . . . Somehow, she'd lost her mind. Utterly and completely. Just as her fathers had with the siren.

"Ebba-Viva?"

She jumped and glanced up at Plank through the latticed rope of her hammock.

"Oh, little nymph," he sighed.

She leaned back, staring at the stick in Plank's hand. "What's that?"

"Nothin'."

"Is that a short straw?" she accused.

Plank hurried to hide the small stick. "Nay, lass. Just some rubbish layin' about."

That was a pirate truth.

He held out his other hand, offering her a goblet. "Here. Locks whipped ye up a little sumpin' to help ye sleep."

That was what she wanted—to slip away into sleep for a while. But each time Ebba closed her eyes, she remembered what had happened. Still shaking, she took the goblet and emptied the contents in two gulps before handing the goblet back to her father.

He set it down and then lowered to crawl under the hammock with her. Plank pulled her into his arms, and she rested her head against his shoulder.

"Ye be recallin' it all then?" he whispered in her hair.

She stilled. Memory loss hadn't occurred to her as an option. Maybe she could take the easy way out with this. Her fathers had to be just as mortified as she was. Ebba winced, remembering how she'd scaled Calypso's body, how she'd torn off his . . . fabric skirt thing. When she thought of Jagger and Caspian in the boat with her, and what she'd said, mortification flooded through her. They saw and heard everything.

The temptation to shrink away, to not talk was nearly overwhelming. And she could choose to bury the truth; she knew all too well how her fathers would go along with whatever she decided. Yet, Ebba didn't want to do that—not when she'd seen how talking could help. She felt sick inside, her soul burdened. Carrying the trouble by herself was a ploy she'd often used in the past. But this time, Ebba feared what it might do to her to bury the turmoil.

"Calypso was a man," she whispered.

Plank tightened his hold. "Aye, little nymph. He was. And we're right sorry for allowin' that to happen to ye."

"It ain't yer fault," she said, feeling her body relax from Locks' drink. "Ye can't always be there to protect me."

"Perhaps not. But we'll always try our best. And we'll never stop wantin' to protect ye."

She blinked. "Grubby was on deck. He told me to go."

"That man ain't Grubby," Plank growled. "Not the one we know and love."

No, he never would've let her go out there, even being a smidgen slower than most. But then, knowing a selkie's nature to be geared around the drinking of tea, Ebba couldn't quite summon the energy to sustain being mad.

"The stuff be kickin' in," she admitted as her eyes grew heavy.

"Then let's get ye into a hammock so ye can sleep."

"Nay," Ebba murmured. "I'd like to stay right here." It was safe.

"We'll stay here then. But little nymph?"

"Mmm?"

He squeezed her shoulders. "Ye know what happened ain't yer fault, don't ye? Ye know he had magic to use against ye and that ye had no chance of fightin' back? I remember how it was with the siren."

"Ye all said ye didn't recall that."

Plank didn't answer immediately. "Aye, we did. Seemed easier at the time. The siren made us feel . . . pained love and want. But that ain't what love feels like, and we all had normal memories to compare the experience to. But ye don't. What ye felt with Calypso wasn't what ye'd feel in real life."

"What about my response?" Ebba asked, giving up the battle to keep her eyes open.

He paused. "Uh . . . well. If ye find the right person, I'd say your, uh . . . that would be similar-like."

"Don't hurt yerself, Plank," she muttered.

Her father snorted. "We thought this talk would be another twenty years off."

"Twenty years?" Ebba yawned, snuggling closer. "I'll be nearly dead by forty."

"Thanks," Plank replied drily. "But serious time, little nymph.

What Calypso did twisted a pure thing. When touchin'—the kissin' and the like—be done for the right reasons, they're beaut'ful. And none o' my co-parents want ye to grow afraid o' explorin' that. In twenty years. Part o' me wishes ye'd already been kissed just so ye'd understand what I be sayin'. It was a shameful way to exper'ence it for the first time."

His words made fundamental sense to her. Because what she'd had with Caspian had felt safe and warm and exciting. Not harsh and all-consuming and anguished.

"I've kissed someone," she said sleepily. "Ye don't need to be worryin' about that."

Plank stilled, and she made a noise of complaint as his grip grew painful. He loosened his hold, and Ebba began to drift, safe in her father's arms.

"Oh?" he replied, an edge to his voice.

She tried to open an eyelid but couldn't. "Mm," she replied.

"Anyone I know, little nymph? Ye can be tellin' me."

A twinge of alarm buried under hundreds of blankets of thick cloud told her otherwise. And so, instead of clawing back out of the clouds to answer him, Ebba sank blissfully into their folds. Into oblivion.

"ISN'T IT UNCOMFORTABLE DOWN THERE?" Caspian bent down to see into the cozy nook she'd created under the hammock.

In the day since her lip fest with Calypso, Locks had piled up blankets to cushion her from the hard, wooden floor. Peg-leg had brought her a fruit platter, and Stubby kept her goblet filled with grog. Grubby hadn't been down to see her, but from a few shouted words that made their way below deck, she'd guessed that her other fathers were barring him.

Cocooned in a blanket with only her eyes showing, she didn't look at the prince. Ebba was burningly aware their last conversation had included several mentions of 'demon.'

"Nay, it's fine." Her voice was muffled.

Her cheeks flushed as he maintained his stare. She could feel his intense perusal like a series of small pinches on her arms.

"You don't need to hide down here, Ebba," Caspian said.

She sniffed. "I ain't hidin'."

"There's nothing to be ashamed of."

She peeked through the tiny gap in her cocoon. His gaze was too bright and, after a few seconds, Ebba had to lower her head again.

Caspian shuffled underneath the hammock to sit next to her. "I knew something was wrong when we were coming up to Calypso. It was too quiet. We could feel the ship changing direction and jerking around. But each of us was remembering what you described with the siren, so we didn't dare come up."

"Ye don't recall?" Her fathers had.

"You pushed me down the ladder, didn't you?"

True.

He continued, "I didn't want to be a hindrance, so though I knew I should go to you, I didn't." His fist curled. "I'm so very sorry."

"It ain't yer fault."

The prince shrugged. "That doesn't stop me from being angry at myself for letting you down." He glanced at her.

Caspian reached forward for the edges of the blanket, and she let him pull it open; she was fully clothed beneath. The prince shifted to sit beside her against the post and pulled her into his side before tossing another blanket over them. Ebba tucked in the edges so they were both cocooned within.

"I ain't ashamed o' my part in what happened," she admitted. "I didn't do nothin' wrong—he did. But I can't get the feeling out o' my skull. His magic made me feel as though I was drownin' in want. And I guess I'm ashamed ye all saw it. I feel sick about that more than anythin'. Because I can't keep it a secret now."

Touch itself, between two willing people, was beautiful. That was what Plank said. Touching for the right reasons was okay. It was Calypso's reasons that were wrong. Yet he was an immortal heeding the call of his nature, driven to fulfil his purpose like all magical beings.

She was confused about that part.

Caspian kissed her temple, and warmth surged within her at the gesture. "I know what you mean. You have no idea how I wish you never saw me in those first weeks after I lost my arm. I could have met you again when I was stronger. When someone hasn't seen you at your lowest, it's easier to pretend nothing is the matter."

She frowned, nuzzling closer to him. "There's nowhere I would've wanted to be than there helpin' ye put yerself back together."

"That's what I feel. I want to help you. Yet I also know from my own experience that a person only heals because they want to—no matter how much a beautiful pirate might be trying her hardest to force the recovery."

Ebba grinned.

Her smile faded after a beat. "I was nervous about seein' ye. I know we talked about yer feelings for me not long ago. I didn't want ye to blame me for what happened with Calypso. Or be upset."

Caspian rested his head atop hers. "If I'm honest, I hated what I saw. I hated seeing you kissing another. That look of passion in your eyes, I want that for myself. I was jealous of Calypso. But most of all, I loathed that he was controlling you. No one has a right to do that to another being. I've only wished to kill someone once before, but I would've killed Calypso without regret."

"Pockmark be the other?" she asked and felt his answering nod.

She thought of the intense fervor she'd felt for the immortal being and shuddered. "I don't ever want to feel that way again, Caspian. It was torture. Even as I was crazy for more, I was tearin' off my skin for the want o' him. That ain't sane or healthy. If we ever have sumpin', I don't wish it to be like that."

Ebba turned her face up to look at him, blinking when she found him already watching her.

"Have you thought more about us?" he asked.

She hadn't thought of anything but the feel of Calypso in the last two days and sincerely hoped the lingering lust would disappear in time.

Ebba sighed, listening to the calls of her fathers on the main deck. "I guess. I ain't sure where to begin. Is there an order to follow?"

"I don't think so," he said. "The ship . . . changes things."

Snickering, Ebba called him out. "Ye mean bein' on a ship with my six fathers changes things."

His amber eyes glinted. "Well, yes. Usually, I would court you. We would go on chaperoned strolls around the castle; I'd ask you to be my partner to a ball or two; our families might dine together. And when we could, we might steal moments in each other's arms in some hidden corner of a hall."

Heat crept along the tops of her cheeks.

"That is the order I know."

She smiled at the picture he'd painted her. "That's a nice order. But all o' yer things involved castles." Pirates didn't belong in castles. Maybe only on occasion.

"What do you think about me asking your fathers if I can court you?"

Ebba's stomach swooped. "I be thinkin' that the Dynami Sea is very black and very deep. And it's a long way to swim back to Zol."

His lips curved. "Yes, perhaps."

"So what? Ye do that stuff—the strollin' and whatnot, and then what? I'm missin' the part where the feelings happen."

Caspian winced.

Replaying her words, Ebba also winced. "Aye, sorry. That sounded bad. I mean, I feel safe with ye. I like to spend time with ye, and—"

The prince arched a brow, and she trailed off.

He traced her face, first her eyes and then her lips. "You've never led me to believe you feel otherwise, so please do not pain yourself. The idea of courtship is that you get to know the other person and that, *if* the stars align, you develop a regard for the other."

But Caspian already held a regard for her, and they hadn't done any of that stuff.

"I see," Ebba lied.

"You have no idea how I felt the first time you asked me to kiss you." He chuckled under his breath. "For a moment, I forgot about my arm, about my father's death, about all the problems in my life, thinking you might feel something for me."

Ebba chewed on her lip, still staring up at him. That was everything she *wanted* him to forget. She didn't want Caspian to feel pain; she wanted him to see what she saw—someone capable of changing the world.

"Ye see things through yer amber eyes I could only be dreamin' o'," she confessed to him.

Slowly, she inched her fingertips to his face and drew light circles around the burning orbs. Caspian closed his eyes, sighing at her touch.

Being in his embrace felt nothing like Calypso's. It was the exact opposite. There were no expectations, no overwhelming desire that obliterated every thought in her head. She could talk to Caspian and knew he would always listen to her, always balance her impulsiveness—just as she might balance his need to think every little thing through.

"Caspian," she said. "Will ye kiss me again?"

He studied her. Always thinking. "Might I ask why?"

"Ye always tend to," she teased. "What am I to think if ye always do?"

The smile slid from her lips at the torn expression on his face.

He searched her face. "You were just taken advantage of. I don't know how okay you are inside. In fact, I highly suspect you're more hurt than you're showing. I don't want to take liberties when you're vulnerable."

"By sayin' that, ye've ensured I know ye ain't," Ebba countered.

Her insides felt slippery with grime. But for once, Ebba wasn't shoving the problem down and wishing it would disappear. And yet, Ebba had to admit that she wanted him to kiss her in order to scrub Calypso's presence away. To replace a bad memory with a good one or, as Plank had said to her, to remind herself that what the immortal had done twisted something beautiful into ugliness.

"I want to." She stopped, blinking a few times. Blasted eyes were like flooding scuppers. "I would like to remember what an actual kiss feels like. All I can feel is what Calypso did."

Caspian's brows slammed together. He ground his teeth so hard that Ebba could hear them complaining. "How I wish I'd hurt him."

She watched the prince, wondering if he'd ever shown so much anger. Ebba felt enough anger and hurt herself right now that she didn't want to see any more. "So? Are ye goin' to leave me hangin' or what?"

A smile trembled on his lips as amusement replaced his rage. "You know I'd never do that. But are you sure?"

Ebba rolled her eyes. "Aye."

"Aye," he mimicked.

Already wrapped in each other's arms, Caspian lowered his head. His warm breath hit her a moment before his cool lips touched her bruised mouth. The smooth chill of them was a balm, and Ebba melded to his body. She kissed him in return, enjoying the gentle feel of their mouths moving. He increased the pressure, following as her head tilted slightly back.

He slid his hand upward to cup the base of her skull.

A pleasant tenderness filled Ebba, and she smiled, feeling Caspian's answering curve of the lips just before they broke apart for air.

Ebba ducked her head and rested against his chest.

She smiled there, a thrill shooting through her as the buzz of silence grew.

". . . I'll never get sick of that," he declared at last.

Ebba closed her eyes. "Thank ye. It was a beaut'ful kiss."

They remained tangled around each other.

Still.

Quiet times aboard a ship were rare, and she was glad for the minutes with the prince to sooth her battered spirits. Actually . . . not a string of three minutes usually went by before someone charged down to grab tools or grog or to cook or clean. But that Plank would let Caspian down here and give them privacy—even if she hadn't told him *who* she'd kissed—told her he'd guessed the truth.

Or hoped.

"I wish I had two arms to hold you with."

Ebba pulled back. He avoided her gaze. "Ye said ye can still feel yer other arm."

"I can."

"And where is it now?" She arched a brow.

He darted a look at her, and she almost laughed at his guilty expression as he confessed, "Around your waist. Sorry."

She shook her head and nuzzled in again. "Then ye are holdin' me, codfish. Just don't be puttin' it any lower."

Caspian's body shook underneath her head as he gently laughed. "I could go a lifetime not feeling sorry for myself in your presence."

And that's exactly what she wanted for Caspian. Ebba never wanted him to feel less.

EIGHT

Aside from Grubby, only one person onboard hadn't been to see her. Ebba dreaded meeting Jagger for the first time since Calypso.

He never ventured below deck if at all possible. That wasn't what worried her. It was that Ebba didn't know what he'd say. Anxiety filled her because the pirate never pretended. He was nice sometimes, and he wasn't *mean* as such. Not really. Not now.

Jagger possessed a natural propensity to call a stone a stone, and the unpredictability of his honesty unsettled her.

Ebba creaked open the bilge door and peeked out. Stubby was alone at the helm. Safety. Pushing open the door, she slid out and shut it behind her, skimming on light feet to her father at the wheel.

"Ahoy."

"Ahoy," Stubby replied, tucking her into his side. "How are yer legs, lass?"

Bending over, she pulled up her slops to show him the scabs that had formed. They'd leave scars, but Ebba wasn't fussed over things like that. "They don't hurt too bad except if the scabs stretch overmuch. Where are we now?"

"We're just goin' in circles until ye had time to recover. Seems about all we were doin' before anyhow."

Ebba remained at the wheel with Stubby as she scanned the deck. She knew Locks, Barrels and Peg-leg were below deck. Plank was showing Caspian how to trim the sheets on the port side. Grubby was nowhere to be seen.

She asked, "Where's Grubs?"

"Over the side, lass. He tends to be out there more than on deck."

"Did ye all tear shreds off him?" she asked. Grubby was changed now, but in no way did that mean Ebba wanted him to leave.

Stubby's hard expression told her the answer to that was yes. "We made it clear-like that he should think twice about his selkie traditions when it came to ye in the future. He's been scarcer since."

When he got back, she'd talk to him and clear the air. The ship was too small to let things fester, and the thought of him leaving sent a tendril of panic through her.

"How're we goin' to catch the next part if it keeps movin'?" she mused.

"We've been thinkin' o' stringin' nets out, but in these seas, we be worried about what immortals we might catch. Still, it's the best idea we've had. Other than that, maybe if we keep chasin', whatever is carryin' the part will tire."

The other parts had been on land and guarded by immortals. Ebba would have assumed a sea creature had the part if they were in their home waters, but the mysteries of the Dynami made it impossible to assume anything. Was it an island that could move? Or some other immortal being? Maybe a human-animal hybrid like the Daedalions? Was the creature evil or good? Was there some trick to making whatever the thing was stop so they could retrieve the part? And what if the part was deep, deep down in the water? Grubby could retrieve it, she supposed, but going in alone was dangerous. They hadn't managed to retrieve any of the parts since the *dynami* without someone dying.

Her attention drifted to the prince, recalling the sweetness of their kiss yesterday evening. A twinge of excitement clenched her insides, and Ebba observed it, wondering if that was the deeper regard Caspian spoke of. They'd kissed before, but last night felt like . . . more. Not new, necessarily, but like it meant something bigger. From what the prince said, if she'd understood right, the feelings game was a wait-and-see kind of deal. Ebba wanted to return his regard, and she was pretty sure that with time, she would.

As though feeling her heavy perusal, Caspian glanced up from Plank's tutorial on the ropes controlling the sails and grinned her way. Ebba waved.

Stubby cleared his throat. "He'd make a good captain, that one."

Ebba lowered her hand. "What?"

The tips of her father's ears pinkened. "Just sayin'," Stubby hurried to add. "A passin' remark. He might not have started out so well, but he learns quick and is eager to know more. Kind to a fault. Aye, he could make a very good captain."

"Aye," she drew out.

Is that what all of her fathers thought? That Caspian would make a good captain? Her eyes rounded. *Oh, shite.* Had Plank shared their discussion with the others?

Ebba cringed, realizing Stubby had just given the prince his approval. Or had he?

Her fathers once made the prince vomit for being without a tunic around her, and now they were giving her two thumbs up? Why the sudden change? She'd altered a lot, so maybe they'd seen that. Regardless, if this was Stubby's way of tricking information out of her, she wasn't falling for it. Her fathers might act like they didn't care for the day, but Ebba knew how overprotective and wily they were.

"He might," Ebba answered neutrally.

Stubby opened his mouth again.

"Where be Jagger?" she blurted.

Her father's pleasant expression dropped into a scowl. "Why do ye ask?"

Because she wanted to avoid him. Ebba shrugged a shoulder.

"I ain't seen him in a bit," Stubby said, adding, "He'd make a terrible captain."

She craned to see up to the crow's nest, but there was no sign of his flaxen hair waving about in the chilled morning breeze. He must be below deck, which was odd. Ebba kissed Stubby's cheek before freeing herself from his embrace.

"I'm goin' to climb the shrouds. Shout if ye need me."

"I will, lass. Do yer spellin' on the way. Barrels is on at us to get ye practicin'."

She snorted. "He's worse than a shark stealin' fish from a line."

Stubby glanced around for her oldest father before answering, "He's like a dried barnacle on the underside o' the ship. But best keep him happy; he leaves ink blotches on my deck when his cravat be in a twist."

He pointed to the deck and Ebba squinted, bending down. "That's tiny!"

Stubby glared at the offensive ink stain on the wood. "Still there, ain't it?"

Ebba knew better than to argue. She slapped the wheel. "W-h-e-e-l in the h-e-l-m," she said loudly. Leaving the helm, she jumped on the deck and said, "D-i-c-k."

"D-e-c-k," Stubby called.

She peered back, copying her father. "D-e-c-k."

Ebba pointed to the center of the ship. "M-a-s-t."

Running to the rigging, she swung herself up and began to climb the "R-i-p-e-s in the r-i-g-g-i-n to the n-i-s-t."

Ebba looked to the right when the sails were happy and full. "S-a-i-l. B-o-o-m. S-k-y. B-u-r-d." She blinked to where the diluted strands of light were punching through the c-l-o-u-d-s, and as she swung into the crow's nest, she shouted, "S-o-n!"

Her foot landed on soft ground.

"Oof." Someone exhaled.

Ebba squeaked as her legs went out from under her and she

landed, unceremoniously, on top of the person, knocking her head on the inner wall of the nest.

"Ouch." She pushed back her dreads, glaring.

"It's s-u-n," Jagger drawled.

She twisted and glanced down. He sat cross-legged in the nest, and she was sprawled sideways across his lap.

Ebba struggled to get off the pirate in the tiny space. "What are ye doin' here?"

"Watch it," he scolded, shifting the unsheathed *veritas* out of reach from her flailing arms.

Ebba abandoned her escape, jaw dropping. "I could've landed on that."

"Ye're the one who jumped in without lookin'."

"I thought *my* nest was empty," she said. "Why are ye in here if ye ain't lookin' at the sea?" She struggled again, and Jagger watched her attempts without a single offer to help.

It occurred to her that he was greatly enjoying himself.

His gaze fell to her legs.

She peered down and saw her slops had worked themselves higher as she fidgeted. Ebba reached down and tugged the trousers back down to hide her injuries.

Jagger gripped either side of her waist and lifted her, depositing her on the nest floor opposite him. He drew in his legs to give her space and shifted *veritas* farther away.

Ebba huffed and pushed her dreads off her face again.

Ice shot through her as she belatedly recalled her plan to avoid Jagger.

"Ain't ye goin' to tell me to get out?" he asked, watching her.

She peered at him, heart pounding in her chest. The sun hadn't fully risen, and his half of the crow's nest was cast in shadow. His flaxen coloring was easily lost in the dark, but his silver eyes glinted more in the absence of light.

Ebba glanced away and quickly realized that the confines of the crow's nest didn't make avoiding someone easy.

"Ye were below deck for a couple of days, so. . . ." He gestured to the nest.

"Aye," she said after a beat, clearing her throat. "It be okay."

His eyes widened dramatically. "It's okay that I'm in yer nest? Viva, just how badly did Calypso scare ye?"

Her cheeks burned. "I knew ye'd make fun o' it." She wanted to meet his gaze and dare him to say more, but whatever Caspian's earlier kiss fixed had run out.

"Ye did call me hideous silver eyes and a lipless stingray. I'm allowed a couple o' digs to earn my dignity back."

She didn't answer, scratching at the grain of the wood barrel.

Jagger nudged her with his foot. "Do ye want me to go back and kill him for ye?"

Ebba frowned and glanced over at him. "What?"

"I'll shove *veritas* right through his black immortal heart. I ain't sure if he'd come back or not, or if that would even kill him, but it'd make ye feel better."

"I'm surprised ye'd offer," she replied.

"Are ye? Then ye haven't been lookin'."

Oh, she'd been looking, all right. Hard not to when he leaned everywhere. Jagger had shown he was willing to go to great measures to protect his tribe. But she hadn't ever thought herself within the number of people he'd strive to protect.

"I don't want ye to kill Calypso." At least she didn't think she did.

"Oh, ye want to take his skirt off again?"

Ebba kicked him, face flaming. "Nay, that ain't why."

"Good. Then tell me."

Good? She glanced away once more, disconcerted by the tilt of his head and the challenge in his eyes that reminded her, in part, of the immortal.

"It was his nature to do that, wasn't it?" she said. "Calypso's? I didn't like it. Well, I wasn't in my right mind for it. That's why I didn't like it."

"If ye were in yer right mind, ye'd be up for it?"

She darted a look back and saw Jagger was grinning. Ebba kicked him a second time.

"Ye ain't allowed to kick me just because ye're sad and hurtin'," he scolded. "And ye didn't answer."

She sniffed. "If I were in my right mind?" She thought about it. "Nay, I don't know or trust him. Why would I wish to kiss him as I did?"

"So trust be the key," he murmured.

Ebba frowned. "What did ye say?"

Jagger sat back, and the tension between them dissipated somewhat. She took a full breath for the first time since leaping onto his lap.

"That's why I didn't kill him—his nature," the pirate said. "I wouldn't kill a creature for obeyin' its instincts, like a sow protectin' her piglets. But the more I think on it, the more I wonder if I should've."

"Eh?"

He ran a hand through his hair, tousling the strands that extended down past his chin. "The pillars are just actin' in their nature, and they're plain evil. Where be the line when it comes to actin' in yer nature? Calypso stepped over the line well and truly. What he was goin' to do is worse than lurin' ye to the rocks to die."

Ebba mulled that over, surprised that Jagger was confused over the same thing as she. "I don't know his story, but ye're right, I ain't sure nature should be an excuse. Was Calypso aware of what he was doin'? Seemed so. And the pillars cert'inly are. The siren had a mindless want to draw men to the rocks for revenge. And Ladon didn't seem to have a choice when seekin' the good half o' his soul over and over."

Jagger nodded. "Ye think the line be det'rmined by mindlessness and abil'ty to reason?"

Did she? "Perhaps. But evil still be ter'ible without reason, don't it?" Ebba thought of what Calypso did and realized that was true of what he'd done to her. Magical nature aside, he shouldn't be allowed to hurt others or take their will away.

She sighed. "What he did to me was plain wrong. Obeyin' yer nature only be okay if it don't hurt anyone else."

"Aye, I agree," he mused and then cursed loudly. "I should've killed him."

How had the conversation arrived here? Why wasn't she shouting at Jagger to get out of her nest? This was . . . nice. Nice enough that Ebba felt safe venturing to a subject that had played on her mind for a while now.

"Hey, Jagger? Ye know when we were in Medusa's Lair, and that sweet-smellin' water made ye spill yer guts out?"

His eyes darkened, and he said warily, "Aye."

The tone of his reply caught her off-guard. She floundered for a moment before matching it as an exact replica to the tone she'd used minutes ago. He felt vulnerable. Just like her when she hadn't known what he'd say to her.

"I've wanted to say sorry since then. Kind o'. When ye returned the beads to me back on Zol, I wasn't sure what ye meant by the gift, and so I couldn't decide how to respond." She stopped and then added, "But in my defense, ye're a secr'tive, moody bugger."

He appeared surprised by her sort-of apology. He blinked. "I ain't sure how I meant the gift either."

Jagger's gaze dropped to *veritas*. She stared down at Caspian's family heirloom.

"Do ye hold that sword to sort between tainted moments and the real stuff then?" Ebba blurted the question and held her breath.

He regarded her and said drily, "How long have ye wanted to ask that?"

"Not long."

Jagger stared at the dark sky. "Aye, I do."

"Aye?" Caspian was right!

"I used to steal it when I couldn't see straight. But since the prince *deigned* to lend it to me, I just hold it all the time. It shows me truth from lie."

Ebba slanted a look at him. "Are ye still holdin' on to killin' Caspian?"

Jagger regarded her. "Not for now. He gave me the sword and saved me from the thunderbird, so I can't kill him just yet."

"That's very . . . pirate o' ye," she ventured.

"I spent a long time with my tribe, but I took to pirate life."

She had to agree. Silently. When they first met, she'd thought him born on the seas. "How long do ye think ye'll need to hold the sword and be above deck for? Ye're an immune. Medusa said ye'll force the taint out."

"If she's right," he muttered darkly.

Pain flickered across his face. He whipped out a hand to grip the hilt of the sword. He froze, silver eyes wide as his lips moved wordlessly.

He was. . . . Was he struggling with the taint? That was all it took to trigger his tainted thoughts? Or was the darkness always present, and he found it harder to distinguish the truth at times?

She'd never seen Jagger lose control like this. Not daring to make a sound, Ebba watched him fight the invisible monsters in his head.

His mouth stopped moving, and slowly his body unlocked. He straightened and met her stare. She eyed the red tinging the sides of his neck and jaw.

"We need to figure out how Caspian and me fit into all this." Ebba changed the subject, tapping her bottom lip.

Jagger shifted though he retained his grip on *veritas*. "Hard to do in the middle o' the Dynami."

She ignored the slight shake in his voice. "True enough. But I wish I knew why all this was happenin' to us."

"Does there need to be a reason? Sometimes shite things just are."

Ebba thought of everything he'd gone through and conceded the point. Mainly because he still looked a bit ashamed after the sword-clutching episode.

"It was shite what happened to me with Calypso." She rested her chin on her knees and hugged her legs.

"Aye, Viva. Bein' controlled ain't pleasant."

When it came to the taint, Ebba had to agree though she hoped to never be in that position again.

She startled when Jagger held out the hilt of *veritas* to her.

"Hold it," he told her. "The sword don't show truth for anythin' ye haven't already witnessed, but it will for anythin' ye did see. Think o' yer time with Calypso and hold the sword. It'll show ye how things really were. The sword'll help even if it be hard to watch."

For the first time since finding out what *veritas* did, Ebba was tempted. And very, very afraid of going back there. She hugged her knees to her chest and stared at the sword.

"Why are all pirates so scared o' the truth?" he murmured. "That be one thing I ain't picked up. Touch it. Go on."

The sword was shinier than the other parts of the weapon they were assembling. She guessed it hadn't been buried away for fifty years and left to tarnish. Ebba answered his first question. "Because we're all runnin'." She changed the subject. "Will it only show me the part with Calypso? I don't want to know all the truths."

"Like?"

She lifted a shoulder. "I don't know. Stuff I be happy not knowin' that I don't know about."

"When I hold it, I keep my mind on the present moment. If my mind drifts, the sword shows me the truth o' other things—replays my memories to show me the truth o' those moments. It shows me truth and lie, too, one as a glowin' light and the other with a shadowed edge. Ye get used to the shock o' it, and seein' the truth ain't bad at all. Not when ye haven't been able to see anythin' in a long time."

A challenging gleam entered his eyes again.

"It will help ye," he pressed. "Trust me."

She'd already decided she trusted him, but part of her still hesitated. Ebba licked her lips, fingertips extending to the sword.

Jagger leaned forward, crowding close, and Ebba's chest tightened.

Dare. Challenge. Promise.

Overwhelming.

Her breath came quick and, eyes wide, she shot to her feet. Jagger snatched the sword. The blade just missed cutting upward through her torso.

Standing, he rested it against the barrel behind him.

"Viva, it's okay, it's okay," he said, turning back, hands out. "What's wrong?"

He stepped closer. Standing over her.

Ebba gripped the edge of the crow's nest behind her, chest rising and falling as she stared at him.

"It's all right, Viva," he said gently. "Shh now. That's just a bad memory comin' up to grab ye."

Her heartbeat thundered in her ears so loudly she could barely hear him. But she inhaled sharply, slowly recollecting herself as he continued to murmur low and soft.

Shoulders sagging, she let go of the barrel lip, avoiding his gaze.

"Ye should touch the sword," Jagger urged.

Ebba slowly turned away, swinging a leg over. "Nay, Jagger. Not today."

He followed her as she placed both feet on the rigging on the other side. "Are ye sure?"

She stared at the rope squares. "Aye."

Desperate to be away, Ebba made to descend. Jagger reached down and covered her hands with his. Peeking up through her lashes, she scanned his serious expression.

"Ye don't need to be afraid o' me, Viva. Not ever. Ye can trust me."

NINE

Ebba thudded on deck, having taken her time on the way down from the conversation with Jagger.

"Everything okay?" Caspian said.

He peered up the rigging, and she heard the ropes creaking overhead. Ebba didn't turn to confirm Jagger was descending too.

"Aye," she managed. "Learn anythin'?"

The unsmiling prince didn't answer.

"Caspian?" she said, confusion filling her.

He ran his hand through his hair and smiled at her. But the gesture was tight, nothing like his usual grin. The prince peered over her shoulder again.

She fidgeted as the silence between them became awkward. Was this the jealousy Caspian talked about earlier? He'd only mentioned feeling it over her with Calypso, not with Jagger. Was this a new thing?

His smile eased, and he said, "Learning the theory is one thing, but carrying out a task is different entirely. Trimming the sheets on a day like this is different to trimming them in a storm."

"I s'pose so," she quickly agreed, eager to be rid of the weird tension.

The ropes creaked overhead again. Closer.

Ebba didn't want to be here when Jagger made it to the bottom; she was still mortified after her panicked moment. And then there was Caspian's weird reaction.

She took a single step away.

In a hissing eruption of water, Grubby burst from the black sea. A very *naked* Grubby.

Ebba yelped and slapped a hand over her eyes. "Sink me, he needs to ring a bell or swim in clothin'."

Caspian replied, "Don't you find it amazing this man was inside of Grubby the entire time?"

"Not when he be naked, nay."

Wet footsteps approached her, and Ebba jumped at a thud from behind as Jagger landed. Sod it.

"Daughter."

She recognized Grubby's voice. "Are ye dressed?"

"I have a towel around my genitalia, yes."

Ebba was glad she had no idea what that word meant, and she'd be taking absolutely no pains to understand it. She dropped her hand and scowled at the towel around Grubby's hips. "What is it?"

He bowed to Caspian and then addressed her. "My co-parents have informed me at length that I did wrong by allowing you to fulfil your lustful urges with Calypso."

Caspian drew closer, and Ebba darted a look at him, taking in the cool expression upon his face.

"Aye, ye did," she said. "He took over my mind, and I didn't know what I wanted anymore."

"Ah, yes. I greatly underestimated how a full-blooded mortal would be affected by his sway. To me, he merely appeared as an attractive individual, and I gleaned nothing more from your response than my usual response to a woman. But I understand he used compulsion, and I apologize for that lapse in my knowledge and judgment," her selkie father said, regret in his eyes. "Satisfying one's carnal appetites is not right without the will of both parties intact."

Ebba wasn't sure she wanted to discuss the matter with two males her age standing within earshot. "But ye impregnate the women who come to the western Kentro cove."

"They ask us to. That is the difference, daughter."

"Well, aye," she said, wrinkling her nose. "I'd ap'reciate it if ye didn't let Calypso near me again. Or anyone immortal who has the same magic. I don't like to be kissin' strangers."

Mr. Grubby's eyes flickered to where Jagger stood and back to her. Twice. "I see."

Uh. "Nay. Not him."

"Are you sure, daughter? I know attraction when I see it."

A sharp tension filled the air.

Ebba resisted the urge to press her hands into her scalding cheeks. *Grubby did* not *just say that,* she thought, mortified. She floundered for a way to escape from the present company.

"S-stubby, we need to keep huntin' the part down, aye?" she shouted. Loud.

"Aye, when ye're ready," Stubby bellowed back over the wind.

Too late, she realized her error. Her ploy to get away from Jagger and Caspian had resulted in the opposite. They'd have to touch to find the direction again.

Sink her. This wasn't her day.

Muscles coiled tight, she muttered to the men at her back. "Come on then." And then shot at the selkie. "I need the *dynami*."

She caught the reluctance on Grubby's face as he extracted the tube from his vest, and she snatched it from him.

"Are ye sure ye don't want to hold the *veritas* instead?" Jagger asked her.

Being near Jagger was about the last thing she wanted. Added to what happened earlier, there wasn't any way he'd missed Grubby's announcement. She darted a look at his face, her embarrassment flaring anew.

"I'll touch the sword when I be good and ready," she snapped. "*If* I'm ever good and ready. And ye can wipe that smirk off yer face."

He quirked a brow. "Ye know it'd make ye feel better."

"Kissin' ye?" she scoffed. "I don't think so."

A drawling grin crossed his face. "I was talkin' o' the sword, Viva."

Her eyes flew to his. He was right. He hadn't mentioned kissing at all. And neither had Grubby. Not directly. Her entire being flamed with a soul-deep embarrassment that struck her mute.

Ebba became extremely occupied with tucking the *dynami* in her belt.

"But it would make ye feel better," Jagger said low in her ear. "Much better."

Uh.

Ebba studied his boots. If she thought about Jagger's boots, there was no reason to look at his face. Her cheeks were still burning, and Ebba knew he'd catch the embarrassment in her eyes if she lifted her head. As would the prince.

Shite, shite, shite. What did Caspian think about all this?

Jagger rested a hand on the top of the prince's stumped shoulder and darted out to snag Ebba's free hand, squeezing tight. She started to withdraw and then decided not to make a big deal out of it. There had been enough awkwardness for one day. She'd play it cool.

Dreading what she might see, Ebba glanced up at the prince.

White-lipped, he met her gaze with flashing amber eyes.

Sink her, that was definitely jealousy. She'd have to talk to him later. After the Calypso talk with Grubby, the word just slipped out. It was all a misunderstanding. Things between her and the prince were new and uncertain, but Ebba never wanted him to feel something as ugly as jealousy.

She held out her hand, pleading with her eyes for him to take it. Relief coursed through her like a cool breeze when Caspian's eyes softened.

"I know, Ebba," he said with a sigh. "Don't mind me."

And yet the tension didn't dissipate one bit with the oversized presence of Jagger.

Caspian interlaced his fingers with hers.

White light erupted, and after the shocked moment of seeing how they were transformed by the radiance, the three of them stared northwest at the beam.

The warmth of the brilliant sheen basked within her, and though Ebba never liked breaking the connection, this time she *really* didn't want it to end. After what happened with Calypso, the link felt healing. Purging. When Jagger and Caspian tried to pull away, Ebba clung tight to their hands, closing her eyes to take several deep inhales.

She dropped the link, and Caspian looked at her in question.

"I needed that." Ebba shrugged a shoulder.

"Northwest?" Plank called.

Ebba and the others strode toward him and Stubby at the helm.

"Northwest," Jagger echoed. "Again."

"We'll have to put the nets out," Stubby said, fist curling. "Or else who knows how long this might go on."

Grubby hummed. "There are a number of creatures with power under the surface who would object to that treatment."

"Like?" Caspian asked, exchanging a look with her.

He bowed to the prince. "Like Capricorn, Eachies, Jendu, and a Shen."

Plank whistled low, adjusting the green bandana holding back his raven curls. "Aye, we don't want to anger any o' them."

"What are they?" she asked.

"An Eachy be a great slimy creature who lives on the sea floor and eats anythin' and everythin'."

Grubby cut in. "The Jengu are usually pleasant and helpful, but they can curse you with permanent disease if angered."

"Shen can make ye see things that ain't real," Plank said. "And Capricorn be nasty buggers in the tales I know—half-goat, half-fish."

There was a time when Ebba would've thrown back her head

and laughed at the thought of a goat-fish. Though even with all they'd seen, the combination sounded strange.

"The net is all we've got," Ebba said. "Unless whatever be carryin' the next part tires. But that could be days or weeks. Or never."

They stood in silence.

"What about him?" Jagger said.

They followed the jerk of his thumb to Grubby, who looked almost sheepish at the attention.

"My name is *Gustafio*," he replied.

Jagger cut him off. "When we round up livestock on Neos, we surround the beasts on all sides except the direction we want the herd to go."

"That's what we aimed to do with the nets, lad."

"Aye," the younger pirate said. "But ye have a selkie who can go in the water. He can help to trap whatever it is we be chasin'."

Everyone watched as Grubby puffed himself up. He glanced around their circle and deflated. "I *suppose* I could do that."

"Ye'd already thought o' it," Stubby accused.

The selkie threw a hooded glare at Jagger.

Caspian spoke. "It would be ideal if we had an island or rocks of some description to direct the creature into. That's what we used to do on a hunt."

"Calypso's rocks?" Grubby offered.

Ebba shook her head, swallowing hard. "Nay, I ain't goin' back there."

Stubby hummed. "So we'll sail northwest and get Grubby to round the thing off at the top and drive it back toward us."

"Worth a shot." Plank scanned them all. "Let's get to it."

EBBA FOLDED the multitudes of blankets that made up her hiding spot under the hammock, shoving them back in her fathers' trunks in the sleeping quarters. The last blanket was hers, and she folded it, kicking back the top of her second trunk—which contained her clothing—to place it inside.

"I can't hear you practicing," Barrels called from his office.

With her, Jagger, and Caspian checking the direction of the part every half hour, Barrels had allowed her to skip her lesson for the day. The condition being she spell words aloud.

"T-r-u-n-k," she called back.

"Well done, my dear."

All she wanted to do was read her scrapbook, but Barrels had tucked the gift away as though sensing as soon as she memorized the scribblings in there, she'd stop lessons. He was canny, her father.

She threw back the top of her other trunk—the accessory trunk—and stared inside.

"Necklace," she said, screwing her face up. "Nn-eek-lah-ss. N-e-k-l-i-c-e!"

"N-e-c-k-l-a-c-e. Very close. I'm glad to see you sounding things out."

Ebba blew out a breath. This language was stupid. "N-e-c-k-l-a-c-e," she repeated dutifully, drawing out a large strand of beads and then letting it fall back in a pooled heap atop her multitudes of bright fabrics and bandanas. She'd dressed in her usual slops, tunic, *dynami* tucked in her belt, and a black jerkin. *Same, same, same.*

She wanted something a bit different today.

Humming to herself, Ebba sifted through the scraps of fabrics. Some were braided; most were frayed.

The bilge door opened.

"Hey, can ye help me?" she called, knowing it would be either Caspian or her fathers.

"Depends what it is."

She glanced up at Jagger. "What are ye doin'? Ye never come down here."

He quirked both brows. "Gettin' a drink. Is that okay with ye?"

Did that mean the taint was leaving him?

Not rising to his bait, she held out her arms and the fabric. "Can ye tie the fabric around my wrists? I only want them about a third o' the way up my arms."

Jagger glanced around the sleeping quarters. She shook the fabric at him.

Sighing, Jagger set down *veritas* and took a short, braided length of fabric from her. He wrapped it several times about her wrist and then tied it off, leaving the short ends free. He reached for another and she tutted.

"The striped one next."

He snatched the striped one, wrapping it about her wrist. He continued, wrapping three more frayed lengths on her right arm and then started on the left.

"Is that good enough for ye?" he muttered.

"It will do," she announced regally, waving him off.

"I'm so glad."

Jagger left, muttering under his breath.

She smirked after him, but the gleaming silver of the sword caught her eye. He'd left it behind. *No.* He'd left *veritas* right next to her on *purpose.*

Bloody sod.

Jagger's words from the other day struck her, and Ebba stared at *veritas.*

Ducking her head to see between the posts, she checked to make sure the pirate had truly left for the hold and then sat back to contemplate the sword again.

Truth.

Something she'd always done without. Happily so, until a bit of pressure was applied. Then, the little cracks she and her fathers had filled in with dirt were washed out and exposed, very nearly to their demise. Maybe they would've always ended up together again, but as much as Ebba feared losing them or being apart from them, her time on Pleo had been the closest she'd come in her life to wanting to leave them behind. Lies and cover-ups had caused that.

Ebba had decided to stop lying to herself—was even becoming pretty good at it. But so far, admitting the truth had remained in her head, a silent thing. She wasn't quite so good at speaking the truth aloud. If she touched the sword, the truth would *still* be just in her head. Others wouldn't see.

Tentatively, she reached out for the blade, but the same fear from yesterday stilled her hand. Would the sword show her something horrible? Truth was important, but there were varying degrees of it. There was good truth, and there was harsh, bitter truth—like the one she discovered on Pleo about her fathers.

Jagger said if she focused on something, the sword would just show her that. . . .

"I can't hear you," Barrels called.

Ebba jolted. And curled her stretching fingers into a loose fist.

"P-o-s-t," she said, heart thudding. "H-a-m-u-k."

"H-a-m-m-o-c-k," he corrected.

She mimicked him, her thoughts on *veritas*.

Boots appeared in her vision, and Ebba quickly sat back on her haunches, shifting her stare to the pirate.

"Did ye get yer grog?" she asked Jagger unsteadily, knowing he'd seen her.

He grunted.

Jagger picked up the sword and disappeared up the bilge ladder. Ebba let out a long exhale, glad she'd resisted temptation. Two embarrassing episodes in front of Jagger in two days would've been too much.

"S-h-i-p," she called for Barrels' benefit.

Digging into her trunk, Ebba paused as her fingers encountered the woven flax pouch Jagger had given her on her eighteenth birthday.

She drew it out and unraveled the fastening, squeezing the pouch's sides to see inside.

"B-e-e-d-s," she whispered.

Her gaze snagged on a wooden bead with a zig-zag design. Her fathers gave that to her when her first tooth fell out. Ebba smiled. And the purple one with gold dots they gifted her when they accidentally left her ashore building sand castles while they rowed back to the ship. She'd guilted them into that one. Ebba chuckled to herself, rummaging through the beads. Even after having them cut from her dreads and thinking she'd never see them again, she could still recall every happy memory contained within.

Crouched under her hammock, the memory of Jagger gripping the sword and muttering wordlessly to himself rose to the surface. He was trying his best. After seeing Jagger's vulnerability, a larger part of her cared about his plight. Though she had selfish reasons for wishing his success. If Jagger could beat the taint, so could her fathers, and so could everyone else. With his immunity, that didn't make real sense. But her hope didn't need logical facts; it just needed *something* to cling to. And part of why he had to win was because, when things like Calypso happened, Ebba didn't always believe *she* would be all right.

Jagger had to keep fighting. For all of them.

Putting these beads back in her dreads would help him. And help her. It would be a belated thank-you, a sign of her gratitude for him collecting the beads.

"O-n-e," she said as she threaded the first bead back into her dreads.

She couldn't use the same dreadlocks. They weren't nubs that stuck upright any longer, but they were short. She'd been encouraging the new growth to form new dreads, teasing and rolling wax into the hair. The three strands would take years to catch up to her other dreads—if they ever did.

Ebba grabbed the gold thread she'd nabbed from her time in Medusa's Lair. Inspired, she picked up a white dread, one of six bleached of life by the *purgium*. Previously, Ebba had stacked her beads against each other in a solid row. But now, using the lengths of golden thread, she spaced the beads through eight of her dreads, including the front two white dreads. When done, she felt over each of them, wondering what they looked like and hoping the reality matched the vision in her mind.

Ebba was glad she'd changed the placement of the beads. Going completely back to how they were wouldn't be right.

"S-h-i-t-e," she said.

In retrospect, her move seemed . . . bold. Everyone would make a big deal of her beads when they saw her. Maybe she'd hide them a bit.

Leaving them down, Ebba placed a red-purple bandana over her dreads and tied the loose back end in a knot to hold it in place. Relenting in part to include some of her usual getup, Ebba tied a black length of silk around her hips and tied it off to the side of her waist. She pinged the golden hoop already in her ear.

"Ebba?" Caspian called down. She liked him calling her Ebba. He should have done so from the start. Mainlanders and their misplaced manners.

"Caspian," she sang back.

As he climbed down the ladder, Ebba skirted from underneath the hammock and straightened her outfit.

His eyes rounded when he saw her. The prince stopped short and surveyed her.

Striding forward, he picked up one of her dreads. "You put your beads back in." He paused, frowning. "Why?"

"Do I need a reason?" she asked. Her decision was too personal to share.

He thumbed the golden thread and two of the beads, sliding down her white dread and tugging on the end. "Please tell me I'm being a jealous fool, Ebba. But can I ask if Jagger has anything to do with this decision?"

"O' course," she replied, scanning his face. "He gave me the beads."

"No, what I meant was: Is there anything going on between you and Jagger? Romantically?"

What? A short laugh burst from her lips. "Ye're kiddin'." She snorted. Lowering her voice, Ebba asked around a chuckle, "Me and Jagger? Ye're bonkers, matey."

"Just a jealous fool then," Caspian said, darting a sheepish look down at her. "I apologize."

Ebba shrugged. "Better out than in. But just so ye know, I don't like it when ye're jealous. If I ever felt sumpin' for someone else, I'd let ye know. Why were ye comin' to get me?"

He started. "Oh, time to check the direction again."

"Best hop to it then," she said, stepping around him.

She climbed up the ladder, but feeling Caspian's eyes on her from below, Ebba glanced back down.

"Ye're lookin' at my butt," she hissed at him, lips trembling.

Caspian's face flooded red, and as he stammered an apology, Ebba's trembling lips gave way to violent, all-consuming laughter. She clutched at the ladder, but as the gales burst from her mouth, the force of it slowly drained her strength.

"Caspian," she gasped as the waves of laughter wracked her frame. "My arms are gone. I'm goin' to fall."

She heard his mad scramble downward and had the presence of mind to double-check he'd reached the bottom before relinquishing her grip on the rungs.

The force of her fall sent them both to the ground.

Ebba rolled off him, snorting and gulping for air. She clutched her stomach, curling in a ball.

"I'm glad that amused you rather than offended you," Caspian said, a wry twist to his mouth.

Barrels poked his head out of his office. "What's going on?"

"Uh," the prince stuttered.

Ebba's laughter only swelled higher and louder, and Barrels lifted both brows faintly before disappearing back into his numbers-and-letters room.

In the chuckling aftermath, she half-crawled to the ladder. "I'm near-on sweatin', I was laughin' so hard."

"Just so you're aware," Caspian said in her ear, "I enjoy looking at your body very much. I hope that doesn't make you uncomfortable."

Did he now? Ebba smiled widely and propped up on tiptoes to kiss his mouth.

"Oops, I missed," she said, pulling back from kissing his chin. "I'm laugh-drunk, I be thinkin'. And nay, I'm okay with that."

She turned from him and climbed the ladder, burningly aware that Caspian would be watching, but not willing to glance down for fear of laughing so hard she cracked her skull open on a second fall.

Shoving open the bilge door, she wavered toward Jagger, her body still weak.

"Why's yer face flushed?" he asked.

"A laughin' fit."

He peered past her at Caspian, and Ebba glanced back to see the prince grinning widely. She giggled and slapped a hand over her mouth.

Jagger stared at her in disgust. "Did ye just giggle?"

He couldn't be more disgusted in her than she was. "Nay, it was a belch. We doin' this or what?"

The pirate made to reply but then froze, his eyes roaming over her hair. He was in front of her in a second, one hand going to a beaded dread.

"Ye put yer beads back in," he said curiously. He dropped a hand down and touched *veritas*.

Oh, right. "Aye."

The urge to dislodge his other hand threatened to overwhelm her. She wanted to itch her scalp, as though a tiny tingle ran from his fingers, up her dreadlocks, and into her skin.

"You can see them perfectly well with your eyes," Caspian seethed from behind her.

Ebba didn't look back. "Nay, it's okay." Whatever Jagger currently felt was strong, and he could touch her dreads if he needed to.

The pirate didn't appear to have heard the prince anyway. He thumbed the beads and golden thread at the bottom of one dreadlock, expression closed off, silver eyes fixed. He didn't just stop there. Gently pushing back her bandana, he let *veritas* clatter to the deck and trailed his fingertips over all eight strands in turn.

Ebba was transfixed by his expression—equal parts wounded and wonder.

"Excuse me, comin' through," Peg-leg said, elbowing between her and Jagger.

Ebba sighed at her father's intervention, her hair swinging back into place.

"We need to find the direction." Caspian walked up to her side, expression closed off.

Jagger took her hand again, but this time Ebba withdrew, opting to clutch his forearm instead. He stilled but reached out to clasp Caspian's shoulder without comment. She grabbed the prince's hand and, in less time than it took to blink, a white beam shot from their glowing trio into the distance.

Peg-leg shouted to Locks at the helm. "It's headed northeast."

Locks altered their course, causing *Felicity* to lurch in the swell.

"Can we assume that means Grubby's turned whatever has the fifth part around?" Caspian asked.

"He's meant to be herdin' it to us, not sideways—" Jagger started.

The beam shifted.

"Northwest," she called to Locks.

Plank and Stubby joined them, standing just outside their glow to watch the beam.

"That's more like it," Jagger said smugly.

The beam shifted again. Northeast. Northwest. The direction changed every ten seconds, then even that whittled away until the beam jerked erratically.

A geyser of water, much like water forced upward from a whale's blowhole, exploded from the Dynami.

"Grubby's signal," Plank said.

"The thing be near," Stubby told them. "Don't break the co'nection."

She wasn't planning on it.

Stubby hurried to the sheets with Plank, shouting for Barrels in the hold.

Peg-leg made directly for the bow.

Ebba tightened her grip on the others, trying to peer through their glowing aura to see ahead. The beam shifted frantically, twisting and bolting like a fish hooked on a line.

"There be sumpin' in the water," Peg-leg hollered, leaning over the bow.

"How far?" she asked him.

They waited, but Peg-leg straightened, scanning the water. He went to port and then starboard to peer down each side of the ship.

"It disappeared," he announced.

"Shite, it's bloody gone past us again," Locks exploded from the wheel.

Ebba stared at the beam, watching as it looped in a lazy circle about the ship.

The beam pointed directly down.

Felicity pitched and fell back to the ocean. Ebba yelled, glancing up at Jagger and then Caspian, and from the horror in their eyes, she could see they'd come to the same conclusion.

There were many things a ship could do, but jumping wasn't one of them.

She choked out the words anyway. "It's under the ship."

TEN

Something huge slammed into the underside of the ship. Ebba's hand was ripped from Caspian's, her grip on Jagger torn away as the ship began to shudder and jerk. She staggered to regain her balance, but then her feet were leaving the deck entirely. She sailed through the air as *Felicity* pitched upward out of the water.

Ebba cried out, arms flailing as she struggled to make sense of which way was up. Sea spray exploded in every direction. Shouts from her fathers heightened her desperation. Her gaze caught on a piece of the rigging and, pushing away her shock at the sudden height, Ebba twisted her body and stretched her fingertips out as far as she could.

By the skin of her teeth, she managed to latch onto the lowest boom.

But the assault from below the ocean's surface wasn't over. Ebba didn't have time to search for her fathers or time to look for the creature attacking them. She clung precariously to the boom, nails digging into the wood, arms shaking as the lurching, plunge and slap of *Felicity* continued.

And then all went eerily, eerily still.

Ebba pulled herself atop the boom. She'd ended up on the lowest boom, close to the mast.

"Where's Ebba?" Plank shouted.

"Up here," she called, peering down.

Grubby burst from the water and landed butt-naked on deck. Stubby was trying to help Peg-leg up. Plank and Caspian had ended up at the bow, and Jagger at the helm.

"Barrels is below deck," she heard Caspian yell.

All of them were accounted for. Ebba allowed herself a shaky exhale.

"What in Davy Jones' was that?" Stubby demanded, limping up to the naked Grubby.

"*Is* it," the selkie corrected. "It's still here."

Plank wasn't the only one to yell, "What?"

Her fathers surrounded Grubby.

"What is it?" Locks pressed him. "Will it attack again?"

She had to get back down to the deck. But as Ebba made to hoist herself up, her eyes caught on something else.

Something bad.

Gigantic tentacles with suckers the size of her head crept over the bulwarks in every direction. Ebba knew the answer to this one.

"Kraken," she bellowed.

The crew spurred into action, drawing their weapons.

Ebba pulled herself upright and ran to the mast in the middle to assess the situation. Taking tight hold of a sheet in one hand, Ebba drew her cutlass with the other and scanned the deck. Which side needed her most?

Caspian was frozen, staring in horror at the huge, slimy arms of the sea creature slithering over the sides of the ship and onto the deck.

Two of the massive tentacles stretched up for the rigging, weaving around the lowest boom where she stood. The tentacles began working inward toward her.

"I'll handle the ones up here," she called to the others.

Ebba had heard enough stories to know what happened next. The kraken would pull them down into the black depths of the Dynami Sea.

As soon as she had the thought, the kraken did just that. *Felicity* lurched downward.

Crying out, Ebba teetered on the boom, nearly dropping her cutlass in the natural urge to hold on with both hands. Recovering, she widened her stance, frantically looking port and starboard as the two tentacles drew closer to her.

They had to do something. But she could only think of the four magic objects in their possession.

"Can ye heal it, Caspian?" she yelled.

The prince twisted to look up at her and nodded. He leaped into action, sheathing his cutlass to rip the *purgium* free. He edged toward the closest tentacle and held one end of the tube, stretching to touch the other end to the beast.

Nothing happened.

"Bugger," she muttered, eyeing the ever-nearing tentacles either side of her.

The *scio* might help if they could get the kraken's head above water. She couldn't see what use *veritas* would be—except as a normal weapon. That left the *dynami* in her belt.

She counted six tentacles wrapped around the deck, dragging *Felicity* down, excluding the two up with her. The kraken's hold on the ship's hull was the biggest threat. Ebba could hack at the other two—and hopefully not die in the process.

"Plank!"

He craned to look up, and she held the *dynami* aloft, letting it drop into his hands.

"Pull off the tentacles," she told him.

Felicity sank farther into the ocean, and she clung to the mast.

Water began flooding in the scuppers.

Plank tucked the tube in his belt. Running to the nearest tentacle, he peeled the suckers off without effort. The ship hauled from port to starboard side without warning as the kraken's grip was dislodged, and Plank sprinted across to the opposite bulwark, peeling off the three tentacles there.

But the kraken was already bringing the first three back.

The rest of the crew sliced at the tentacles, trying to prevent the creature from regaining its grip.

Hands on his knees, Plank passed the *dynami* to Locks, who took over, moving to the bow and the helm on repeat.

It was working.

As the nearest of the tentacles on the boom slithered closer, Ebba adjusted her grip on her cutlass.

"We'll be havin' kraken for dinner," she said through clenched teeth.

With a yell, Ebba slashed at the nearest limb, smiling ferally as it retracted. She could almost hear the creature's hiss of pain. She didn't wait for the immortal to attack, relinquishing her grip on the sheet to follow up with another slash and another.

She chased it back to the tip, jabbing and thrusting savagely at the tentacle as she shuffled along the boom. When the kraken drew the tentacle off the boom and below the surface, she hollered, "Ye ain't havin' our ship."

"Grubs," Peg-leg called. "Can't ye help it see reason?"

Panting, Ebba turned away from the water to glance down as Grubby dove overboard. She struggled to hear the rest of their conversation over the pouring and hissing water.

When had that started?

It sounded a lot like when she stood from a bath and water fell off her body in torrents. Except much, *much* louder.

Swallowing, Ebba pivoted as a shadow fell over her.

She swallowed a scream.

The kraken sat at eye level with her. Its eyes, the size of barrel ends, glowed an ugly and sinister red. The blazing orbs sat within the head of an octopus twice the size of their ship. The creature had a beak—was that normal?

She frowned at the sharp edges of its mouth. The kraken snapped, and Ebba jumped.

Her hold on the rigging slipped. She windmilled her arms, crying out wordlessly as she toppled past the point of return.

And began to fall.

Air rushed past as she hurtled toward the deck, eyes blurring. The scream torn from her lips cut short as she came to a jarring halt, her head whipping back against a soft, slimy surface.

She'd stopped falling.

She hadn't landed on the hard deck.

Ebba glanced down at the thick tentacle wrapped tight about her middle. The kraken caught her. Phew.

The kraken caught her!

Ebba shrieked, kicking and thrashing as the sea creature drew her to its snapping beak. Yellow teeth, the size of short swords, appeared each time the kraken opened its mouth.

Her crew shouted her name.

She couldn't spare another breath to scream.

Her cutlass was gone; her arms were trapped at her sides. In her peripheries, she was aware of the kraken's other tentacles beating down on their ship. Wood splintered, shards flying past her face and bouncing off the monster's bulbous head.

Its grip was so . . . very . . . tight. Ebba dragged in a breath, but it wasn't enough. She stopped kicking, her thrashing weakening, weakening, until she couldn't keep it up.

Ebba slumped, resting her head on the creature's tentacle.

Scales larger than her hands covered the kraken's tentacles. Innumerable hues of purple and blue and silver folded together creating a masterpiece. She flopped her head back as black crept into her vision. Droplets of water and the kraken's blood were everywhere, chaos reigned, and her vision tunneled on the kraken's burning eyes. "Yer scales be so beautiful."

So tight.

The creature reared, but Ebba couldn't keep her eyes open any longer. She listened to the droplets of water returning to the ocean surface with a hiss. She smiled as the splintering of wood stopped and as the anarchy faded to calm.

The tentacle loosened around her, and without conscious effort, she sucked in a massive breath, coughing pathetically. She didn't even have the strength to lift her head.

The monster shook her, and Ebba's teeth rattled.

"What did you say?" The words were barely discernable through a series of clicks.

Ebba gulped in more air, clinging to consciousness. The wind whooshed in her ears as she was moved downward in a blur and carefully laid on a wooden surface.

Hands clutched at her.

"Give her room to breathe, ye dolts," Locks said.

"Make her talk." The clicks came again.

Had she died and gained the ability to speak kraken? Or was the kraken one of the immortals capable of speaking pirate?

"Uh . . . we'll be tryin', great kraken, but it may take a while. Ye cut off her breathin'," Plank said.

Her father understood the creature. Unless Plank had the *scio*, the kraken could definitely speak pirate.

Hands rolled her, and she continued to breathe through the dizziness assaulting her. Slowly, her inhales evened out, and some strength returned to her body. Ebba opened her eyes to see her fathers. Or four of them.

Their joyful expressions turned into alarm as tentacles flicked them away like flies.

The kraken loomed overhead, blotting out any trace of the sun. Her eyes widened as it hovered right above until its eyes were once more on level with hers.

"What did you say about my scales?" the kraken asked, beak snapping with every word, *very* close to where her innards wanted to stay inside her body.

Ebba opened and closed her mouth. "W-what?"

"My *scales*," the kraken said. "You said something about them. What did you say?"

Did it . . . just roll its eyes?

Ebba tried to recall her delirious thoughts, a wrinkle between her brows. "I said that I thought them right beautiful."

The creature reared back and clapped two of its tentacles together. "You said they were soooo beautiful."

What. In. Davy. Jones'. Locker?

Turning her head to the side, she locked eyes with Stubby. He appeared as baffled as her.

Ebba peered past him and took in the ship. The deck was *destroyed,* cracked and pitted all over. The mast was still up but on one side, and where the kraken had caught her, the lower boom was demolished. Water sprayed up in several places from holes in the hull.

She struggled up. "Barrels," she rasped through her sore throat. He was below deck.

Caspian heard her and inched toward the bilge door. "I'll find him."

"Why is your face like that?" the kraken demanded, bringing its head down. She fell flat again as it poked her in the side a few times with its tentacle.

She wheezed, "Like what?"

"All horrified. That's all I ever see," the kraken said woefully.

The creature had just destroyed *Felicity*. What did it expect?

Ebba managed to prop onto her elbows. "I'm not horrified at ye so much as horrified at what ye've done to our ship."

The glow of the creature's eyes dimmed as it pulled back and surveyed the ship. Then the glow blazed again. "You were chasing me. Hunting me down like so many before you. And do you know what I did to them, female mortal?"

She gasped, quickly nodding.

The kraken stilled. "You . . . you do?"

"Aye," Ebba rushed to say. "Ye latch onto the ship and pull them to Davy Jones'."

"I would *never*," the kraken said, holding a tentacle to its chest.

"She means the deep sea, Mr. Kraken."

The creature glared at Plank. "I don't like that name."

Ebba sat up. "What's yer name then?"

"You're only talkin' to me because ye don't want to die."

"Aye, but also because yer much di'ferent from what I thought ye'd be."

The kraken flopped across their bow, a tentacle over its eyes. Two of his tentacles crashed down on their bowsprit, snapping the jutting point clean off. Stubby groaned low.

Ebba glanced around the ship again. Was the water level of the ocean that close before?

"Tis my curse to be misunderstood," the creature said, sighing heavily.

Ebba got to one knee. "Well, if ye'd like to convince us otherwise, ye're more than welcome. My name be Ebba-Viva Fairisles."

He lifted the tentacle and studied her. "I don't have a name. People always call me kraken."

"But ye said ye don't like that name," she said. "We'll just have to pick ye one sometime. It ain't nothin' to be destroyin' things about."

"You seem nice," the creature clicked. "I've never really stopped to talk to one of you before. How do I know you're not mean? You were hunting me."

Ebba got to her feet and stepped toward him. "Let me clear the huntin' thing up. We weren't after ye. We were lookin' for part o' a weapon that we need to save the realm. Is there any chance ye have it?"

"A weapon?" the kraken's eyes popped, and he covered his mouth with a tentacle tip, only dropping it to say, "A *quest*. Do tell."

Locks murmured in her ear. "The ship be sinkin', lass. Is there anythin' ye need?"

"What are you speaking about? Are you plotting against me?" the kraken roared, making her arm hair stand on end.

"Hold on a minute," Ebba said, her heart sinking. "Our ship be goin' down, and my father's askin' if there's any keepsakes I need."

"Oh . . . sorry. I'll wait."

She couldn't even think about losing *Felicity* right now. The ship had always been in her life. But with a kraken before her, sinking down to cry or running about in a panic wasn't an option. Ebba's thoughts went to her beads, but they were back in her hair. "Just the scrapbook if it ain't already damaged and the bangle Marigold gave me. It be in my port trunk."

Locks nodded and hurried off.

Jagger approached on her other side.

The creature's eyes sank to what he held. "You hurt me with those sharp things."

"Sorry about that," Jagger answered. "We were tryin' to save the ship. But this one is special. It makes a person tell the truth."

"You lie."

"Then let me lay it upon ye and ask ye a question," the pirate said plainly.

The kraken narrowed his eyes but dangled a tentacle before Jagger. She and her crew had done a number on the sea creature. Cuts marred the length of all his limbs barring one.

Jagger laid the flat of *veritas* against a sucker. "What be yer saddest memory?"

The kraken's eyes bulged, and the answer rushed from his beak. "My mother was killed by hunters seeking a trophy. Five ships. I watched it all from below. She sank down past me afterward. They'd cut her beak and eyes out and taken three of her tentacles."

Ebba covered her mouth. "I'm so sorry," she whispered.

"My mother and father were killed," Jagger replied quietly.

The kraken studied him. "Your sword works. I tried to resist and couldn't. Rest it on Ebba-Viva Fairisles, please."

Jagger did as bid.

"Ask her if she really thinks my scales are beautiful," the kraken demanded.

Ebba was beginning to think the creature might have a vain streak. But something about him reached in and squeezed her heart. To her, he seemed unbearably lonely. And she feared that fate enough to not want another to suffer it. Even if he'd destroyed their home.

Jagger reached forward and gripped her arm, making her realize she was weaving on the spot. "Are ye okay?"

Felicity was sinking. "Aye," she replied.

He let go but hovered close as he rested the flat of the blade on her palm. "Do ye think this creature's scales are beautiful?" Jagger asked her.

The urge to tell the truth was undeniable.

"Aye," she answered. "They be made up of so many purples and blues and silver; I know there be too many to count, and I can't sort them into just one color. I could look at your scales all day."

The kraken turned away and appeared to wipe his eyes. He didn't turn back but said, "Ask her if she was hunting me."

"Were you huntin' him?" Jagger asked softly.

"Nay," she obeyed the *veritas*. "We were tryin' to catch ye but only to find the next part o' the weapon."

The kraken spun around, sending water pouring over the deck. "A weapon? I don't have a weapon. You've got the wrong guy."

Ebba sighed. Great. But that was a worry for when the ship wasn't sinking.

The kraken wiped his face again. "Are you mad at me for breaking your ship?"

Jagger repeated his words.

Ebba glanced around. "I ain't mad so much. Though yer nature don't give ye the right to hurt others. I'm mostly just sad, and I don't know what life will be like now *Felicity* be sinkin'." Her breath caught. "I've spent most o' my eighteen years aboard her. She's my hhome." She blinked back tears, trying to remember there were more pressing matters.

Jagger lifted the sword, and when she stumbled, he wrapped an arm around her shoulders.

"We can heal yer cuts for ye," Ebba told the creature, sniffing hard.

She turned and saw Stubby and Peg-leg still stood there, silently watching in case the kraken turned ugly again. Locks was readying the rowboat—Plank, too, she assumed, considering he was nowhere in sight.

They'd brought out five barrels. She watched as they disappeared below deck again and scanned for Caspian.

He crouched by the bilge door over a motionless Barrels. She gasped, and the prince glanced up.

"He's okay. Breathing," Caspian called softly. "Looks like he was knocked out by something in the hold."

Ebba sighed in relief.

"Where's Grubby?" she blurted.

Pushing away Jagger's arm, she shouted her question, spinning in a circle. "Where's Grubby?"

The kraken lifted a tentacle. Wrapped inside the slimy limb was her father.

"You mean . . . this one?" he asked her.

"Grubby," Ebba choked, clutching her chest in the panicked second it took to remember her father could breathe under water.

The creature appeared a smidgen guilty as he laid Grubby on the butchered deck. "I was hoping you wouldn't notice. Sorry, I don't like selkies."

"I'm with ye there," Stubby called over their heads.

Grubby was pale. His head was covered in blood.

Ebba whirled on the kraken. "What did ye do to him?"

Peg-leg and Stubby dropped down beside her.

"Knocked in the noggin'," Peg-leg declared.

The creature's tentacles lowered. "I stopped killing him when you spoke to me. I was going to tear him in two, but I didn't."

Heat crept up her neck.

"On tiptoes, little nymph," Stubby muttered under his breath.

Right. They could still be torn apart.

"He's breathin', but his eyes be all wonky. Look," Stubby said.

Ebba turned back. Grubby's pupils were different sizes. "Will he be okay? The *purgium*"

Peg-leg shook his head. "After last time, I'm not sure, lass. I say we keep that for a last resort."

She deflated. But he was right. They had no idea if the *purgium* had just healed Grubby's head last time or the taint as well. Did it heal one thing or both? And if the taint wasn't gone, and the *purgium* healed him, Grubby might die.

Ebba rubbed her temples.

"Is the *purgium* what you were going to use to heal my cuts?" the kraken said. "Because I'd appreciate that. My flesh doesn't knit together; I'll just form big scars, and it'll be harder to move. You should've seen my grandfather in the end. He was practically immobile." The kraken shuddered.

Jagger answered, "Aye." He glanced at Ebba.

Still seething at the kraken for hurting Grubby, Ebba nevertheless strode to Caspian and held out her hand.

"Are you injured?" he asked.

"Nothin' that won't heal itself," she said. Which meant the *purgium* wouldn't bother. It only dealt in the permanent and terminal.

She gripped the tube but gasped as a buzz akin to lightning struck her momentarily dumb. In a daze, she pulled up the leg of her slops. Before, scabs had covered them. *Now*. . . . "Forgot about those."

"What did it take from you?" Caspian said, frantically searching her limbs.

The prince turned over her right hand and they stared at her blackened fingernails, leached of the usual fleshy pink color. As though hammers were brought down on each one in turn.

Ebba turned over her left. The same. "That be right fierce," she promptly decided.

The prince hummed. "Uh. . . ."

"Ye don't like them?" she asked, holding both hands out to study her darkened nails. "I do. The shanties about me just became next level."

Not waiting for a reply from Caspian, she approached the kraken. "The *purgium* will only work if ye've had an injury, inside or out, that will leave ye with a perm'nent change. And ye should be warned that—"

The creature was darting peeks at her, its eyes just visible over the splintered remains of the bulwark.

Ebba sighed at the sulking kraken. "Ye have to understand that my fathers be the most precious-like thing to me in the realm."

"How many do you have?" the kraken squeaked.

"Six," she said, glancing at the unconscious Barrels and Grubby. "And I don't know what I'd do without them."

"Six?" the kraken asked as he held out a tentacle to her. "Is that normal?"

"Nay," she said. "And I'll tell ye how it happened another time, if ye should like."

The creature's cheeks lifted in what Ebba assumed was a smile.

She pressed the *purgium* against the kraken's cuts and watched as the creature jolted. Ebba's mouth dried as at least half of the creature's suckers disappeared.

"Sink me," whispered Peg-leg.

The cuts healed. Ebba rotated in a circle, watching as all of the kraken's cuts faded . . . and more suckers disappeared.

"Whoa," the creature said with a click.

Ebba gripped the tube tight, ready for his wrath. "Uh . . . some of yer suckers be gone."

"I wish the rest would go." He scowled.

Peg-leg and Stubby shared a relieved look.

Felicity lurched, and the kraken jolted in alarm, lashing out a tentacle. There was a mighty *crack,* and Ebba watched their figurehead—the mermaid that had always rested on the bow—sail through the air and hit the water in the distance with a faint splash.

Her heart plummeted to the bottom of the sea.

No ship could survive without a figurehead. Every pirate knew that.

"Abandon ship," Stubby called dully.

The order was a physical blow. Ebba squeezed her eyes shut and absorbed the pain of it. She couldn't think about losing her home until everyone was safe.

Jagger spoke to the kraken. "We need to get in the rowboat now, but will ye wait?"

Ignoring the kraken's reply, Ebba strode with the others up to the starboard side where Grubby was being lowered into the smaller vessel.

An escaped sob had her turning back.

Plank stood in the middle of the ship, his feet far too close to the top of the greedy water. He stared into the black sea, face wet from the torrents of tears spilling from his eyes.

"Plank?" she asked, taking a step in his direction.

Did he hear her?

Ebba's legs unlocked. She hurried back, taking her father's hand. "M'hearty, I know it be sad, but we need to get off the ship."

Though Plank cried, his dark eyes were vacant. "Nay, I'm with her until the end. All this time, I should've been with her."

She reeled from him, lips numbing. "Ye don't mean to go down with the ship. Ye don't mean that."

Ebba spun away, searching the deck. "Locks."

He glanced up, one leg over the bulwark.

"Plank said he ain't comin'."

It wasn't clear if Locks heard her words, but those still on deck turned back at the panic in her voice. Two of her fathers slipped down the slanting deck to join them.

Felicity groaned, and the helm began to steadily submerge. Huge bubbles erupted around them. And *still*, Plank didn't budge.

Ebba gripped his wrist. "Ye're comin' whether ye like it or not," she snarled at him. Why was he doing this? Everyone else was as devastated, but no one was stupid enough to take it to mean they should drown along with the ship.

"Nay, little nymph." Plank shook her off. "I'm stayin' here."

"Ye fool. Get off the ship. Right now."

He knelt. "I was never meant to be parted from her. I know that now. Leave me here. I'm ready."

Ebba gripped his belt and pulled in earnest as *Felicity* began a steady descent. "Then ye'll kill me too. I ain't leavin' without ye."

That roused him. But only to argue the case. "Ye can't stop this."

"I can," she said.

Locks and Stubby reached for her father. Ebba gasped, staggering back as Plank swung at Stubby, nearly connecting with his jaw.

Locks tried something different, wrapping his arms around the other man. "We know, matey. We know what she means to ye. But ye can't be doin' this."

"I told ye I'd only stay until the ship sank."

"And we told ye that was fine, but we were lyin'," Locks said gently.

Water crept up over their boots, and urgency clawed at Ebba's throat. There wasn't any time for this. She turned to the kraken who watched with rapt attention. "Can ye put him in the boat for us?" she asked.

The kraken stirred uneasily. "I don't want to get involved in family drama," he hedged.

"Ye're clearly content-like to watch it. He's only sad because ye damaged the ship." Ebba hurled the accusation. "Please, can ye help instead o' watchin'?"

The three of her fathers were struggling. Plank fought to free himself from Locks as Stubby shoved both of them in the direction of the rowboat. Ebba stared around what remained of *Felicity*'s slanted deck and swallowed. The others were already over the side and shouting for them.

She placed her hands on her hips and faced the kraken, who rolled his eyes.

"Fine," he said, puffing out a breath.

The grunts and yells of her struggling fathers turned to yelps of surprise as the kraken wrapped all three in a great tentacle and lifted them over Ebba's head.

She climbed up the deck and peered over the side, scanning the rowboat. "Barrels, Grubby, Peg-leg, Caspian, Jagger, Locks, Stubby." She glanced at her last father. "Plank."

"Get in," Jagger said, jaw clenched.

"Have we got all the parts?" she asked.

Caspian held up the *purgium*. Ebba could see the *veritas*. The *dynami* was still tucked in Plank's belt. "The *scio*," she shouted. "Where is it?"

Stubby righted himself from where the kraken had dumped him unceremoniously in the rowboat. "I have it on me, lass." He felt in his vest and drew out the tube.

"*Now*, will ye get in?" Jagger said.

Ebba swung her leg over *Felicity*'s bulwark and hardly needed the rope ladder's help, so far keeled was the ship as it sank.

Her feet made a hollow thud as she descended and accepted Jagger's hand to steady herself. He immediately flipped her hand, studying her new dark nails, and grunted before releasing her.

"I can paint yers if ye want," she shot at him.

She avoided looking at Plank, who was pinned under Locks on the boat floor and struggling to throw off the larger male, glancing back at the ship instead.

Her chest squeezed to near-unbearable levels. *Felicity* was sinking.

This was really happening.

"Let's row, lads," Peg-leg said, face pale and drawn. "We want to be out o' here to escape the tow."

Jagger and Stubby grabbed the oars and Ebba took a seat at the front of the rowboat by herself, staring at *Felicity*. The pace was slow-going with their load, and a leaden quiet settled heavy upon the occupants of the vessel.

As the distance increased between them and their destroyed home, so too did the oppressive silence.

She'd crawled upon those cedar decks. Then she'd stumbled, walked, run, jumped, climbed. The wood there was smooth from her presence; the rungs of the ladders, the posts holding her hammock, the lid of her trunk, and the edge of the crow's nest. She *knew* that ship. If Ebba had six fathers, *Felicity* had always been her mother.

Just the bow of her mother was visible now. It was as if a real person drowned before her very eyes.

Ebba's chin trembled as she remembered *Felicity*, the rock of her, the rich worn smell, sitting out on the bowsprit as the sea spray washed over her. She remembered years of happy times, of climbing the rigging, of listening to Plank's stories, of singing bawdy shanties to pass the time. Of hiding below her hammock when she was sad or afraid or upset.

Of the first time she navigated the ship.

Swinging upside-down from the rigging to scare her fathers.

Believing she was climbing the rigging into the very stars.

Ebba watched as her home, her *memories*, and all the warm familiarity that came with it was forced vertical in the black waters of the Dynami. Their home began the final descent, and she looked at the bulwark for the last time, the bilge door, the bow.

Her beloved rigging.

She choked on a sob as *Felicity* went down, down. As the very tip of the bowsprit disappeared.

Down.

And when only bubbles remained, Ebba hung her head.

She hung her head and let the tears fall.

ELEVEN

How quickly the tide turned.

For hours, they'd taken turns rowing, unspeaking in the shocking wake of their loss. Eventually, they stopped. Their aimlessness felt right, a reflection of their grief, perhaps.

The kraken swam next to the rowboat. After trying to engage each of them in conversation to no avail, the creature had taken the hint and settled into silence.

. . . If she'd known upon waking that *Felicity* would be gone by the day's end, would she have acted differently? Would she have taken more of her possessions?

That was useless thinking now.

Felicity was gone.

The sun's rays had disappeared long ago. Ebba doubted anyone had slept. She hadn't slept a wink.

Now, as the weak sunlight transformed black to charcoal gray again, Ebba inhaled, twisting to scan the rowboat's occupants.

Plank sat in the middle of the boat on the floor, dark circles under his eyes, hardly blinking. Since his crazed words about going down with the ship, he hadn't made a sound. For the first time in her life,

Ebba was afraid of one of her fathers. Or for him—of what he might do. That man back on *Felicity*. The one willing to drown. She hadn't known him. Plank had slipped out of her reach in that moment, and Ebba was yet to regain a grip on him. Whatever sat behind his panic and despair was unfathomable—and currently too much to contemplate with her own grief.

Barrels regained consciousness sometime in the night for a few moments but quickly slipped back into slumber. He had a multitude of cuts on his face and clearly hadn't fared well in the hold when the kraken first attacked. Caspian was right. Something must have struck Barrels unconscious. Or he would have burst up onto the deck shortly after the initial attack.

She skimmed her eyes over Stubby, Jagger, and Locks. Caspian lifted his head when she turned his way, but Ebba quickly glanced away, not ready to see whatever might rest in his amber eyes.

There was a new distance between them. Perhaps just in her mind, but right now, Ebba didn't want to talk to someone who didn't understand. And Caspian didn't, *couldn't* truly know how losing *Felicity* felt. Even when he'd lost his home to the six pillars, he'd worried more about his people. She understood that, having been just as worried for her fathers. But he'd never had a home he depended on for survival. He'd never worked in tandem with a ship to navigate the seas. Ebba didn't want to look in his eyes or hear his sympathy.

She wanted *em*pathy. True understanding.

Grubby lay at the center of the rowboat, under the benches so he could be flat and in relative comfort—as much as could be had while laying atop coils of rope and tools. She pivoted on her bench seat at the front of the rowboat. Grubby's feet were at her end, and she peered between two of her fathers to the opposite end, trying to see his head. Her part-selkie father hadn't awoken yet.

"Is he breathin'?" she whispered to Stubby, seeing his eyes were open.

Stubby bent down. "His pupils be the same size now. What does that mean?" His voice was hoarse from disuse. Or from hours of crying, like her.

"Not a clue," she answered.

He sighed heavily and straightened. "Could ye pass me some grog?"

Ebba nodded and swiveled back to the bow. Grabbing one of the four ropes there, she heaved. Moving hand over hand, she pulled in the string of barrels bobbing out over the line. Her fathers had managed to haul ten barrels up from the hold to bring with them. Three contained food, one contained their prized possessions, and the rest were filled with grog.

The first barrel on the line was grog. She worked at the cork, holding the barrel still with her arm. She swiped up a goblet from the bottom of the rowboat and carefully rolled the barrel, holding the goblet flush so the nutmeg mixture could trickle in.

She passed the goblet back to Stubby.

"Want one?" she asked Plank.

He didn't reply.

"I will," Jagger croaked from the bench next to hers.

She filled another goblet for him and then Peg-leg and Locks before grabbing one for herself. She corked the barrel again and let it drift back out to join the others.

"Where are we?" Caspian asked as everyone began to shift in acknowledgment of morning.

Everyone glanced to the sky, but the Dynami always had been dark and cloudy, and it was no different just because they now needed the stars to navigate.

"What's that you're drinking?" the kraken called from where it swam lazily twenty paces to their right.

Ebba held up her goblet, finally feeling sorry enough for him to answer. "Grog."

The kraken drifted closer. The glow from the creature's red eyes had faded entirely, and Ebba watched as he observed their exhausted and dispirited group.

"You're all so sad," the creature said, his tentacles drooping. "I really made a mess of things."

Allowing her sadness to become anger would be easy, but Ebba wouldn't resent the kraken. She'd regret what they could've done differently. She'd play the 'maybe' game. But they'd cornered a live being. If cornered, Ebba would fight too. The kraken wasn't to blame. None of them were. Was that why she felt so unsettled inside? She wanted to rant and rave but had no real outlet for her anger.

"It weren't yer fault," she said. Reaching out a hand, she patted a tentacle drifting by.

The creature sniffed, blinking rapidly. "You're just being nice," he said, harsh clicks punctuating the words. "You probably don't want me around anymore."

The ocean didn't belong to their crew, and she'd never felt any right to tell the beings within it, fish or otherwise, that they couldn't live in certain parts. "Nay, that ain't the case at all, matey," she replied. "Ye're welcome to keep us company. Just don't destroy this rowboat. It be the last vessel we have."

"I want to stay. But do you want me here?" he asked.

Ebba glanced at her fathers.

Locks replied after peering at Plank. "We don't begrudge ye for the ship. Ebba-Viva be right. There ain't no one to blame for what happened. Just a . . . misunderstandin'."

The rest of her fathers, barring Plank, mumbled their assent—Stubby's more of a choke.

"Thank you," the immortal said, his eyes shimmering. "I never knew people on ships could be nice. I might've stopped to get to know a few before devouring them."

"Uh, ye're welcome," she said weakly.

"I'm so glad I met you, Ebba-Viva Fairisles."

"Me too," she grunted.

The kraken held the tip of a tentacle to his chest. "In fact, I'm so very glad I'm going to tow you all to the nearest island."

They stared at the creature.

Stubby blew out a breath. "That'd be right good o' ye. We have no idea where anythin' be in these seas and only so much grog and food." His eyes narrowed. "But what would ye be wishin' in return?"

"Nothin', nothin'," the immortal assured them with flapping tentacles.

The crew relaxed.

". . . But now that you mention it, there are a *couple* of things."

Ebba withheld her groan. Great. The offer was too good to be true.

The kraken held up two tentacles either side of his head, sucker side up. "The truth is: I eat ships. And a lot of other things. But my temper has been worse recently. I have some debris stuck in my teeth, and I've tried everything to get it out."

Caspian said, "You want us to get it out? How did it get in there?"

"I was swimming along, thinking about devouring ships—I get carried away sometimes when that happens. Makes me really mad. I was distracted and mistook a bit of debris for a fish. So, here's my deal with your crew: take the debris out of my mouth, and I'll take you wherever you want."

She exchanged a long glance with the others.

"And you have to give me a name, just whatever you think suits me," he gushed.

That was easy enough. It was the first part of the deal that seemed dangerous.

"Oh, and you all have to be my friends."

They didn't really have a choice. After checking in with the others, Ebba turned to the kraken. "Ye have yerself a deal."

"Let's get to it then," Jagger said.

Everyone turned to watch him, including the kraken.

Their ship had just sunk. There wasn't anything *wrong* with getting down to business, per se, but it just came across as so . . . so cold.

"We don't need to do that just yet, I think," Caspian said to the pirate in undertones.

Jagger shrugged. "No time like the present. Not like we're doin' anythin' else."

Ebba sucked in a breath.

"Have some decency," the prince scolded him. "They just lost their home."

And here she'd convinced herself that a mainlander couldn't understand. Ebba met the prince's gaze, and they stared at each other, his amber eyes filled with sorrow and regret—hers no doubt bloodshot and red-rimmed.

"Aye, they did. And they'll find another."

Her fathers stirred, and Ebba clenched her teeth alongside their low rumblings of disapproval.

"Do ye hear yerself?" Peg-leg asked him. "There be strength, lad, and then there be plain cruelty."

Her father had twisted on the third bench so only a few handspans separated his face from Jagger's.

Jagger didn't shift back from the cook's harsh expression.

"I be hearin' myself just fine. But ye listen, all o' ye. Do ye know how many people don't have a home at all? Do ye know how many spend their life searchin' for one, never content with what they find? Do ye know how easily a person may be ripped from everythin' they know? What yer feelin', that deep achin' loss, that can be a madness, too. That urge to remake what ye once had, to never be happy without it. I've seen it happen. I've felt it more times than I can count. And so aye, be sad. *Felicity* was yer home for a long time. But don't let it become madness because walls don't be makin' a home; the people inside the walls be the essence. If ye lose sight of why we're here, then ye'll risk yer home in truth because ye're playin' with the lives of yer loved ones."

Ebba couldn't tear her eyes off Jagger in the wake of his speech. Oddly, despite the harshness of his demeanor and initial comments, his words *righted* something within her.

A quick glance around told her the others were as affected as she was. Plank's face was wet again.

Jagger's lips were pressed together so hard they were drained white in some places. His shoulders moved with his impassioned breaths.

She leaned forward and touched his knee. He'd opened his mouth to continue, but whatever he'd been ready to say halted on his lips at her touch.

"Ye're right," Ebba said softly.

The pirate closed his mouth and jerked his head in a shallow nod.

Barrels groaned, and Locks leaned over to pull the older man's hands from the cuts on his head.

"None o' that, matey," he scolded.

"I feel like shite," Barrels moaned.

If he was speaking pirate, he really felt bad.

Locks helped him sit and, in short succession, helped her father chunder over the side. Ebba didn't envy the nausea or the headache he likely had from whatever had struck him.

Her eldest father leaned away from the water after, wincing, his eyes crinkled in pain. He reached into the top pocket of his vest and drew out a handkerchief.

The simplicity of the action tickled her fancy and Ebba cracked a smile. "Only ye would bring a handkerchief along with the ship sinkin' behind ye."

She chuckled, Peg-leg and Stubby adding a few quiet chortles as well.

Barrels didn't seem to appreciate the joke. "It was on me, my dear. I got hurt retrieving your scrapbook when I realized the ship was sinking."

Ebba was glad to have it. But her crew's safety was the most important thing. "Thank ye," she said. "But I don't like that ye got hurt gettin' it."

"It was a tad foolish," he replied. The boat rocked gently as Barrels tied his peppered hair in a fresh ponytail and tucked his handkerchief away.

"Sit tight, now," Locks told him. "Let's look at yer cuts."

Barrels sat still as Locks prodded at his head. "What did I miss? I only remember snatches. Did we run into an outcrop or something?"

The kraken groaned, and Barrels peered over his shoulder. The color remaining in his face drained in an instant. Barrels swayed where he sat, and Locks wrapped an arm about his shoulders to stop him toppling backward out of the rowboat.

. . . Her eldest father was yet to glimpse the kraken. *Oops.*

"Don't panic. This be. . . . Well, we need to name him yet, but this be the immortal who sank our ship." She trailed off into a mumble.

"Oh." Barrels puffed the word, swaying again.

The kraken lifted a tentacle out of the water and waved.

She released her pent-up exhale, wondering if her father would collapse in a dead faint. But despite his pallor and clear horror, Barrels wheezed, "A pleasure."

"The pleasure is all mine," the creature replied.

Ebba glanced at him. "How is it ye speak our tongue? Some immortals we meet don't."

"Depends how much magic you have, but I taught myself," he said, lifting up in the water. "It gets boring out here. Not many people visit, and those that do, I eat. But you can only listen to the smaller creatures under the surface for so long before craving some change. The rest of my kind were pretty stodgy and refused to speak in the mortal tongue, so I used to sneak up and listen to mortals. Took a while to perfect," the creature clicked, and Ebba focused to separate the words. "But," the kraken continued, snapping away, "I barely have an accent anymore."

Stubby cleared his throat. "Ye know the Dynami Sea fair well then, matey?"

Jagger perked up and Ebba glanced at him.

The kraken inspected his tentacle, brushing it on his vast octopus head. "I may know a few places."

"Where are we?" Jagger pressed.

"In the water."

"Aye, but where in the water?"

The kraken's tentacles drooped. "I mainly specialize in what's under the surface."

There was a collective sigh from the boat. He'd kept *that* quiet during their negotiations. But maybe he could still dive down and get his bearings.

Jagger stood, knees bent as the boat rocked. She watched the muscles in his legs move to keep him stable. He wasn't overly muscular, erring more on the side of sleek grace than brute strength, but no one could think Jagger's body was anything other than powerful.

Ebba blinked, realizing what she was doing.

"Right," the flaxen-haired pirate said, silver eyes gleaming. "The sooner we get to land, the better. So open yer mouth, and give us a look at this debris."

"My mouth?" the kraken said. "Like, just one?"

Ebba's mouth dried.

Caspian asked, ". . . How many mouths do you have?"

The creature's beak opened slightly. She glimpsed his massive blue tongue feeling around as he checked. "Hmm, four? Five? I'm all teeth inside aside from my tongue, so it's hard to put a definitive number on it. All just feels pointy to me."

Peg-leg laughed. Without a speck of humor.

She'd cursed the deal by thinking of how easy it would be.

She shot a look at Plank, waiting for him to interrogate the kraken further. Her daydreaming father didn't utter a word; he wasn't even looking at the kraken. He sat facing in the opposite direction, staring at the vast black sea.

Jagger paused and then shrugged. "Well, open all o' them, I suppose."

"Okay. Sure."

The kraken reached out and stilled their sideways drift with a tentacle at either end of the rowboat.

"Gentle with her," Locks said. "This be our last ride. I know ye're only haltin' us, but break this one, and we're goners."

The kraken drooped. "I promise to be careful."

They didn't have much of a choice but to accept that as the immense magical being lowered his head until his beak was directly before Barrels and Stubby. The kraken opened his beak, and Ebba craned to see. She stared in mounting disbelief as, like the petals of a Venus fly trap, the first mouth unlocked. Through it, the second mouth unlocked in the same manner, and then the third, fourth . . . fifth . . . *sixth.*

Six mouths! Her jaw dropped.

Between the first and second mouths was enough space for a small person to stand, but the space between the mouths grew smaller and smaller as they disappeared into the kraken's beak. The inside of the creature's cheeks—at least that's what Ebba assumed the inner walls of his mouth were called—were embedded with the dagger-like teeth, too. In fact, only the kraken's flat blue tongue interrupted the pointy daggers he used to chew who knew what.

The kraken's oral cavity was like a dark, wet cave embedded with daggers, with six trapdoors made of swords that could scissor shut at any time. His tongue was the only pathway to the back.

"Sink me," Locks whispered.

"Aye," Stubby chorused. "That's about the size o' it."

Size.

Everyone turned to peer at Ebba, and she gulped.

Her voice was strangled. "Can ye feel where the thing is in there?"

They watched the teeth surge and ebb as the kraken replied with all his mouths open. "Ahh, righ at the back, I fink."

"We could use an oar to loosen it? He might be able to work it forward himself after." Peg-leg got the idea ball rolling.

"Bang on the outside o' him?" Locks added.

Ebba stood and propped a hand on Peg-leg's shoulder, brushing past the still-upright Jagger. Careful not to jostle Grubby, she balanced in front of the kraken's mouth and held a hand over her mouth and nose to ward off the smell of decay.

"Wah's hapnin?" the kraken asked, swallowing. The back teeth snapped together like clashing cutlasses.

"Shite," she muttered, the blood draining from her cheeks.

There was only one way to get the debris out, and that involved a person small enough to climb inside the creature's mouth to retrieve it. Her crew ranged in size from Grubby, average pirate height, to Jagger, oversized. No one even came close to her petite stature.

"Nay," Plank said.

It was the first word he'd ventured, and for some reason, hearing his voice annoyed her. She ignored him, addressing the kraken. "The only way to get it out is for me to climb inside o' yer mouth."

"Wah?" the kraken squeaked. ""Cun y'see it?"

"There be sumpin' at the back," Jagger said. He was also standing, squinting into the dark depths of the kraken's mouths.

She followed his gaze. "Where?"

"At the back. Right upper corner."

Ebba peered into the darkness. Scanning left to right at the back. He was right, something *was* shining. All of the kraken's teeth gleamed but were yellowed. The debris wasn't yellow, it was—

"Silver," she gasped, turning to Jagger.

He nodded, eyes flashing with excitement. "Aye, Viva. I think we just found the next part."

"What's goin' on?" Locks demanded.

Ebba faced the others. "We think the fifth part be wedged in his teeth."

The gasps of her fathers and Caspian rang out.

They'd known the part was moving around. The beam of light had shown them that the kraken had the fifth piece of the root. But when she'd seen him and then questioned him, Ebba had assumed the beam was pointing elsewhere. This was why the immortal had no idea what she was talking about.

She'd been so shocked after the attack and the sinking of *Felicity* that she hadn't put two and two together when the kraken mentioned debris in his teeth.

Stubby looked into the immortal's mouth. "I can't see anythin'."

"Ye're sure, lass?" Peg-leg called over.

She glanced at Jagger. "Nay, I'm not. Are ye?"

Jagger pressed his lips together. "It'd make sense, wouldn't it? Why the part was movin' around. Even if it only be a theory, we still need to check it ain't the next part."

Her thoughts exactly. And if the debris was a piece of the root of magic, walking into a kraken's mouth seemed like a breeze compared to all the other things they'd done to win parts. Every other part they'd encountered was guarded by an immortal. Had the kraken eaten the guardian of this piece?

She wouldn't put it past him.

"Whu ah yu sayn?" the immortal asked.

The creature closed his beak, and whatever blood had remained drained from Ebba's face at the guillotine sound.

"We're thinkin' the debris in yer teeth be one o' the parts we're lookin' for," she said to him gravely. "But the thing is that yer teeth be awful sharp, matey. Can ye swear not to swallow or close any o' yer mouths while I'm inside gettin' it out?"

"I swear not to eat you. Hold on," the kraken said, swallowing several times. "I want to start fresh. Now that you've said not to, swallowing is all I can think about."

Great.

Caspian gripped her arm. "No, Ebba. It's dangerous. I can probably fit in there."

She looked away from where the kraken still swallowed and regarded the prince in doubt. "I don't know what space ye're lookin' at. And it be dangerous for anyone goin' in. I'll be fine." She rested a hand on the kraken's beak and looked into his huge eyes.

"Ye won't hurt me, will ye?" she asked, feeling like a mere droplet in front of an entire ocean.

The kraken darted its eyes to where her hand rested on his beak. He swallowed again, hard, and gazed back at her. "I won't hurt you, Ebba-Viva Fairisles. I swear it."

"There," Ebba said, casting another look at the prince. "Ye heard him."

Peg-leg nudged her on the other side. "Stay in the middle, on his tongue."

Well, she was hardly going to roll across the cheeks embedded with teeth.

"We should wrap her forearms in case she falls off the tongue into the teeth either side. It might help," Jagger said, studying the kraken. "And sumpin' around her torso. Unless he swallows her, she should be okay."

Should be.

"Belts," Stubby said, already drawing his off. He reached around the back of her and looped the belt above the one she had on. He pulled it tight, far beyond the last hole in the leather, and sighed. "Look at ye, ye scrawny wee thing. Ye only need a quarter o' my belt. Makes me feel right fat, that does."

Ebba grinned and scratched his stubbled jaw before leaning into kiss his cheek. "Ye are fat, m'hearty. But ye're over thirty, so that's nothin' odd."

"Ah the disillusionments of youth," Barrels sighed. "I remember, in my teens, believing my life would be truly over by thirty."

It would be. Everyone knew that was what happened. Ebba stayed quiet, however—due to the number of over-thirties onboard.

"Here's mine," Locks said.

His belt was secured above Stubby's, and then Barrels' and Grubby's and Caspian's. She was covered from hips to the underside of her chest. Jagger leaned in with his belt in hand and smirked at her as he made to secure it above her breasts.

Peg-leg snatched it away, whacking the pirate with it. "I'll be doin' that."

Her father secured the last belt higher on her chest, over her heart and breathers.

"I kind of feel like Marigold," she said. "Ye know how she's always trussed up to look skinnier?"

"Yes, my dear," Barrels said. "Perhaps don't mention that when you next see her."

Seeing Marigold again seemed optimistic given their current predicament.

Next, Stubby removed his sashes and wound them about her forearms. He peered into her face. "Ye be careful, lass. Walk on tiptoes, and put those sea legs to good use."

"I'll watch my step," she said, hoping that was a promise she could keep.

Squaring her shoulders, Ebba turned to face the kraken.

"Ready?" the kraken asked.

What in Davy Jones' was she about to do?

Mute, she dipped her head, but her eyes rounded as the creature unlocked its six mouths again, each gate peeling outward in four sections like the petals of a flower. Jagger and Stubby held her hands as she stepped into the kraken's beak. Once she was stable, she let go of them and stepped forward onto the immortal's large blue tongue.

She gulped and glanced left and right at the teeth of his first mouth. Wicked daggers extended from the purple-pink of his gums. Ebba stepped through the first lethal mouth into the small space on the other side.

"Naooo," the kraken said. "Tickles."

All light disappeared. The creature's teeth snapped together, ringing high like the hiss of two clashing blades. Ebba shrieked, hearing her fathers' yells outside. She only had an instant in the stinking pitch black before the kraken's mouths opened again.

Her exhale shook—for good reason. If she'd been a hand-width farther in or out, she'd be mincemeat. And all because the sea monster was ticklish.

"I'm okay," Ebba called.

"Are ye sure?" Peg-leg's frantic voice echoed back.

She chose not to answer that and instead took another three steps past the second row of teeth, pausing with bated breath in the relative safety of the next gap. The space here was smaller than the last. If she was unlucky, that trend would continue.

Although used to fishy aromas, Ebba still gagged at the smell drifting up from the kraken's throat and stomach. But forcing that to the back of her mind, she hunched and shuffled forward through the next set of teeth.

Three down.

The piece had twinkled from the back, but she wasn't going in any farther than she had to. Ebba glanced around her, squinting to see in the darkening space.

Nope, not here.

Hunching, she continued through the fourth mouth. The gap between the kraken's mouths now wasn't large enough to protect her if he decided to shut them.

A cursory glance told her the fifth part wasn't here either. Not wasting any time, she bent in half to get through the fifth.

Something arrested her movement. Ebba tried to step forward again, but was jerked to a halt.

"I'm stuck," she hissed.

The third belt around her torso tightened under her chest.

"Are you hooked on a tooth?" Caspian called in. "Try moving backward a bit."

She attempted that, but the teeth were crisscrossed like a rigging made of swords—a way to ensure none of the kraken's prey escaped, no doubt.

Ebba shook her head—there was nothing for it. She undid the belt and turned, working the leather off the sharp tooth it had caught upon. The belt slid free and she wrapped it back around her waist, fingers fumbling.

"Ye may wish to hurry a scant bit, lass," Peg-leg called. "His eyes are waterin' sumpin' fierce."

The part had to be in the last mouth.

She'd need to get onto her hands and knees to get through the last mouth—no easy task with a belt corset on. If the tube wasn't there, they were screwed because beyond the sixth mouth was the pitch darkness of the kraken's throat. Her breath echoed, alerting her to the steep drop ahead. And Ebba could imagine the fall into the kraken's throat would only be interrupted by yellow dagger teeth sticking out in all directions.

Ebba crawled forward to the sixth mouth, breath held and nose scrunched. Even on her hands and knees, the teeth of the mouth scraped against her back and wrapped arms. She winced as the razor-sharp protrusions scratched the unprotected outsides of her thighs.

It was too tight.

She'd have to peer through the sixth mouth instead. She took shallow inhales to limit the effect of the smell and poked her head through the mouth. She glanced left, squinting into the grimy teeth, and skimmed her eyes across the teeth bordering the top, searching for what she'd glimpsed from outside. Nothing.

Carefully moving her head to peer right, Ebba tried her best to otherwise remain still.

There.

Up in the right corner. She'd never fail to recognize that silver glimmer. The part had wedged itself in a small gap formed by three teeth.

"Shake a leg, Ebba-Viva," she whispered.

"Anythin'?" someone called in.

"Aye," she replied under her breath, unsure if shouting would tip the precarious balance.

Ebba reached up, and her fingertips slipped against the pointed end of the tube. It wasn't enough to get a grip. And it'd need to be yanked out. She really didn't want to think about what that might make the kraken do.

She had to get in there.

Ebba drew her legs underneath her and huddled in a ball to inch through the sixth mouth, pressing her lips together as teeth scraped along the belts covering most of her back.

Once inside, she very carefully lifted her hand to encircle the tube's spiked end. Ebba tensed her arm and then halted.

"Can ye warn him that I'm about to pull hard?"

Voices murmured, and Caspian's voice was strained as he answered, "He's ready."

Ebba yanked. Her elbow jerked into the teeth behind her, and she let go. Swallowing her shriek of pain, Ebba took a few deep breaths before sliding her arm off the teeth behind.

She gasped at the sting, cursing loudly.

Glancing up again, she cradled her elbow. The tube had barely budged.

"Flamin' sod," she muttered.

Arm aching, she reached up again and twisted instead. The tube had gotten in there; surely that meant it could come out. Ebba twisted to the left and froze when the resistance lessened. Ebba tugged and the tube slid out a little. She pulled again and gained some more. Ebba settled for small jerks on the object, ignoring the mounting burn in her bleeding arm.

"Come on," she grunted.

Any outside sound was muffled by her harsh breathing. Ebba worked the tube, twisting and pulling, just as fearful of the part sliding free as she was of it being stuck for good.

Her yanks were weakening, and Ebba dropped her hand to shake strength into her limb.

The kraken groaned, and Ebba ducked into a ball as the teeth constricted, grazing her thighs and belted hips. She bit back on a scream.

He settled again, and forcing her aching arm up, Ebba gripped the protruding end of the tube and jerked it roughly.

This time, her arm didn't wrench back into teeth. Instead, her entire body toppled with the force of her pull as the tube slid free.

Doom filling her, Ebba held her arm down against her torso and screwed her eyes closed as she fell against the row of teeth to her right. She cried out in a pitiful wail as multiple teeth entered her side, some of the sharp points finding a way between the stacked belts.

Dots filled her vision, and Ebba focused on the pain, forcing them away.

She couldn't lose consciousness in here.

Too scared to make a move without taking stock, Ebba peered down. Her heart stopped as she realized she'd dropped the part.

Felicity was lost because of this silver cylinder.

There was nothing for it.

What came next would hurt regardless.

Ebba gritted her teeth and, with a low moan, pulled herself off the spikes. She swayed in a ball from the throbbing pain, shaking her head to be rid of the ringing in her ears.

Where was the fifth piece?

She stilled as the kraken's tongue moved and the piece began rolling away.

Abandoning all caution, Ebba threw herself flat as the tube began to tip down the kraken's throat.

TWELVE

She let her head sag onto the kraken's blue tongue, no longer worried about the smell or the teeth or *being here*. She'd nearly lost the fifth part.

Her fingers complained at the tightness of her grip on the tube, and the injured muscles at the back of her upper arm ached in protest. Ebba placed the tube sideways between her teeth and began to shuffle backward out of the creature's many mouths. She didn't dare slow her pace.

On her stomach, digging in her bleeding arms and legs, she worked her way back through the sixth and fifth mouths, through the fourth and third mouths.

Hands grabbed at her feet.

"Ugh," the kraken said, back mouths snapping closed. "Augh!"

Ebba tore the part from her mouth, gripping it tight as she quickened her backward wriggle. "Don't ye dare!"

An inch from her face, his second mouth snapped shut.

"*Augh-choo*," roared the kraken.

The helping hands of her crew were ripped away as Ebba *flew* from the kraken's mouth. She was sneezed over her fathers' heads.

Their shocked faces barely registered before Ebba realized the kraken had sneezed her *beyond* the security of the rowboat.

Well beyond.

Ebba broke the surface of the Dynami Sea with a slap that would have her smarting for days, but the stinging heat was lost as black water closed over her. Bubbles erupted in all directions, stealing her sense of up and down, and still the force of the kraken's sneeze shot her downward into the abyss.

She held her breath as her uncontrolled hurtling through the water slowed. Not for a second did she relax her death grip on the weapon part. But she unfroze enough to draw the cylinder to her chest and cradled it tight.

Peering around, she released a bubble and watched the direction it rose in, and then began kicking in the direction of the surface.

Something brushed against her leg. She ignored it.

. . . Probably nothing.

Please be nothing. The mind played tricks underwater. The whir of a current or floating seaweed grew in the skull to become sharks, rays, and sea monsters.

A hand clutched her foot.

Harder to ignore!

Her chest had tightened already, and Ebba's remaining air left her breathers in a bubbled expulsion. Her legs worked double-time, yet as she neared the surface, her muscles ached from lack of air. Her heart stormed in her ears. Her kicks became feeble. The thing beneath her grasped her feet in an unbreakable hold.

Ebba's chaotic upward surge ground to a halt. Until. . . .

She was *pushed* up.

Not just pushed. As her eyes began to close, her arms were extended and wrapped around two bodies who supported her to the top.

Ebba broke the surface and dragged in a breath that was half water. She choked and coughed, strung out between *who knew what* as her body demanded she focus on survival. Spluttering, drawing in painful gasps, she cracked open her eyes, wincing as salt water stung them.

Blinking, she looked side to side in tired bafflement at the creatures under her arms. Ebba stared. And when the pressure under her feet disappeared and a third creature popped up, Ebba stared some more. At what she believed to be . . . a mermaid.

Their form resembled *Felicity*'s sunken figurehead, yet their hair wasn't smooth and flowing but matted with shells and seaweed and piled atop their heads like one of Pillage's hairballs. Their skin, where it showed on their faces, arms, and part of their chests, was a faded red like a dying sunset. From the waist down, their bodies were covered in deep red scales the size of Ebba's dark fingernails.

Glancing down, she caught sight of their large fish tails waving languidly beneath them.

All three of the mermaids were smiling, their teeth square and spaced apart and their eyes watchful—though crinkled in a similar way to Barrels' when his numbers tallied up right.

Ebba cleared her throat. "Ahoy."

The creatures jabbered at her in unison, melodious voices clamoring in an echoing ring. The one to her right patted her, clucking, the sound like the peal of a bell. The one on the left pursed her lips, shaking Ebba's forearm in an admonishing kind of way. Meanwhile, the third spoke at her as she continued swimming in a wide circle. Inspecting her?

They could've been calling her fish lips, and Ebba wouldn't have known, but their kindness and worry seemed plain. Her fright dispersed somewhat. "It's been a helluva day," she told them.

The two mermaids touching her melted into her sides, hugging her tight. Impossibly, Ebba could almost *feel* their love for her.

. . . Odd.

Shouts and splashes pranced across the black surface, and Ebba squinted into the distance for her fathers, silently hurrying them along. Who knew what else lurked in the depths.

"Over here," she shouted to her crew.

That kraken had a bloody strong sneeze.

A large swell rolled in from her left. Ebba glanced back and nearly screamed. The kraken peeked above the surface, just his eyes showing. Which was to say his entire forehead too. So a mass about half the size of a ship was visible.

"Ye didn't chomp me." Ebba attempted to console him.

The kraken emerged a little more. Not enough to fully show his beak, so as well as the clicking, a loud gargle accompanied his reply. "You got the thing out. I can feel it."

He sighed, and water sprayed from his mouth as the gargle turned into a geyser. "My mouths close properly again. Hey, how many mouths do I have?"

"Ugh." Ebba's mind stalled as she recalled the seven-inch daggers he called teeth. "Uh, s-six."

"And that's it? You have the thing?" he asked, staring at what she still clutched in one hand.

Ebba shifted her gaze, warmth hitting her chest. The mermaids either side of her sighed and nuzzled in.

"Aye, it be the fifth part," she said.

"It felt a lot bigger—"

The mermaids listened to the conversation, heads tilted to the side as they swiveled between Ebba, the kraken—who they didn't seem to fear—and the approach of her fathers.

Ebba inhaled, suddenly exhausted. And only a speck of her fatigue originated from almost being eaten, punctured and drowned. The rest was simple heartache.

"Matey," she called to the kraken. "Can ye introduce me-like to yer friends here? They saved my life." Or nearly killed her, but considering there were three of them and they really liked her, it was in Ebba's best interest to go with the former. Especially seeing as they held her up in the water. She couldn't feel her wounds from the kraken's teeth through the cold of the sea, but no doubt they'd make themselves known soon enough.

The kraken slapped a tentacle to his forehead several times.

"Where are my manners? These are the Jendu." He lowered his voice. "Sorry, they're so annoying. I sort of have a deal with their kind."

Ebba stared at him as she processed that. One, seeing as the Jendu didn't react to that comment, they clearly couldn't speak pirate. And two. . . . "How long have they followed the rowboat for?"

"Since we became friends."

Was that what he called destroying *Felicity*?

"Ebba!"

She waved at her fathers, attention still fixed on the kraken. "So what's yer deal with them?"

The monster dropped his gaze, swishing a limp tentacle through the water before him. "I protect them from the Capricorn."

He continued swishing the tentacle, avoiding her eyes.

"And. . . ," she prompted.

"And they don't curse me with disease for that one time I accidentally ate one of their babies."

The kraken wailed at her shocked expression, the thick tops of his tentacles shaking like shoulders as he sobbed. "I didn't know," he clicked, chopping up the word. "I thought it was a red fish. We get those here."

The kraken was one accident after the next. Perhaps the Jendu had cursed him with bad luck instead.

"They have one of my scales and say they'll work their magic unless I'm their constant bodyguard." The kraken sniffed.

"Why don't they just curse the Capricorn instead o' threatenin' ye?" she asked him.

The kraken rolled its eyes. "Did you even hear a word I just said? They have *my* scale, not one of the Capricorn's. Plus, their curses stick better on land-beings. Being out of water makes me feel fat, but I can cross an island if I have to whereas Capricorn are confined to water. Makes me more curseable."

Ebba stared at him, briefly distracted by thoughts of him slithering across land. What would that even look like?

"Lass." Stubby leaned over the lip of the boat, reaching for her. "Are ye okay, lass?"

Her crew's faces showed alarm, barring Grubby whom she couldn't see. Even Plank had roused himself, concern rampant on his face. Caspian was pale. And dare she even think it, but was there a flicker of apprehension in Jagger's silver orbs?

"Aye, a few wounds in me but nothin' too serious, I'm thinkin'." She was definitely bleeding, and who knew what her blood would draw to this spot? She should get into the rowboat now.

"Let's get ye in." Peg-leg's throat sounded clogged.

The Jendu either side shoved her down under the surface, their hands raking her skin and scalp, tearing at her clothes. They wrenched her up again and Ebba emerged to yelling and swinging oars. The Jendu's eyes were huge as they backed away, dragging her with them as though she were a prized doll.

"Wait," Ebba spluttered.

When the yelling faded, she repeated, "Wait. Who has the *scio*?" No way was she trusting the yet-unnamed kraken to smooth this over, considering his ability to attract drama and his unchecked interest in witnessing it.

Barrels stretched out to hand her the *scio*, and Ebba briefly noted that she was yet again holding two of the weapon's parts before turning to the Jendu she was clamped against.

"What was that just now?" Ebba asked.

"You stink," the one who'd been circling earlier sang.

Ebba's brows lifted. Maybe the kraken was right about them.

The patting Jendu clucked again. "What Emphamiza is trying to say is, you were in baby-slayer's mouth."

It certainly hadn't smelled like good things in there. "That's fair enough then, Emphysema."

"We were cleaning you, mortal," the third Jendu said, flashing her the half-apologetic, half-admonishing smile.

Ebba cleared her throat after noting the heightened concern on their faces. Did Jendu always get this attached? She called to her fathers, "They were cleaning me."

Locks threw his hands in the air. "Can ye tell them to make it look less like they be drownin' ye next time?"

"My fathers thought ye were drownin' me," she explained. "That's why they were swingin' and cussin'."

All three of the Jendu appeared mortified. One of the creatures holding Ebba swam to the rowboat and clutched Caspian's hand. "But please," she said to the baffled prince, "we would never kill your daughter. We, we. . . ." The Jendu blinked. "We love her."

What now?

The Jendu who was speaking appeared to be as confused as Ebba. She shook her head and said, "I mean, we revere our young too." She accompanied that with a scathing look at the kraken, hissing, "Baby-slayer."

"You have terrible hair," the kraken replied flatly.

Ebba had to give him that. She repeated the Jendu's words for the rowboat—the amended version, not the 'we love her' weirdness. She watched Caspian stammer away the title of father and the way Jagger's lips spread in a wide grin the longer it went on.

"Thank ye for yer help," Ebba said to the sea people as her fathers' outrage simmered and then extinguished altogether.

"Pass it here, would ye?" Locks took the *scio* from her and then faced the Jendu. "Thank ye," he said simply. "Our daughter is our world. We owe ye a debt."

She sucked in a breath. Her fathers didn't hand those out every day.

The Jendu spoke to him, their voices intertwining in pleasant song that was just a jumble to her now. The *scio* really was underrated, she realized. So much could go wrong without the ability to communicate.

Ebba removed her arms from over the two immortals' shoulders and then grabbed the lip of the rowboat with her free hand. Plank reached down and hooked his fingers around one of the many belts still layering her torso and heaved her inside.

Ouchie, ouchie, ouchie.

She brought half the Dynami with her, but that was the least of her concerns. Sprawled over Grubby's limp feet, Ebba didn't immediately move, now keenly aware of every wound she'd received in the kraken's mouth.

"Yeouch," she gasped, shifting her hand to hold the wound over her right ribs as Locks kept up his conversation with the Jendu.

A hand shook her shoulder. "Are ye okay?"

Ebba lifted her eyes and merely looked at Jagger.

His eyes raked her body, settling first on her thighs and then on the hand she'd pressed against the belts—more importantly, against what lay beneath them.

"Ye're hurt," he said in a low voice. Jagger leaned down and picked her up, his feet either side of Grubby's.

With her in tow, Jagger stood on one foot and—in what had to be one of the most impressive displays of sea legs she'd ever experienced —used his other foot to nudge her unconscious father's legs out of the way.

Jagger barked at Peg-leg to move and then deposited her carefully between two benches—her head on one bench, butt on the bottom of the rowboat, and legs propped over the next bench seat.

"I'm all right," she complained, flustered by the lingering feel of Jagger's arms on her body. "Don't make such a fuss."

Locks appeared in her vision. "I'll be the judge o' that."

Jagger sat next to her as Locks began unbuckling the corset of belts.

She glanced down. Her slops were stained pale pink from where her thighs bled. The ocean had washed away most of the red, but she could see fresh blood oozing up through the material.

One stab wound high on her right haunch was making itself known, along with the one on the back of her elbow, but the worst pain was all for her right side. She relayed this to Locks, who grunted.

He left the belt underneath her hand in place and freed his dagger to slice through the bottom laces of her jerkin. He lifted the bottom half of her tunic.

The faces overhead gasped, the kraken joining in as he blotted out all trace of the sky above.

"Ye've got a lot of scratches, lass. But the one under the belt be the only one that worries me. I'll leave the belt there for the moment. It be stoppin' the better part of the bleedin'. Are ye breathin' okay?"

Ebba inhaled. "Aye, think so."

"Let me know if that be changin'." Locks lowered the tunic and returned to her legs.

"Are the Jendu gone?" she asked as he hacked off her slops into shorts.

"Aye, little nymph," Plank said. "From our sight at least."

She lolled her head toward him, searching his face. "Are ye back then, m'hearty?"

He swallowed and smiled but made no answer.

The smile was forced. The dreamer's glaze to his eyes had peeled away and left behind rotting deck boards. Ebba had no idea how to fix a deck with only rotting boards to work with.

Her attention was stolen by Locks' prodding fingers. She bit down on her lip.

"He got ye good a few times, lass," he said quietly, directing the others to rip the lower half of her ruined slops into strips and wash them in the seawater.

"Brandy," he ordered.

Silence reigned.

Locks glared over his shoulder. "Stubby, ye hoardin' sod, give me yer brandy. I know ye brought some. I need it to a'hygiene her wounds."

Pain was coming.

Ebba braced herself as Locks uncorked the bottle of brandy with his teeth. Her eyes found Caspian's for an instant before her father took a long swig and then tipped the alcohol into the wounds on her thigh.

One hand was pressed against her deepest wound, but Ebba lifted her other hand—gripping the new part—and pressed it in a fist against her mouth. She shrieked behind closed lips, and her blackened nails cut into her palm as Locks continued, dousing both of her bare legs.

He squeezed her shoulder. "Those be done."

The gentle peal of bells rang across the water.

"The Jendu say we should put this under the binding," Barrels said, holding up a bunch of flaccid purple seaweed, the *scio* in his other hand.

Locks stared at the sea plant. "What is it?"

Barrels turned back to ask the Jendu, saying after, "It will draw out any infection from the baby-slayer's teeth. And help the bleeding stop. They seem insistent that their 'dearest one' must stop bleeding as soon as possible."

Aye, the rum belonged in her body, not out. Ebba shrugged as Locks glanced her way. "Sounds like we better use it, then."

Her father placed the seaweed over her wounds, keeping back a few pieces for the punctures on her stomach and right arm. He took the strips of her ruined slops, soaked in seawater, and bound the seaweed in place. She sighed at the instant cooling on her skin. Some of the ache leeched from the stab wounds.

"That seaweed feels good," she said. "Say thank ye to the Jendu, please."

Barrels repeated her message. "They just keep saying no blood, no blood."

"Why?" Jagger asked. He glanced at her father, making her aware he'd been staring at *her* beforehand.

"You got the next part, Ebba?" Caspian called from the opposite end as the others conversed.

The part was in the fist she'd held against her mouth. She lowered her arm. "Aye, I did."

"Read it then," Peg-leg urged. "What does it say, lass?"

Barrels straightened. "Yes, my dear. Read it aloud."

"Ye're kiddin'?" Jagger said. "Ye want to do a readin' lesson? Now?"

Her father's eyes narrowed, but he didn't answer.

Ebba stared at the writing on the new tube, but as Locks tied off the last of the rag bandages on her thighs, she gave up.

She slapped it into Jagger's palm, and his eyes flew to hers, widening into huge circles. He gasped and she jolted at the shocked sound.

The part tumbled from both of their hands, rolling over Grubby to land on the bottom of the rowboat.

"What's wrong with ye? What happened?" she demanded, staring at him. "And why are ye pantin'?"

Jagger's throat worked several times before he tore his attention from Ebba and bent to pick up the tube.

He read the word etched on the side of the part, still breathing heavily.

Ebba exchanged a look with Stubby. "Jagger? Are ye okay?"

He glanced up at her, shoulders tensing. "*Amare*," he said. "It says *amare*."

"*Amare*," Caspian said, scrutinizing the object. "Love."

The prince lifted his chin to regard Jagger. "What did you just see?"

"Nothin'," Jagger said shortly, shoving the tube at Peg-leg.

"Sink me, I don't want it." Peg-leg surged to his feet. The boat rocked violently.

Jagger tried to shove the *amare* at Barrels next. *He* held a hand to his mouth and waved the thing away.

"I'd rather not," Barrels said.

"Don't even think about it," Stubby growled at the pirate, hands lifted defensively.

"I'll take it," Locks offered over his shoulder.

"No!" several of her fathers yelled in unison.

Jagger shoved the part at Caspian. "Take it, landlubber."

The prince whipped his hand behind his back. "I can't hold it; I only have one hand. I need it."

"Good lad," Peg-leg said with an approving nod. "Told ye pity could get ye things. It's a currency of its own. But turn up the sadness a mite."

"Ye're usin' yer arm as an excuse," Jagger grated. "The *purgium* be in yer belt. Put this one in yer belt too."

"Aye," Caspian said in relief. "I can't hold two at once. I'll be blasted away. Might destroy the rowboat."

"Viva can, maybe ye can too." Jagger's eyes darkened as he leaned to slip the part in the prince's belt.

"I'll take it," Plank said quietly.

"Uh," Barrels replied after a beat. "Are you certain that's wise?"

Plank raised his head, reaching out a hand without further comment.

Jagger shrugged and thwacked the tube in her father's palm.

"I'll fix up yer chest wounds now," Locks told her.

He rolled the bottom of her tunic higher, winding back the wet material to the only remaining belt that covered the deepest of her wounds.

Locks tapped the hand she kept pressed over the belt and wound. "Give me a look then, lass."

Sighing, Ebba lifted her hand, and with nimble fingers, her father undid the last belt and hurriedly directed Jagger to press down on the bared wound.

He did so, picking up some of the seaweed and the last of the rags from her torn slops. He placed this over the jagged, flapping wound just under her ribs and pressed down firmly.

"Yeouch," she spat at him.

"Would ye rather bleed to death?" he shot back.

If it would prove him wrong? . . . Maybe.

Ebba averted her eyes, except rather than ignoring his presence as she'd intended, she glanced down her body, realizing just how little she was wearing. Her slops resembled some odd version of shorts that stopped at the top of her thighs. Across her chest, her tunic and jerkin were in place, but below? Bare skin.

Torn skin, but bare nevertheless.

She changed without a thought below deck. But here . . . on this rowboat . . . with Jagger's hands on her stomach, it was . . . different.

Ebba watched his hands on her stomach and chicken bumps erupted over her tummy. She shivered violently.

Brandy sloshed over her, and she yelped, taken unaware. She tensed, toes curling, jaw clenching until the stinging pain began to ebb.

"All right, lass, now the big one."

Ebba glared at the brandy bottle. "Aye, go on then."

Jagger lifted his hands, and Locks poured. The burning brew hit the edges of the torn skin, and Ebba cried out, beads of sweat breaking out on her forehead.

As the pain dissipated, she relaxed her head back with a thud on the bench behind her. "That hurt."

"The wound be shallow," her father said, inspecting the injury as he cleaned it. "Just long and ugly. I'd usually sew it up, Ebba, but I don't have my supplies. I'm afraid it'll be a ropey scar."

"There's the *purgium*," Stubby said.

Caspian folded his arms, peering between him and Peg-leg. "Is using the *purgium* on a whim wise?"

"Mayhaps not." Peg-leg pursed his lips.

Ebba was happy with just six white dreads, and she could handle black nails. The rest of herself could stay as it was. "I'll just heal natural-like, I think."

Locks tore the bottom of her tunic off. Washing the strips in seawater, he bound the seaweed in place against her wound.

Bells sounded again from the water. The mermaid creatures were back.

"The Jendu are very adamant that we must not put more blood in the sea," Barrels called when the immortals' bell-like voices faded. "They look irritated."

Jagger shook off his hands from where he'd washed them in the Dynami.

"They say why?" Ebba asked, eyelids heavy as Locks finished his ministrations.

"They're gone again. They seemed afraid."

"Ye know," she said with a yawn, "they were actin' right weird before. Sayin' they loved me and huggin' me close and all sorts. If the new part be love, do ye think that was the *amare* workin'?"

She glanced at Plank, but his gaze was fixed on the *amare*. He gripped it with both hands, his eyes a million miles away. While daydreaming wasn't unusual for him, the anguish reflected there was.

And unwanted.

Ebba didn't want any of her fathers to feel pain. When they felt pain, she felt pain.

"Seems likely," Peg-leg said, scratching his chin. "I mean, they didn't do the same to any o' us. Though, we are men." He froze and darted a look at her.

"True." She nodded, not bothered by the mention of her gender. "I hadn't thought o' that."

Peg-leg relaxed and jerked his head at the *amare*. "Did it make ye feel love, lass?"

Ebba thought back. "Nay, I don't recall so. Though the third Jendu, the one not touchin' me, didn't seem affected. Just the ones huggin' me were actin' odd-like."

Barrels hummed. "So the bearer must be touching another person to make them feel love."

"But I didn't feel love while in the kraken's mouth, and I was touchin' him," Ebba trailed off, darting a look at the kraken bobbing beside the vessel.

This gave her father pause.

"Where was the *amare* in his mouth, my dear? Was it just touching tooth or flesh?"

"Just tooth."

"Perhaps then," he said excitedly, "we can assume the *amare* must be touching flesh to influence another."

"I held the *amare* in my teeth on the way out." Ebba recalled. "Until he sneezed, then I put the piece in my hand."

Maybe Barrels was right.

Jagger scoffed. "I thought this thing we be buildin' was meant to be a weapon."

"Aye," Ebba said. "What use is the *amare*?"

Plank turned to look at her with red-rimmed eyes. "Love is a weapon, Ebba-Viva."

He never called her Ebba-Viva, always little nymph.

Something deeply disturbed him. She hadn't forgotten the conversation as *Felicity* disappeared. Plank had a deal with her fathers that had ended when the ship sank. Though she'd seen him ready to go down with their home, Ebba couldn't accept that he'd wanted to die back there. Why would he want to leave? His words didn't connect with her. That they originated from pain, she was sure. But how could love be wielded?

"Aye?" she whispered.

He broke their stare. "It's the strongest part we've collected yet."

The *dynami* could crumble an entire castle passage. The *veritas* could drag truth from any person it touched. The *purgium* could bring you back from the taint itself. The *scio* had shown its use with both the Daedalions and the Jendu. But love?

"I don't see it," she admitted, watching him closely.

"Who knows what the Jendu would've done to ye if they hadn't been swayed by the *amare*."

Ebba remembered when the creature first grabbed her. She'd thought they were drowning her. Really, she couldn't be certain they weren't. "I s'pose."

"I be thinkin', in the wrong hands, false love could be very bad indeed—if that be what this part does," Stubby said, arching to stretch. "Imagine bein' forced to love yer enemy?"

The few minutes she'd spent locked around Calypso were enough for her to agree.

Maybe Plank had a point.

Yet a whispering, fearful part of her said he meant something else entirely.

THIRTEEN

"What about Jerald?" Ebba called up.

She was dressed in the only spare tunic, courtesy of Barrels, who'd appeared mournful at the loss of it, and her hacked-off slop shorts. Her legs were bare from the tops of her thighs, aside from the bandages covering them.

Time moved slowly as the kraken, a rope looped around the base of his tentacles, tugged them toward the closest island.

The kraken glanced back. "No, that's too stuffy. Like I host intimate dinners no one wants to attend."

"Berty?"

"How old do you think I am? There's a difference between collecting antiques and being an antique."

Considering he was probably hundreds of years old, she thought Berty was about right. "How about. . . ." Ebba glanced at the others, but no one else was interested in their conversation. Honestly, neither was she, but there was nothing else to occupy her mind, and she'd already annoyed half of her fathers.

"Do ye like Rory?" she asked. "I'm runnin' out o' names."

"No."

"Stanley?"

"No."

"Matey, ye need to choose at least a few ye like." Ebba sighed.

The kraken stopped and twirled in the water. Ebba lunged for a handhold, crying out at the pull in her wounds.

"Matey," he declared, huge eyes wide.

"Aye?" Stubby said, exhaling loudly as the boat settled.

"No, *Matey*," he said.

Ebba scrunched her nose. "Nay, what?"

The kraken snapped his beak. "I want my name to be Matey. You guys say it all the time."

There was a reason for that. It was a term of informal endearment. One the crew often said. And Ebba could tell that, like her, her fathers were envisioning how annoying that could get.

"Ye don't like Marty?" Ebba asked in a last-ditch attempt.

The kraken scratched his bulbous head with a tentacle. "Nah. Pretty set on Matey."

Peg-leg groaned.

"Aye then," she said. "Then yer name be Matey. Meanin' we've fulfilled our promise to ye, just like we said we would."

"You have," the kraken choked. "I've never had someone keep a promise before."

Probably because they hadn't got the chance to make one, but Ebba kept her mouth shut.

"I wouldn't do that," the kraken said to Caspian before turning to set off once again.

The prince was washing her bloody bandages in the sea because when Ebba tried, bending over hurt. He straightened, peering at Matey's back. "Why is that?"

"Capricorn. They can sniff a drop of blood a mile away."

Barrels lowered his hands from the limp cravat he was trying to breathe dignity into. "You didn't think to mention that before?"

Matey kept towing them. "I don't know what you don't know."

That seemed a reasonable explanation.

She shifted her leg over Grubby to ease the mounting numbness in her butt. Grubby's state was no better or worse than the days prior. She'd decided to hang on to that as a good sign. Locks said he might be getting stable inside before healing, and surely if he were in real trouble, he'd be on the decline? As long as one of them watched him around the clock, they still had the *purgium* in their back pocket.

"I know exactly what I don't know," Ebba declared proudly.

"Always a good thing," Stubby said.

Caspian smiled. "And just what is it that you don't know, Mistress Pirate?"

They were back to Mistress Pirate again? Why? Was he angry at her?

She glanced at him in question, but he either hadn't realized the change or was working hard to *pretend* he hadn't noticed her reaction. He'd only called her Ebba a couple of times, but the informality had made her feel like they were getting closer.

Switching back made her feel like he was pushing her away.

She pushed aside that dilemma to focus on his question. What didn't she know?

An awful amount was the answer.

She didn't know how the root of magic was meant to be used to defeat the six pillars. She didn't know if touching the sword was something she should do. The whole courtship thing with Caspian still confused her a smidgen. She didn't know why Plank was so devastated, nor why Jagger had treated her like she had the plague since he touched the *amare*.

And she didn't know. . . .

"Hey," she said to Matey. "What do ye know about the six pillars?"

Matey gasped, jerking in the sea and sending a small wave of water into their rowboat.

"Watch it," Peg-leg said. "The swell's already three meters high and ye're fillin' us up."

A few of her fathers grabbed goblets and set to scooping water out of their boat. The small vessel was streamlined at one end to cut through the waves. The smaller bench she sat upon—able to fit two pirates—was situated there, with three wider benches spaced out through the rest of the rowboat. Large enough to survive in but not much else.

If they didn't have immortal help and barrels of grog, their odds of living would be dismal. And the grog would eventually run out.

Ebba shivered as the cool water soaked the bottom of her tunic, and spared a thought for Grubby, who was nearly submerged in the bottom of the vessel.

"What do I know?" Matey screeched. "*What do I know?*"

Ebba rolled her eyes and waited.

"I know that my grandfather never got over being taken by their taint. That's why kraken have such a bad name. Because of the things he was forced to do."

Plank stirred and glanced up. "Yer grandfather had the taint?"

"A lot of magical beings did during their last reign. It wasn't until the pillars were defeated that we reverted back."

Caspian straightened. "You mean we'll be able to save those currently under the pillars' power?"

"The taint works differently with immortals." Matey spun around again. "They have to be trapped and drained. Our magic battles against the pillars' power. If the pillars are weaker than the immortal they're draining, they lose. If they're stronger, the other immortal will slowly be taken unless it can escape. And why? Why do you want to know about them?"

Jagger eyed him. "I worked on their ship for two years."

The kraken drooped and didn't utter a single word. "Everyone knew they'd returned to this realm when the wall began to crumble. After last time, we thought they'd be dealt with immediately. Though the powers of oblivion *did* call the magic folk back to the immortal realm last week."

"They did?" Barrels asked, exchanging a leaden look with the rest of them. "Why didn't you go?"

"I know this is a mortal realm, but for many immortals, this is our home. We were locked away from it for hundreds of years. I don't want to be locked away again. I'm not going back."

Ebba reached out a hand to pat his tentacle. "Ye should, Matey. The pillars have taken the throne, and their taint be spreadin' through the waters west o' here."

Matey scoffed. "Ugh, the west waters. I can't stand that side of the realm. Too fake. The mortal sea creatures there spend their lives trying to look younger. It's ridiculous. And the gossip! Don't get me started."

He was judging others for gossiping?

Jagger's silver gaze narrowed on the kraken. "How do ye know so much about the taint?"

"I'm not sure I like you," Matey said. "You seem a bit full of yourself."

Jagger appeared genuinely amused by that. Taken off-guard, Ebba threw a grin at him, which he returned.

The kraken sniffed. "I grew up on stories from my grandfather."

He had? Ebba straightened, ignoring the twinge in her side.

Locks beat her to the question. "He was open about the taint then, yer grandfather?"

"Super open," Matey replied. "Even when the taint left him, he found it hard, remembering what he'd done. But he always said the best way to heal is to speak of your troubles. He said that only idiots keep it all inside."

Ebba glanced at her fathers, biting back on her snicker.

Stubby scratched his chin as he cleared his throat. "Aye, and how long did it take for him to begin speakin' o' it?"

Matey stopped towing and floated with them. "I wasn't born then, but I know it was three months because he kept journals."

Three months. Her fathers took twenty *years*. Ebba grinned as she observed their sheepish expressions. Peg-leg knocked her ankle with his peg.

"Idiots," she declared happily.

This time all of them glared at her. Except Grubby. She glanced down at his legs that were now cleared of the water Matey had splashed in.

Ebba blinked as his foot twitched. She waited with bated breath, but nothing else happened.

Her eyes were playing tricks on her.

"Your grandfather kept a journal? In the water?" Caspian asked.

"Our ink is water-resistant," the kraken said, chuckling. "Though don't ask where it shoots out of."

. . . She wasn't planning on it.

"I don't suppose we could read that journal?" He glanced at Ebba and Jagger. "The thing is, we are tasked with putting together the root of magic that will defeat the six pillars and rid humans and immortals in the Exosian realm of the taint."

"Impossible," Matey declared. "Humans can't be cured of the taint."

What? Ebba jolted, listening to the shocked exclamations of the others.

"Tainted mortals died when the pillars were defeated last time," Matey said.

"But . . . we've left our friends and family back in the realm," Caspian said urgently. "That can't be right. There has to be some way to save them."

Ebba watched her friend closely as her fathers exchanged worried murmurs. Saving his people was what Caspian had held onto since his father died. He couldn't lose hope again. And neither could she. Her fathers *could* be freed of the taint, regardless of what the kraken said.

"—Verity—"

"—Sherry—"

"—Marigold—"

Ebba turned to look at Jagger, who'd squeezed his eyes shut. The pirate had only come with them to ensure the pillars would be defeated and his tribe would be safe.

"We'll figure sumpin' out," she said in a firm voice, unsure if she was attempting to convince herself or everyone else. "There *is* a mortal that can survive the taint."

She jerked a thumb at Jagger on the bench opposite her. "He can. He was on their ship for ages, and he's gettin' better."

He was the immune, yes, but maybe his natural resistance could be mimicked somehow. Magically. Ebba had no clue; she only knew they couldn't give up hope of saving their friends back on Zol. If Jagger could be saved, they had to believe others could too.

The bags under Jagger's eyes were long gone. The sinister shadow behind his previously darting silver eyes had changed. Always too tall for a pirate, he'd gone from wasted to the muscled side of lean. Not only were his clothes and body different, Ebba had to admit—to herself—that the way he behaved now was a far cry from what the taint had made him do months ago. She was yet unsure as to where his exact moral compass pointed, but she knew when the compass needle moved—when his tribe was threatened. His threats to Caspian had steadily dropped off, and though Jagger put his change of heart down to 'owing the prince for the loan of *veritas,*' she wasn't so sure about that. He'd helped out on the ship, saving her life when he probably wouldn't have bothered once. Were these all signs of his immunity forcing the taint out for good?

Ebba jumped as the kraken screeched.

"Shut. The. Clam. Door," he said, swimming back and forth before them and slapping the surface with four tentacles. "*No!* I won't believe it. I *can't* believe it!"

Ebba watched him in mounting concern. "Believe what?"

The kraken wrenched to a halt before Jagger and sank down into the water until his beak was just above the surface, his glowing eyes fixed on the pirate. "You're the immune? The only mortal able to resist magic? I'm your biggest fan. Seriously. You were always my favorite in the stories."

"I thought I was full o' myself," Jagger replied, face impassive though his lips twitched.

Matey ignored him, already running his eyes over the rest of the rowboat. His clicking voice trembled as he asked, "Please do not tell me all three watchers are on this rowboat. I'll die. Right now. I'll just die if you tell me that."

"They're on the boat," Jagger said flatly.

Locks snorted, throwing the pirate a wide smile.

"You're one," the kraken said, jabbing the tip of a tentacle at the prince. "For sure. You just have a real regal look about you."

"Aye, he's always sat too straight-like," Ebba teased. Caspian arched a brow at her, and she arched one right back.

"And then. . . ." The kraken scanned the others, shaking his massive head as he passed over Stubby, Peg-leg, Grubby, Barrels, and Locks. His glowing gaze rested on Ebba and Plank. "You," he said to Plank. "Broody. You're the third."

"*I'm* the third," Ebba said in a clipped voice. She'd only worried about fulfilling her duty before, but now she didn't even *look* the part?

Jagger and Caspian laughed, and Ebba silently dared her fathers to join in.

"That's what I said," the kraken insisted. "The current just moved my body and made it appear like I was looking at your dad."

Ebba folded her arms, and Matey trailed off.

"I can't believe it," the sea monster whispered. "My grandfather would have been so honored to meet you all."

Caspian half-stood. "Then you know something about the three mortals who defeated the six pillars hundreds of years ago?"

"*Do I know about the three mortals,*" the kraken said derisively. "Only everything. The three heroes rose, bathed in their white glow to defeat the pillars of six. I've said it once, and I'll say it again; the three watchers did more for us in that battle than any immortal."

Ebba thought Matey might be quoting his grandfather word for word. She also agreed wholeheartedly on the 'more than any immortal' part. So far, the all-powerful magical beings who supposedly ruled immortalkind hadn't lifted a finger to help them fight the pillars. The Earth Mother had seemed torn between killing them and not. The thunderbird *had* tried to kill them. Ebba didn't know if there were any other powers of oblivion, but if they were anything like the first two, she didn't want to meet them.

She said, "We know the watchers saved the realm."

"Do ye know what the other two are called? Or what they do?" Stubby asked.

Matey faltered. "Other two?"

"The other two watchers," Peg-leg said. "We know Jagger be the immune. What do Caspian and Ebba do? Do they have a title?"

The kraken blinked several times, bobbing in the drift. Ebba frowned, glancing about. Was he paying any attention to their direction? She pushed the thought aside to watch Matey mutter to himself. It was no secret she'd burned to know this answer for a long time. Really, since all the way back on Pleo though she hadn't known she was a *real* part of defeating the pillars back then. Ever since they'd discovered she was one of the watchers, Ebba had burned to understand just what she was meant to do. Not just to answer the question but to decide whether or not she was up to the task. She didn't have any special skills. She couldn't fight the taint, and without the tubes in her hands, Ebba didn't have any magical punch.

What if she failed her crew?

The kraken's muttering went on.

"I thought ye knew *everythin'*," Locks said, emerald eyes blazing.

"I do," Matey snapped. "It's in my head somewhere. But we always call them the three watchers in the main stories, and I told you the immune was my favorite. I know the watchers were super-exclusive and elite. Kept all the inner workings to themselves. And I do know their individual titles. I just need a second."

"Are those details that would be in your grandfather's journals?" the prince asked.

"He never skipped a detail. But I know it, I'm sure. You just put me on the spot."

Caspian wet his lips. "Of course. I don't suppose the journals are close by?"

The kraken glanced around. "Uh. . . ." He twisted the other way. "Uhm. . . ."

"Ye're lost," Jagger accused.

"No," Matey said hastily. Peering at the black sky and rolling sea that was the same in all directions, the kraken stabbed one of his tentacles. "Northeast is this way," he declared.

Ebba narrowed her eyes. "And how can ye tell that? Ye said ye're always below the surface."

The kraken didn't answer.

"We need to get to the nearest island as soon as po'sible," she pressed. "You know why we're here, Matey. This is an urgent quest."

He glanced back. "I know. Serious. This is the way."

"But the journals," Caspian called as the kraken made to turn around again. "Are they close?"

"Tell you what," the kraken chirped. "As soon as I get you all to the nearest island, I'll grab my grandfather's records for you, but I'll have to read them. They're written in krackalaken."

Ebba exchanged a long look with the prince.

Finally, they might get some answers.

"You have no idea how ecstatic my grandfather would be to meet you," the kraken jabbered as he began tugging again. "*No* idea."

FOURTEEN

Cracking open her salt-encrusted eyelids, she stared at the shining blade before her. The instant she recognized the *veritas*, her breath lodged in her throat.

Ebba glared down the length of her body at the slumbering pirate who'd top-and-tailed with her overnight. He was placing the truth sword near her on purpose, all right. What if she'd accidentally touched it as she slept? She would've had dreams of all kinds of truths.

Maybe.

And only maybes kept her from touching the sword.

Still, Ebba didn't shift, staring at the hilt before her. No one else in the rowboat moved. Her other fathers, if awake, weren't by any means alert. Even the kraken was silent. She lifted her head and caught sight of Matey spread out atop the surface like seaweed, huge eyes closed.

They were drifting. *Again.* At this rate, they'd never get anywhere.

A wave slapped against the side of the boat, water spilling inside. The seawater ran in rivulets down her legs, soaking the sawn-off bottoms of her slop shorts. It reminded her of the last time she'd worn less clothes—during the heated frenzy with Calypso.

She stared at the truth sword. The flaming thing had played on her mind since Jagger mentioned it might help her with the Calypso thing. And before then a little. Her fathers felt better for spilling their guts, she could tell. Peg-leg had told her his story, climbed the rigging, and then served three-course dinners until *Felicity* sank. Stubby bore the loss of *Felicity* incredibly well though he was deeply saddened like the rest of them. Locks was a far cry from the man he'd been months before—though some of that was thanks to Verity.

Ebba glanced once more down her body to the other occupants, just shadows in the weak dawn. Something moved against her back, and she glanced behind her at Grubby's foot.

. . . He'd moved.

She'd chalked the last time up to wishful thinking, but he'd definitely kicked her just now. She watched him, breath held, but her unconscious father didn't shift again. Another wave hit, and Ebba shielded her face from the spray.

Grubby twitched again.

And then stilled.

Her eyes shifted from her father to the sea and back again.

Careful not to rock the boat overmuch, Ebba propped herself up and stared at Grubby. Her *part-selkie* father.

Squinting in the space around her, Ebba couldn't find a goblet to test her theory. She grabbed the ends of the bandage around one of her smaller puncture wounds and tugged them. Her blood had congealed, making the rag stick to the wound. She gently worked it off, wincing as the material tore free from the apex of the forming scar.

She leaned to dunk the rag overboard, rubbing the material against itself for a while to clean it in some measure. And then Ebba let the bandage soak with water, bringing it back to Grubby.

"What're ye doin'?" Plank croaked.

Ebba squeezed the rag, pouring water over Grubby's legs.

"Tippin' water inside the boat," Locks murmured, shifting. "Makes sense."

Grubby kicked.

". . . Did he just move?" Plank asked after a beat.

Ebba repeated the experiment, and this time Grubby's knee bent.

"The water is doin' sumpin' to him," she whispered in the dark.

Jagger roused.

She went back for more water, but Locks hands on hers stopped her. "Okay, lass, but don't be fillin' us with water. We'll dip him over the side to see if the sea does him any good."

"I'm thinkin' the sea heals him because he be part selkie," she said, pulling herself up to sit on the bench.

"What're ye doin'?" Jagger glared at her, his blinks more like mini-sleeps.

"Shh," she answered then said to the others, "Let's toss Grubby over."

Grubby was stored under the four benches, the only completely flat position onboard. Awkwardly, they push and pulled him out, waking the rest of the crew in the doing.

His dead weight was too much for Barrels and Peg-leg to maneuver in the rowboat.

"Rope," Caspian said, awake too. "We'll lower him in."

Coiled ropes covered the bottom of the rowboat, along with a few tools. She grabbed a coil and lobbed it to Caspian.

The prince formed a large noose, using his arm and feet, and threw the noose over Grubby's head, shifting it to rest beneath her father's arms. Caspian drew the free end around his back, holding it taut against his right hip. "Place him over the side; I'll lower him into the sea. He can breathe underwater, but we don't want to lose hold of him."

"All right, lad." Peg-leg squeezed the prince's forearm, and Ebba's heart filled with warmth at the pleased smile that spread across Caspian's face.

They lowered Grubby into the water.

Curse the tight confines; she couldn't see a thing. "What's happenin'?" she urged, fidgeting on her bench. "Make sure to secure him tight."

"What?" snorted the kraken, surging upright from a dead sleep. He regarded them through dazed eyes. "Too right."

Ebba sighed. They needed to figure something out to replace the kraken. His heart was in the right place, but they had places to be. In fact, instead of going to an island that might not have any food or water, they should probably just continue on toward the sixth part of the root.

At least she might be on to something with Grubby. And if the water accelerated his healing, her crew would be whole and well again. Plus, Grubby could scout ahead and perhaps find an inhabitable island anyway.

She turned to Peg-leg and Barrels to relate her plan, but a glow in the distance caught her eye.

. . . What was that?

"Oi," she said to Jagger. "Can ye see that?"

He rested a hand on her shoulder to peer in the same direction. "Nay. What do ye see?"

Ebba didn't respond, squinting into the darkness. The glow tugged at a memory. As though she'd had the memory when very young or that time she decided to try Stubby's brandy. The glow called to her like a long-lost friend. Like a lover.

Her mind screamed out a warning, but she couldn't stop looking. There was something else there.

"Ye can't see someone on those rocks over there?" she said dreamily.

Jagger swore suddenly. "Matey, get us out o' here."

"What?" Matey slurred.

"Ye've let us drift back to Calypso, ye fool."

Calypso? Ebba's heart began to race.

The kraken came awake. "Back to Calypso? I wasn't there the first time, but he isn't so bad for a chat."

Jagger cut him off. "Just get us away."

The pirate surged forward to clamp both hands on Ebba's wrists as panic filled her foggy mind.

"I don't understand," the kraken said.

Locks snapped, "Ye don't have to. Just take us in the o'posite direction. Ye said ye knew where land was."

"I did," Matey said, though his voice sounded farther away than before. "But I only really swim between my three spots. When we drifted, I got lost, and I didn't want to tell the three watchers I messed up. I—"

Jagger exploded. "Just. *Swim*."

Ebba's throat worked as peace filled her body. Yet her chest tightened, disturbing the heavy warmth. She frowned. She'd leaned forward over the lip of the boat. When did that happen?

Jagger shook her. "Viva, nay. Ye need to focus on me."

She tore her gaze from the person on the rocks to whom she so desperately wanted to go. She needed to save the person. Ebba looked into Jagger's eyes for a moment, but then, as though physically pulled, her gaze returned to the glowing rocks.

Locks upturned a goblet of seawater on her head, and Ebba spluttered, the cold cutting through the warmth encompassing her shivering frame.

"What did ye do that for?" she demanded.

Jagger shook her hands. "We're comin' up to Calypso. Ye need to focus until we're away again."

Dread flooded down through her, pinning her stiffened frame to the bench. Her gaze flew to Jagger's.

"Nay," she whispered. "I can't go back there."

"Aye," he said, squeezing her hands tight. "Ye ain't goin' back."

Ebba shook him free only to grab back at him. "Ye need to stop me goin' there. Tie me up or all o' ye sit on top o' me. I ain't goin' to those rocks!"

Her entire body wracked with terrible shaking.

Plank was there. "We won't."

But Ebba could feel the warmth creeping back in like poisonous smoke. Fear choked her. "It's comin' again."

Matey sped up, but knowing Calypso was there, Ebba was attuned to the fog shifting, spreading and expanding to cloak her reason. It filled her with a burning dread.

"Jagger," she cried. He was the only one she'd spoken to about this. He knew how scared she was.

"Take the sword," he said, clamping an arm around her waist and pulling her against him.

The heat sweeping through her took on a new direction. She released Jagger's arms to run her hands up his muscular chest.

His words echoed through a long tunnel to reach her. Ebba's lips were numb. "What?" she said thickly.

Silver eyes bore into hers. They belonged to a person who wanted her—she could tell.

"Take hold o' the sword," he said. His voice made her shiver.

The fiercely handsome man didn't really want her hands to stop roaming his chest. *She* didn't want to do that. This felt right. But part of her said otherwise. That part said that the sword was of no consequence; that her life, her everything stood on the rocks awaiting her.

And yet touching this man felt incredible. Real.

"Damn ye, Viva! Ye can be angry at me later."

Her arms were yanked down. She was far too warm—panting from the heat.

Her clawed fingers were pried open by hands far stronger than hers. They were hands she'd decided to trust recently. A cool object was placed in her palm. Her hands clawed again as soon as the person released her, but at the same moment, a cool wind swept through her.

It was as though a blindfold had been removed. One instant, she'd stared through thin material and the next with unobstructed eyes. The man in front of her, Jagger, possessed a shining white quality. And as she looked at him, her mind still lingering on her last thought about trust, surety burst from deep within. She *could* depend on Jagger. Totally and completely.

Ebba blinked and tore her eyes from him. The world possessed a vibrant quality now—an inner glow. The rowboat, the water, the giant monster next to her. Everything was so beautiful.

"Calypso," Jagger whispered.

No. . . . The smile faded from her lips.

Not everything.

As she scanned the sea, Ebba's eyes fell upon shadowed rocks in the distance. The outcrop was jagged, the kind of eroded rock found in shallow pools on the shore that would tear her feet after no short time.

What stood on the outcrop filled her with rage. Now she shook for a different reason.

A mostly naked man stood there. He wasn't cast in the brilliant glow like everything else. In fact, a shadow hung over him like a blanket. From what she knew of this immortal's power, Ebba could guess that the glowing signified truth, and shadow signified a lie.

"Calypso," she growled, her grip tightening on the sword.

His lips curved, and he beckoned her.

Disgust twisted her face, and Ebba surged to her feet, sword in hand so her mind remained clear.

She erupted into a string of curse words, hurling them across the water at the immortal.

Ebba stopped for a quick breath, seeing the gap between their rowboat and the rocks was growing, and launched into a second round of choice cuss words. Throwing her hands in the air, she yelled every bad word she'd ever heard at Calypso, and when that barrel dried up, she settled on some hand gestures.

Her fathers gasped as she started from the top again—even after Calypso blanched violently and leaped from view. Even when the rocks were tiny pinpricks in the distance.

Throat raw, Ebba sat with a huff and stared at the bottom of the boat.

"Ye're the one she learned all that off," Stubby bellowed at Peg-leg.

"How many for the swear jar?" she grunted.

She rested the sword next to her, equal parts grateful to it and still afraid. She'd always thought the truth would rush through her head like pictures. Upon touching the sword back in the castle, she'd seen a memory of her fathers, which confirmed their love for her. But this time was different; the truth appeared to her with a shiny quality, the lies as shadows.

Ebba was just happy the sword hadn't told her anything she hadn't wanted to know. And that was only because her thoughts were on trusting Jagger when he shoved *veritas* in her hand. Still, seeing the truth really wasn't as bad as she'd built it up to be.

In fact, Ebba was truly glad for the tidbit on Jagger.

Really glad, actually . . . almost joyful.

"Uh," Barrels said. "Considering the swear jar is at the bottom of the sea and you don't have any coin, I'd say we just start another . . . down the track."

"I said it wouldn't stop her learnin' the good words," Stubby said loudly. "And I was—"

Peg-leg turned back from where he'd checked the ropes holding Grubby to the vessel. "If ye say ye're right, I'll shove the *veritas* down yer throat so ye talk truth for once."

She tried to ignore Jagger, who had sat next to her and regarded her without expression. Her cheeks burned at his steadfast perusal. She'd taken the liberty of feeling him up while under Calypso's thrall, and yet . . . though Jagger's eyes often glinted with intense challenge and daring, she didn't feel any shame or fear over touching him—except for not knowing if he'd wanted it or not. Not like when she'd touched the immortal back at the rocks.

Jagger's challenge enticed in a thrilling way. Touching him hadn't been a twisted, ugly thing.

Ebba was just surprised her fathers hadn't tossed him into the Dynami Sea.

"Sorry," she muttered at Jagger.

"Don't be ashamed," he said low in her ear so the others couldn't hear. "Ye were under his power. I know that."

He wasn't going to tease her? That was surprisingly nice. Ebba lifted a hand to her head as it began to ache. That was the thing: she didn't feel ashamed. Not at all. In fact, while touching Jagger—though her urges were augmented by magic—she'd felt *alive*; burningly attracted to the flaxen-haired pirate beside her.

That was a problem for a whole other reason that sat on the opposite side of the boat.

She peeked at Caspian, who hadn't said a word. Her furtive gaze bounced off his hard, accusing amber stare.

Flinching, Ebba's mouth dried as the prince glanced away to look out over the ocean. Usually, he became jealous over Jagger's shite-stirring antics. When that happened, she felt awkward, but not guilty. *This* time she was certainly in the wrong. Kind of. Calypso started it, but *she'd* enjoyed the feeling when it transitioned to Jagger. That felt like a betrayal of sorts.

Ebba sighed heavily, dropping her hand. She'd have to talk to him. And that wasn't a conversation that could happen in a rowboat filled with nine people. Even if one of those people was tied to the side of the vessel.

Shaking her head, she looked to where Grubby's head of hair was just visible. "Any change with Grubs?"

"The wound on his head be closin'," Peg-leg replied, patting Grubby gently on the shoulder. "And his color be better. I say we let him stew until he wakes."

Locks peered past her at the sword. "Ye know, Peg-leg, maybe that ain't a bad idea."

"Stew never be a bad idea," Peg-leg said with a smile. "Good for the soul."

"Not the bloody stew—the sword-down-Stubby's-throat part."

Stubby's jaw dropped.

"Not shovin' it down yer throat as such," Locks amended. "But for ye to hold it."

"How about *ye* hold it?" Stubby countered, an evil glint in his eye.

"I will." Matey lifted the tip of a tentacle.

"Locks be havin' a point, though," Ebba said, ignoring the kraken. "I've touched the sword. It wasn't that bad. Just confirmed that. . . ." Blast it! "T-that Jagger be trustworthy."

The pirate jerked, and she cleared her throat, refusing to meet his gaze. Her stomach erupted in drunken sprites as his eyes bore into the side of her face.

"Mayhaps we should all touch it. I'm thinkin' there ain't nothin' about truth to be feared. It shows ye lies and truth too. That'll be handy-like." She tensed, waiting for their laughter. When it didn't come, Ebba peeked up through her lashes.

More than one of her fathers had paled.

"Go on then," Locks said. The words were so quiet, Ebba wondered if he'd intended them to hear.

"Really?" she asked, stumped.

"Go on, afore I change my mind."

Ebba licked her lips, stomach twisting as she reached for the sword. What if Locks didn't see what he needed in order to keep being happy? Ebba was completely certain of their hearts and souls. They were good people, mostly, and the best fathers she could ask for even with the mistakes they'd made. But the truth surely wasn't affected by the love she held for them. It wouldn't dress anything up. There hadn't been any grays when she'd held *veritas*, just shadows and that shiny glow, and that worried her. If there was a word for her fathers' moral compasses, gray would be it.

She picked up the sword, her mind on her fathers.

Ebba looked at them and gasped. Deep within each of her fathers in the rowboat was a swirling cloud of shadow. The ugly black lingered in the middle of their chests, disturbing the otherwise radiant glow around their bodies.

The taint. It had to be. There wasn't any shadow inside Caspian.

Aside from the *purgium*, there was no way to be rid of the taint. But if they touched the *purgium,* they'd die. Ebba suspected Grubby had just scraped through because of his selkie blood. Was hoping her fathers could be healed a fool's game?

Was she stupid for believing Jagger's immunity might mean her parents would one day be happy and whole?

The answer to both questions was a resounding no. When it came to her fathers, Ebba wasn't a fool. She wasn't stupid.

They would be happy again. Ebba knew it in her gut.

An image flashed in her mind. She closed her eyes, swept away by the shimmering image. In the image, Locks was smiling, the truth sword grasped in his hands. Ebba watched as the darkness within the future version of her father lessened, some of the ugly shadow within him washed away as though doused by a bucket of water.

Opening her eyes, Ebba held out *veritas* to her father, a joyful smile upon her lips. She nodded at him. "It's goin' to be all right, matey. I just saw. Ye'll be fine just like I knew ye would."

Knowing the truth loosened the taint's grip on a person—it didn't just help them differentiate truth from lie. If Jagger's attachment to the sword was any indication, it worked on others, too, not just her fathers.

Locks stared at the sword, chest heaving. He lifted his gaze to her and studied her smile. Then he swallowed, reaching out to grip the weapon.

His back arched slightly, and he gasped in what sounded like pain, resting a hand on the side of the boat.

Her father didn't move from the spot after. Was that a good sign? His expression slowly cleared of the pained wince. That . . . seemed okay?

Folding her arms, Ebba left Locks to whatever his truth was and looked at Stubby. "Are ye goin' to touch the sword then?"

"What?" Stubby asked. "Is this a thing now? I thought it were just Locks."

As slippery as a sodding eel.

Ebba studied the occupants of the boat. "Caspian and Jagger have touched it. And me and Locks. That be near-on half."

"Four-ninths, my dear."

She rolled her eyes at Barrels' numbers. "Aye, but I think ye should all do it. When I hold the sword and look at ye all, I can see a shadow swirlin' about in yer chests. I'm thinkin' it be the taint. And just now, when Locks touched the sword, the shadows inside o' him lessened. If the shadows be the taint, then knowin' the truth helps lessen it."

Silence reigned.

"Ye can see the taint inside o' us?" Peg-leg asked.

"I ain't sure if it really is the taint or not."

"It is," Jagger interrupted.

Ebba turned to him. "Ye knew?"

He nodded.

"Why didn't ye tell us?" she asked through gritted teeth.

Jagger glanced at her. "I didn't want to upset ye. I wasn't aware truth lessened the taint and thought there was naught to be done about it. Tellin' ye seemed cruel."

Her anger faded. When the flaxen-haired pirate said things like that, it confused her. Greatly. And warmed her. Which added to her confusion.

Stubby scratched his chin. "But haven't ye looked at yerself, Jagger?"

When Jagger looked at her father, Ebba sagged.

She studied the smoldering heat that had just erupted within her while looking at Jagger. Damn Calypso. Now she was far more aware of men's bodies and how they could make her feel. She hadn't felt lingering lust after the second encounter with the immortal, not like last time when Ebba actually touched him. Seeing as they were away from the immortal's lusty magic, she realized apparently the attraction she felt for Jagger was real.

Ebba was far too aware of the pirate's body for the tight confines of this vessel.

"The sword takes longer to work with me," Jagger said. "Bein' the immune, I guess. It can take a few minutes focusin' on one thing to see the truth and lie o' it. It ain't instant like with the rest o' ye. And I never saw any shadow in myself. I don't think that part works for me."

"Or ye're rid o' the taint," Peg-leg countered.

Jagger's face darkened. "Nay, I'd feel di'ferent if that'd happened."

But he was acting differently. Couldn't he see that?

"If I do touch the sword, I don't want to be rushed," Stubby said, lifting his hands in front of him.

"The taint within ye could lessen, though." Ebba desperately wanted her fathers to be happy. If the sword helped, they needed to touch it.

"I will," he said, fidgeting. "Just not right now."

She narrowed her eyes. "Wimp."

"Good try, lass," he replied. "I ain't takin' the bait."

Ebba smiled slightly, covering her disappointment at his reply. Just because she'd been ready to touch the sword, it didn't mean others were.

"I might do it," Peg-leg said, head tilted as he watched Locks, who still held the *veritas*. "He seems okay. I thought it might kill us if we touched it."

And he'd let Locks touch it?

"I have to say, that concerned me too," Barrels said, speaking over her. "But Locks has lied a great deal more than I. If he's still alive, the rest of us should live too."

Jagger spoke. "That ain't how it works. It just shows ye the truth ye ask."

"It showed me a future truth just afore, though. Does it do that for ye?" Ebba asked him.

He furrowed his brows. "I'm usually focused on the here and now."

"What about you?" she asked the prince.

Caspian didn't look away from the ocean as he replied, "I'm mostly focused on the past. But seeing the truth in the past or future is likely limited by our experiences, too. I tried to see my father before I was born." The prince glanced at Jagger. "But could not. Yet I was taken to a moment I never witnessed when I thought of my mother's love."

"So ye can't navigate the sword for a truth ye don't know?" Plank asked.

Ebba stared at him, wondering if he'd touch the sword.

"Not that I could tell," Caspian said. "I set my mind on our predicament to figure out how Ebba and I fit into this. The sword merely showed me the tubes we'd collected, giving them the truthful shine."

Maybe Ebba should give that a go and check if it worked. They needed all the answers they could get. "Then why'd it show me the taint within Locks gettin' smaller? I hadn't seen that. And ye hadn't seen that moment ye mentioned o' yer mother."

The prince finally turned to look at her.

She braced herself, but his expression was smooth . . . and cold.

"You were certain of the outcome already," he said. "It's the only connection I can find between me seeing the new memory of my mother and Ebba seeing Locks in the future. Barrels?"

Her father pursed his lips. "Ebba knew Locks would feel better for holding *veritas*. And you were certain of your mother's love. Perhaps."

"In which case, the *veritas* is able to show truth or lie in the present, to show you the truth of a moment you've witnessed, and to confirm a truth you already know in the past or future," Caspian said.

From her experiences with the sword, that added up.

"Ye saw the taint in me gettin' smaller?" Locks asked her. He sat straight, his eyes wide.

"Aye," she said, nodding. "The ball o' shadow in ye shrunk for knowin' the truth." That's how she'd interpreted it, anyway.

"Huh, I felt that," Locks grunted. Slowly, a beaming smile spread across his face.

Peg-leg knocked his leg with his peg. "Well, don't hold out, ye codfish. What'd it show ye?"

Locks glanced knowingly at Jagger and Caspian and then at her. Ebba bit back on her laughter, returning the arched, secretive look.

"Ye're jokin'" Stubby said. "Ye ain't goin' to tell us?"

"Perhaps only the brave be deservin' to see the truth," Locks said sagely.

She threw a grin at the prince whose stony expression melted into a tight semblance of his usual smile.

"Tell us," Barrels demanded.

"Nay," Locks said. "Grow a pair and hold the sword for yerself."

Peg-leg groaned. "Oh, go on then."

Locks snickered and grabbed the blade tip to extend *veritas* back to the cook.

"Shite, okay." Peg-leg ran his fingers over his bald head and then snaked out a hand to grip the hilt. "What did ye see?"

Locks, holding the blade of *veritas,* was forced to answer truthfully. He blurted, "Verity loves me."

Everyone groaned.

Peg-leg smirked and removed the sword from Locks' hands. He grunted and doubled over as the sword's power overtook him.

They watched him for a time, and then Plank began to laugh.

The hard sound sent a chill down her spine and everyone but Peg-leg turned to him.

"Love," Plank spat at Locks, his mouth twisted. "Ye don't know what love is."

What? She reared back. Where had that come from?

Locks appeared as nonplussed as the rest of them.

Jagger nudged her foot and tilted his head. Ebba followed the direction to where Plank clutched the *amare* to his chest with both hands. She caught Stubby's attention and dropped her gaze to the tube.

"Matey," Stubby said to Plank. "Pass the *amare* over to . . . Locks."

Plank huddled tighter around the part. "Why?'

"I ain't thinkin' the love piece be healthy for ye," Stubby said, adding, "And there be seven o' us here to make sure ye do as I've asked. Or . . . can ye not let go o' it?"

"O' course I can," Plank withered.

They waited.

His grip on the *amare* loosened in increments, and eventually he extended the tube to Locks.

In the wake, Plank hunched over again, bowing his head to gaze out at sea.

Barrels said, "I don't think anyone should hold the *amare* for too long."

She murmured her false agreement. The *amare* hadn't affected her like that, but she'd keep an eye on Locks anyway.

"Aye," Locks said, staring at the pointed tube in his hand. "We'll keep switchin' it around. Thorns o' a puffer fish, I truly love Verity more than life itself."

"Here we go," muttered Barrels.

"But that's interestin'," Jagger countered, a wrinkle between his brows. "So when a person holds the *amare* and thinks o' someone they love, their love be confirmed." He trailed off, staring at his hands.

"And when I held the *amare* to the Jendu's skin, it was influencin' their feelings for me," Ebba added.

Barrels hummed. "Does it do that for everyone?"

Without preamble, Locks leaned over and pressed the *amare* to Barrels' bare arm.

A wide grin broke out across her eldest father's face. He leaned over and hugged Locks tight. "I'm so glad to have a friend like you."

Locks snickered and hugged him right back. "Right back at ye, m'hearty." He pulled back. "Aye, it works all right. I didn't feel any di'ferent, though."

Barrels glared at him, leaning away.

Stubby whistled. "So the *amare* only works on the person it touches, not the person holding the tube."

"I didn't feel love, though," Barrels said, shaking his head. "I felt intense friendship."

Ebba thought back to the Jendu. "What if it reveals what ye feel for a person? It showed Barrels the love friends share. With the Jendu, it showed motherly love? I bet if Locks touched it on me, I'd feel love for him as my father and parent. Caspian would feel brotherly love for his sisters."

"Pass it here?" Caspian called.

Locks passed the tube back.

The prince held it for only a second. "Yes, Ebba's right. This part shows you how you feel."

Interesting. She wouldn't mind a private moment with the *amare* when they got off this sodding boat. Ebba scanned the vessel and stilled.

She couldn't see Grubby's hair over the side.

"Check Grubby!" she said, half-rising.

Stubby peered overboard. "Sink me," he gasped, jerking back.

"What's wrong? Is he loose?" Ebba tensed, ready to dive in the water.

Stubby clutched at his chest. "Just sunk down a bit. His bloody eyes are open. Thirteen stitches o' a hammock, that near-on stopped me heart, I tell ye. Creepy selkie bugger."

A laugh worked up her throat as her heart hammered. If they ever got to land, she'd reenact Stubby's reaction.

"Any change?" Barrels asked.

Stubby looked again. "Wound on his head be gone. How long should we leave him in here for?"

However long it took for Grubby to wake? Her gut twisted. *If* he woke. "How about we leave him in the water until night falls?" She didn't want him in the water when night fell. That was too much like tempting fate.

A loud thud made her jump.

Veritas fell to the wooden bottom of the boat.

Peg-leg lifted his head, rage distorting his face. Her mouth dried as she received her share of the fury. He'd seen the time she'd dented his pan killing a rat. Or the time she'd sprinkled dried ship scum in his grog when he said she couldn't go ashore. Or—

"None o' ye like my fish stew," he bellowed.

Her eyes widened. Even Plank blanched.

Shite.

FIFTEEN

After lowering the still-unconscious Grubby into the water when the sun first rose, she'd clasped hands with Jagger and Caspian to find the way to the sixth part. Making headway and then drifting off-course while the kraken rested was grinding on her last nerve, but until Grubby woke, that was their reality.

Without freedom to move about a ship, the endless canvas of black water was draining everyone of good humor.

"Let's check the d'rection again," she told Caspian.

Peg-leg glared at her, and she grimaced but didn't offer an apology. It was about time he knew his fish stew tasted like mud.

On the bench opposite her, Locks said, "Here, lass. Let's check yer wounds then."

"They feel pretty good. Just itchy." Sucking in to account for the presence of the *dynami* and *purgium* inside her belt, Ebba pulled the bottom hem free of her belt and sawn-off slops and peeled the tunic upward.

She untied the bandages around her torso, complaining as the bandages tugged at her tender skin. Ebba wrinkled her nose at the stench of dried seaweed beneath. Once she'd unwound the last binding, she balled the lot up and deposited them into Locks' outstretched hand.

"Some o' the smaller ones are healed," Locks said, leaning forward. He glanced at the seaweed in his hand. "Incr'dible. It be a shame there ain't more o' this about."

The prince shifted between Jagger and Locks and took the place next to her. Something tightly coiled within her relaxed at Caspian's warm presence by her side. For three days, he'd sat on the opposite end of the boat, but he'd felt so far away emotionally. With Grubby inside before, moving had been too hard.

Ebba smiled at the prince, eyes searching his face for the anger she'd glimpsed all too frequently of late. He bumped her shoulder and smiled back.

Her stomach twisted with nerves, ruining the moment. Talking to him about her change of feelings wasn't going to be easy. She'd rather eat a barrel filled with Peg-leg's fish stew. But her friend's feelings mattered more than her fear of the conversation. Before, Ebba had waited to feel some kind of deep regard for him. But now, she was certain that regard wasn't coming and never would. She had to be totally upfront about that.

There was barely enough room for her and Caspian to sit side-by-side on the front bench. In the cramped space, his leg pressed against her thigh and a fierce warmth bolted through her chest. Emotion robbed her of speech for a second, and Ebba swallowed back a thick lump rising in her throat.

She threw her arms around the prince and buried her face in his chest.

"I'm so glad to have ye, Caspian," she said tremulously. "Ye've always been there for me. I'll always be there for ye too."

She was surprised when he didn't hug her back. But what Ebba felt didn't lessen as she released him, and the smile she sent the prince left him blinking.

"Keep yer hand to yerself," Jagger snarled at the prince, interrupting the moment.

Ebba stared at the pirate in shock. Why would he say such a thing?

She would have ventured a guess at jealousy except *Jagger* had uttered the words. He'd never displayed jealousy before.

Caspian jerked his thigh away from hers, and the warmth drained away from her chest in a flash.

"It ain't nothin' to ye what his hand be doin'," Ebba hissed at Jagger, flushing after the comment and sincerely hoping her fathers hadn't heard.

"I mean. . . ." She trailed off and returned her focus to pulling off the last bandage.

Jagger was still glaring murderously at the prince, who fidgeted on the bench next to her.

"What if you put the seaweed in the water for a while? It might work again," Caspian said to Locks. His tone was off.

He wasn't bothered by what Jagger had said, was he?

"Ye think?" Locks asked, darting his eyes to Caspian.

The prince shrugged. "Worth a try."

"True enough," Locks said. "I've got to wash the bandages and wounds anyway."

Jagger's eyes were hooded. He was staring at her stomach.

"Ye all right there?" she shot at him, still angry over his remark to the prince.

Silver eyes raised to hers. A smirk crossed his face. "Best view in the boat."

Locks shoved her bloody bandages in his hands, and Jagger's nose scrunched.

"Wash those," her father snapped.

No, Jagger wasn't washing her bandages! Embarrassing. Ebba ripped them from the pirate's hands and began washing them herself. Jagger holding them felt . . . too personal.

"I'll do some." The prince took one and washed it on the other side, placing the *amare* between his knees to do so.

"Ye don't think that we're riskin' notice by the Capricorn?" Jagger said as they worked through the pile.

"I was thinking the same," Barrels piped up. "But Grubby's wound was washed away in the sea as well as Ebba's wounds and bandages multiple times."

Locks shrugged. "Makes no matter, does it? Ebba's wounds have to be cared for. Anyway, they'll take Grubby first."

She whacked him lightly, snickering. "He ain't bait."

Locks waggled his brows at her and settled into cleaning the wounds on her legs and torso, reapplying the soaking seaweed and bandages. He was right; the smaller cuts were healed and gone. The larger cuts had formed hard scabs.

He sat back, dusting his hands.

"Hey," Matey said, breaking the quiet after. "I think I remembered more about the three watchers."

Everyone faced him.

"The titles at least," he continued. "I—"

The kraken stopped swimming abruptly, and Ebba toppled backward with a yell.

"Drunken starfish on a roulette table," she blurted, picking herself up from the bottom of the boat. "Why'd ye stop?"

The kraken bobbed in the water, ignoring her. As everyone reseated themselves, Matey turned in a slow circle, his eyes glowing menacingly.

Ebba raised her hands. *Uh-oh.* "Easy now."

"Capricorn," he growled.

"Where?" Plank asked. "How far away?"

Matey blinked. "They're surrounding the Jendu. I've got to go." He sank down but popped back up, the rope no longer around the base of his tentacles. "But I can't leave you guys," the kraken fretted.

"How far away?" Plank urged.

"Five hundred meters beneath us," the kraken wailed. He stilled again. "They're calling me. The Capricorn have them trapped."

"How can ye tell?" Jagger asked.

"Through my suckers, how else?"

Ebba's hands were still raised. "Matey, it's okay. Just calm down. We'll figure this out."

Stubby stood. "Ye need to keep yer oath to the Jendu."

She stared at her father. If the Capricorn were close, the pirates wanted the kraken on their side. He was their ticket to the next part.

The kraken was panting. "Only if you're sure?"

"We're sure," Barrels said suddenly. "Go now. And hurry back after you defeat them."

Matey nodded. "I'll come back for you guys. I swear."

He sank out of sight, and Ebba hissed, "What're ye doin'?"

Plank was helping Peg-leg to draw in Grubby from the water and spoke. "He sank *Fel*— The ship. Even if he means well, his size makes him clumsy. He's more dang'rous near us than away."

True enough. The kraken threw himself around without thought.

Grubby groaned as he was pulled back into the rowboat. Soaked, Peg-leg and Plank awkwardly maneuvered him between two of the benches.

"Grubs." Stubby shook his shoulder.

Her father moaned again.

"That's a good sign," Locks said. "We'll get him back in the water once the Capricorn leave."

"I hope the Jendu are okay," Ebba said, thinking of their pleasant smiles. They'd given her the seaweed, after all.

Barrels cut her off. "One of the bandages is floating over there."

"Sorry," Caspian replied, picking the *amare* up off the wooden bottom. "That was me."

"Well, let's get it in, smart-like. If it was what drew the Capricorn here, we don't want the Jendu to find out and curse us," Peg-leg said, passing an oar to Jagger. Stubby took up the other, and they rounded to collect the piece of torn and bloodied tunic floating off the port side.

"Want the *dynami* to help ye row?" she asked Stubby. "Who has it?"

"Ye do, lass," Peg-leg told her.

Ebba glanced down to her belt. So she did. And the *purgium.* Hard to keep track, the way these things switched hands.

"I'll be fine," Stubby grunted, pulling the oar back through the water.

"Someone else should take the *amare,*" the prince said. "I've had it for hours." He handed the tube to a grimacing Peg-leg.

She gave Caspian the *purgium* after, keeping the *dynami* for herself.

Something splashed to the left. Everyone whirled to look.

Grubby groaned, but they ignored him, scanning the sea.

"What was that?" she whispered.

Another splash came from the right. Half of them turned, the rest staying put so they had eyes everywhere.

Plank held his cutlass in both hands. "I don't have a good feelin'."

Grubby groaned and slurred, "What happened?"

He was awake.

Her heart leaped, and Ebba struggled to look at him between the bodies of her other fathers.

Peg-leg bent down. "Grubby," he said. "Are ye back with us, m'hearty?"

"My head be hurtin'," he said weakly.

She held her breath as he groaned again.

"Aye, ye took a blow to the noggin'. Again."

Grubby didn't reply.

"Is he okay?" Ebba fretted.

"Don't ye worry, lass. He's just gone to sleep."

Her shoulders sagged. "But he'll wake again?"

"If he did once, I don't see why he wouldn't a second time," Locks answered. "The seawater worked. It must be his selkie side. Ye saved him, Ebba-Viva. Right smart move that was."

She smiled and tucked her dreads behind her ear. "Thank ye."

"That's another splash," Stubby said. "But whatever it is, it ain't breakin' the surface, or it be too quick for me to see."

Ebba returned to her vigil over the side. "What do ye know about Capricorn, Plank?"

They were all facing outward now, seated on the benches with their weapons drawn. Ebba heard her father take a breath and waited for his ominous story-telling voice.

"They be half-goat, half-fish, and take honor in the triumph of a hunt," he replied without a trace of his usual passion.

She cast a frown at him, but apparently, he was done. "That's it?"

"The crux o' them, aye."

Barrels expelled a breath. "I never thought I'd say this, Plank, but I prefer the long-winded, embellished version of your stories."

The lack of interest on Plank's face twisted the strings of her heart. She turned from the sea and rested a hand on him. "Won't ye tell the full story? Ye know I enjoy them."

He didn't look at her. "Nay, lass. I've not the heart for it."

Not today? Or not any day? "Ye've been like this since *Felicity* sank."

Plank flinched at her comment.

"What's wrong with ye?" she demanded. "Why are ye actin' this way? Like ye. . . ." She stuttered to a halt and then squared her shoulders, pushing on. "Why are ye actin' like ye wanted to go down with the ship?"

He turned from her, closing his eyes. His voice was ragged when he answered. "Because I did."

To hear him say such a thing when they weren't surrounded by the chaos of the sinking ship hurt more than the first time. Shock stole her voice, and she worked to find it again.

"Think o' what yer sayin', man," Stubby said fiercely. "Think o' who ye're speakin' to."

"Nay," Ebba choked. "Don't pretend for my sake. I'm sick o' that and have been for a long time." Her voice rose. "Is that what ye've done my whole life, Plank? Pretended to live? Is that where ye go in yer daydreams? To death?"

Plank faced her again, and she could see by the roundness of his eyes that something she'd said had reached him. Ebba could pull him out of this. She could—

"Aye," he said.

Her hope withered. "W-what?" She sucked in a harsh inhale. "Pretendin' to live or daydreamin' ye're dead?"

He returned his gaze to the water.

"Answer me," she boomed. Since Locks had first told the story of his past, Ebba hadn't made such a demand, but she made it now.

Why would Plank want to leave them? To leave *her*? He had to know she couldn't live without him.

He wouldn't look at her, and black rage blasted through her chest. She stood and leaned down in his face, pure terror steering her words. "I told ye to answer me."

"Ebba. . . ," Locks started.

"Nay. He doesn't get to be like this when we all need each other. Be sad, cry or scream, but don't sink into oblivion without a fight."

Plank glanced up.

"Fight for us," she repeated, hoping that her words had hooked his attention.

A speck of awareness entered his eyes. It grew until he blinked, as though really seeing her for the first time since *Felicity* sank. His throat worked, and he jerked his head in a nod.

Ebba whirled away and sat with her back to the others. She felt sick at the thought of how he'd just spoken. Near tears, she rested her elbows on the side of the boat, staring at the blurry wrinkles of her reflection in the sea.

"That was three splashes," Peg-leg whispered.

"And another," Stubby added a scant second later.

She had to get ready to protect the vessel—just in case the splashing was the Capricorn—though a part of her held out hope that Matey had sent the Jendu up here.

Taking a final breath, Ebba made to lean back but stopped as her reflection changed. She peered closer as her moss-green irises morphed to horizontal slits.

Funny. It almost looked as though she had. . . .

"Horns," she burst out, rearing back.

Water exploded in front of her. The boat tipped violently from the other side, and all she glimpsed was a mesh net flying over her head before it closed around her body.

She was yanked forward into the water.

The cries of her crew were lost as Ebba sucked in a large breath a scant second before hitting the ocean. She was towed deeper into the water and kicked frantically, hands flailing to figure out where the attack was coming from.

Her clawing fingers found the net to either side. The mesh pulled in against her back, stopping her movement up to the surface.

They were trying to drown her.

She opened her eyes, squinting through the bubbles. A goat's head reared before her, and she screamed, releasing most of her air. The immortal had the head of a goat, the arms and torso of a man, and the tail of a fish. There was more than one, and each held a spear.

The *dynami* warmed at her hips, its tingle spreading through her. She wasn't about to be drowned by goat-fish. Gripping the net still dragging her down, she pulled with all her strength. The netting parted easily.

Ebba began to tear at the mesh in earnest as her chest tightened.

Plank appeared before her, and her eyes rounded as she tried to silently convey her panic. He held a dagger in his hand and slashed at the net tangled around her legs.

She kicked off the rest and jerked her legs through the water beside Plank, making for the surface. He pressed his dagger into her hand as they swam.

A Capricorn appeared in front of them, and Ebba shouted out the rest of her air as Plank was ripped away.

Her chest tightened in warning. She was no use to her father dead.

She broke the surface, breathing hard. The boat was overturned. Everyone was in the water. And fighting, judging by the water flying in all directions. Capricorn launched from the water in every direction, bearing down to the surface, spears in hand.

Something gripped her leg and she kicked hard. Whatever it was didn't return a second time.

Plank hadn't resurfaced.

Taking another breath, Ebba ducked her head under, eyes stinging at the salt in the water. Dagger still in her hand, she kicked in the direction he'd been taken.

Bubbles erupted in a flurry ahead, and she swam hard for the chaos. Plank was in the midst of the bubbles, both hands around the staff of a Capricorn's spear. He fought for possession of the weapon.

Ebba swam up behind the beast.

The Capricorn could clearly hear underwater, for it turned and dismissed her with a glance, facing Plank again.

A mistake.

A tingling sensation spread out from beneath her belt. Ebba wrapped an arm around the thing's chest, driving her dagger up beneath its ribs with as much force as she could against the drag of the sea. With the *dynami*'s help, that was a lot. The dagger slid under the Capricorn's ribs without resistance.

She pulled the dagger free, ready to go again, but the creature went limp, aqua blood oozing from it into the water.

Plank pushed the Capricorn away and grabbed her hand again. They swam for the surface once more, Ebba lugging him the last three feet as his kicks weakened.

He gasped for air as they emerged.

"The boat," she panted.

Ebba helped him to the overturned rowboat and clung to the hull as she took stock. "Caspian, Peg-leg, and Barrels," she said between breaths. "We need to find them first."

Grubby was the most injured, but he could also breathe underwater.

As though hearing her thought, Grubby burst upward from the water. For a moment, fighting ceased as they watched his glorious arc.

Her father's face was twisted in hatred, a sight she'd never seen. He directed his descent toward the Capricorn surrounding Peg-leg, and a switch was flicked. The battle resumed.

"I see Barrels." Plank coughed, leaning his head against the boat.

She followed his finger. "On it."

Ebba swam as hard as she could through the swell, grateful it was smaller than in recent days so she could see over the top. Ahead, Barrels slashed at a sole beast, but his strikes were slow and weak. The Capricorn swam around him, waiting for the moment her father exhausted himself.

The Capricorn turned at her approach, water dripping off the white hair of its goat head. Horizontal pupils regarded her and dismissed her, like his friend just did.

"I shoved my dagger in a buddy of yers down there," she shouted at the immortal.

The Capricorn slowly turned. Ebba couldn't tell if he understood her, but the creature's eyes rested on her dagger as it inhaled deeply.

"He bleated like a little kid," she called louder.

"Ebba," puffed Barrels. "Don't."

The beast neared her, and Ebba readied herself, saying to her father, "Swim to the boat, catch yer breath. Plank be there; we're regroupin'."

That was a stretch, and Barrels must've sensed it. He hesitated.

"I can't be worryin' about ye drownin'," she scolded him.

Relief lit within her as he nodded, making for the rowboat.

The beast turned to follow.

"Oi, goat face," Ebba yelled, splashing the water. "Ye're a right ugly thing, ain't ye?" She'd never get over some of these magical combos.

The Capricorn lazily drifted her way and then, without warning, launched at her with vigor. Ebba gasped and blindly thrust her dagger out.

The beast collided with her, and Ebba flew up and out of the water, arms and legs flailing as she soared backward through the air.

The dagger was gone. That was her only thought before she bombed into the ocean.

The *dynami*'s tingling power pulsed through her in waves, and with a few short, strong strokes, she broke the surface again. Where was she? On the other side of the rowboat? She couldn't see it.

Ebba swam in the direction of the yelling and splashing, knowing her crew would be exhausted by this point without the help of the *dynami*.

A Jendu popped up in front of her. Ebba flung out her arm instinctively and just managed to stop herself from punching the creature.

"What are ye doin' here?" Ebba hissed.

The Jendu began to tug her away from the noise, and Ebba jerked her arm free.

"Nay," she said, knowing the mermaid couldn't understand her. Ebba pointed at her heart and then back at the boat.

The creature sighed and shook her head, pointing at herself.

"I don't expect ye to come," Ebba told her. "But I must save them."

The Jendu nodded and swam aside to let her pass.

. . . But the way was barred.

As Ebba spun in a circle, Capricorn rose from the water all around, some of them missing spears, some of them bleeding aqua blood, but all of them staring at her and the Jendu with burning eyes.

"This ain't good," she whispered to herself as the mermaid began to cry, the sound like chimes. If Jendu had cursing magic, now was the time to use it.

Ebba glanced down at her belt, double-checking the *dynami* was there. It was all she had to protect herself.

Treading water, she spun in another circle as the Capricorn advanced. "Let the Jendu go," she said loudly, pointing to the young woman. "Let her go."

The Jendu cowered against her back.

"Blimey," Ebba muttered. "At least help yerself."

She whirled in time to see a beast launch at them from behind. Ebba threw a punch, wincing as the Capricorn's cheekbone collapsed inward with a loud snap. The beast dropped—whether unconscious or dead, she couldn't tell.

Ebba struggled to stabilize herself after the punch, briefly bobbing underwater.

The other Capricorn stopped, and Ebba glared at them. The largest of them pointed his spear at her and then at a net in his hand.

"I ain't gettin' in anythin' that'll drown me," she said. "But I will come with ye *if* ye let the Jendu go." She jerked her thumb at the Jendu and made a shooing gesture with her hand, hoping that was enough to convey her meaning.

If the Jendu was allowed to leave, maybe the immortal would tell the kraken what had befallen Ebba. She couldn't see her fathers but could hear them shouting for her. Which meant they weren't fighting for their lives any longer.

Hold on. Were *all* the Capricorn here surrounding her and the Jendu?

Fear twisted her insides. It better not have anything to do with the fact they were both female. Her throat closed over, the image of Calypso popping into her head again. She fought it off, teeth gritted.

"The Jendu goes," she called loudly, hoping her fathers would hear her. "I'll come with ye if the Jendu goes."

"She's over there," someone called. "I just heard her."

The Capricorn glanced in the direction of her fathers. Was it their urgent tone the creatures reacted to, or did they understand pirate?

The beast contemplated her and nodded.

These creatures definitely understood the mortal tongue.

Behind her, their circle broke apart, and Ebba shoved the Jendu in the direction of the opening. The creature peered back at her with wide eyes.

"Go," she shooed her.

As soon as the mermaid made scarce, she'd attack to stall a while longer. She'd told a pirate truth. She was only going with the Capricorn for one second.

The Jendu's lip trembled, but she turned and fled through the gap, disappearing under the surface.

"So. . . ," Ebba said, facing the Capricorn she assumed was the top goat.

The circle tightened around her.

She sized the beasts up.

As the leader shifted, the net in his hand emerged from beneath the surface. She'd thought it empty before, but horror struck her when she saw the tarnished silver tube within.

One of the root parts. The Capricorn had stolen it from one of her crewmates.

Ebba scanned the immortals with new eyes. Four had nets. Considering there were five objects and Ebba had one of them, the presence of four nets was too much of a coincidence to be disregarded. But she had to be sure.

Taking a breath, she dropped under the water and squinted at the closest net. The tell-tale glisten of tarnished silver winked back. Ebba wailed under the water and surfaced once more.

Even if the beasts had *one* part, she had to do everything possible to get it back. But if her gut was right, they had four parts. And if she went with the Capricorn, they'd have five. What was more, the creatures appeared to have deliberately collected the items. They knew what the parts were.

What *that* might mean, Ebba wasn't ready to contemplate. Her choice had to be the same either way.

She stared at the leader, heart sinking. Dipping her head at him, Ebba made no movement in the direction of her frantic crew.

The Capricorn closed in on her, and she didn't fight back. She didn't resist.

Ebba had to go with them.

SIXTEEN

They'd barely stopped the last two days. The longest break occurred shortly after the Capricorn took her hostage, once they'd put some distance between Ebba and her crew. And then, it was only to snatch the *dynami* from her belt.

The slimy wooden raft they carted her through the sea on was just large enough for her to curl up in a ball. Rusty nails protruded from the boards around the edges of the raft. There weren't sides to offer any protection from the water or spray.

In short, Ebba had been soaking wet, thirsty, hungry, and aching for two days.

"If I don't get water soon, I'll get sick," she croaked to the closest Capricorn, who bleated at her and then swam ahead to the top goat.

Should she take that to mean they wanted her alive? And *why* did they want her alive?

In two days, she'd thought of nothing else but how to get away with the parts. Trying to guess why the Capricorn wanted the five parts in the first place. If they knew the parts formed the root of magic, did they know what the root was meant for?

That the Capricorn had no idea what they carried was impossible, considering the care they'd taken to keep the parts separate.

She didn't budge as a wave broke over her head.

The continuous whirl of her thoughts between the snatches of sleep she'd managed to grab had left her exhausted. At least, she knew their direction. A few glimpses of the morning sun yesterday told her they were taking her northeast. Exactly where her crew had been heading before the beasts attacked—toward the sixth piece.

That seemed awfully coincidental. . . .

The situation threatened to overwhelm her, but she had to remember that the end game hadn't changed. Ebba had to get the parts back and somehow find her crew. The latter seemed impossible, so she focused on the first step. Yet that seemed impossible, too, because to take the five parts meant she had to *hold* five parts. She'd managed two but hadn't attempted more.

Ebba shifted her cheek against the slimy wooden board, blinking a few times as the waves smoothed out.

Pushing up on her elbows, she peered ahead to a long, shadowed mass in the distance. She had little idea of the time or whether it was night or day, but the darkness shrouding the island sent a foreboding shiver up her spine that had nothing to do with the cold.

The swell continued to smooth as the Capricorn towed her to shore.

Ebba scanned the creatures for any hint, noting the way they bunched together as they got closer to the island. Their spears were now lifted before them, their eyes scanning the shoreline.

They were afraid.

Which made Ebba afraid. If the Capricorn were meeting someone here, the creature had to be more powerful. Had Medusa been freed? Were the Capricorn working for *her*? Or was there a new foe behind the attack that they were yet to come across?

She set her attention to scanning the shore for any clue of what was to come. No boulders littered the dark beach. The landmass itself seemed relatively flat. She couldn't make out any treetops in the dim light, which added to her sense that the place was generally inhospitable. The island stretched far out to the north, beyond what her eyes could track.

What was this place?

The Capricorn slowed after the break, and the raft Ebba was on sank down into the water slightly. The closest one beckoned her off with jerky gestures.

Careful of the nails, Ebba obeyed, forcing her stiff limbs to move. They weren't inclined to. Ebba rolled off the raft and went under, her aching legs scrambling for purchase as she windmilled her arms through the sea.

The beast gripped the neck of her tunic and hauled her up. Her feet found purchase. Apparently, the water was shallow enough to stand. She grunted her thanks to the creature before recalling she was their hostage.

"Are we goin' in or what?" Ebba called to the top goat. Being a pirate, she was well used to being wet. But after two days of being soaked to the bone, she wanted to be dry. Even for an hour.

One of the Capricorn splashed, and she remembered their fish tails.

"Oh," Ebba drew out. "Ye can't go on land."

They were definitely meeting someone, then. Judging by the empty beach, their boss wasn't here yet.

She straightened. The Capricorn were restricted to water with their fish tails.

The beasts were twice her size, and the water reached her waist. This had to be as close as they dared go. Which meant she only had to get a little in front to escape. Ebba edged forward in slow increments.

Sod it.

She stopped with a weary sigh. They still had the parts. Those things were going to be major seaweed on her rudder.

The Capricorn bleated to each other, casting furtive glances at the beach, but their fearful conversation halted at a deep, echoing thud.

Several thuds.

Ebba shrank back into the water with the rest of the beasts at the sound, instinctively feeling for the weapons no longer on her body. What was making that noise? It sounded like a stampede of horses or cows. She braced herself to meet another magical species, however, knowing domestic farm animals could never instill such tension in the Capricorn.

The two closest immortals gripped her elbows and shoved her forward.

Ebba waded forward until she was just out of their reach, in water to her hips.

The thundering of hooves grew louder, interrupted by yips and shouts, and Ebba struggled to hold her ground as a horde of galloping creatures flooded over the beach toward them.

At first, she could only make out horned heads that reminded her of the Capricorn.

These creatures stood upright, which she found hard to correlate to the galloping noise. As they reached the water and started into the shallows, Ebba saw the new beasts did have hooves. In fact, their entire bottom halves were goat though they were human on top. Various colors of goat hair—white, shades of brown, and black—covered their bodies up to their waist. They were at least five heads taller than her and stood on two legs that bent the opposite way to Ebba's. Around each of their necks hung a small wooden windpipe.

What were these things? Did it mean something that both magical beings were half-goat, or not?

The goat-men surged into the water and Ebba lost the battle to face them off.

Rearing back, she yelped as a spear jabbed her in the back. Glancing behind her, she found the Capricorn's weapons raised in a pointy wall so she couldn't retreat.

Swallowing, she turned to face the latest threat to her life.

Usually, the biggest creature was the leader, but the opposite appeared true here. In the middle, the smallest of the goat-men stood, arms folded against his chest, slightly ahead of his herd, in clear dominance of the situation.

He opened his mouth. "You have the parts, brethren?"

Brethren. They were related?

She jerked as, one by one, the mesh nets containing the parts were thrown to the standing creatures. The spear jabbed her in the back again, and Ebba glared over her shoulder at one of the Capricorn. They held *veritas* out to her.

Wait. They wanted to give her a sword? Sure.

Ebba reached back and grasped the net holding the weapon. She wasted no time grabbing the hilt, focusing her thoughts on one question: What were these immortals going to do to her?

She waited for the sword to answer, but no image appeared in her mind as it had with Locks. Caspian was right. The *veritas* didn't show you the future; it only confirmed what you already knew. And she knew nothing right now. But as the leader of the standing beasts beckoned her forward, Ebba gripped the *veritas* tight and glanced around with the extra sight the sword lent the bearer.

. . . The island possessed a dull glow as did the water around her.

The Capricorn glowed, too, but a ball of shadow swirled deep within them. A dark cloud that was very similar to the taint Ebba had glimpsed inside of her fathers.

She peered down at herself and saw she possessed only shiny radiance. She glanced up at the new immortals.

No light.

None whatsoever. The hooved creatures were drenched in shadows. The cloud of darkness wasn't just a ball inside their chests—it consumed them.

Her mouth dried. The Capricorn were a little tainted like her fathers. But if Ebba was correct, these new immortals were saturated with the evil.

She squinted along the rows of them, trying to make out their eye color in the dim light. If they were contagious, Ebba had to be very, very careful.

Shite.

The sword was ripped from her hands, and Ebba jumped, coming eye-to-chest with the leader. Tilting back her head, she felt her mouth dry at the glow in the beast's yellow eyes. The knot within her loosened at that; yellow, not black with taint. This one wasn't contagious, at least.

"This is the right girl?" The leader spoke over her head while inspecting her. He had horizontal slits for eyes just like the Capricorn.

He lifted a hand to her cheek and Ebba slapped it away.

"Keep yer hands to yerself," she snarled.

The beast ignored her, addressing his herd. "Then the others shall come as expected."

Her heart dropped into her boots.

This was a trap for her fathers? *She* was the trap? But how had they known that would work? How could these creatures 'expect' anything? That meant they had information on her crew.

"What are ye plannin'?" she asked him, jaw clenched.

The leader gestured and two more approached, yellow eyes fixed on her.

She braced herself, watching their movements. "Where are ye takin' me?"

Pain exploded across her face as the back of the beast's hand spun her sideways, submerging her in the water once more. Lights exploded before her eyes, and her ears rang as she was hauled gasping from the sea again.

This time, she was dragged to the shore, and by the time they'd heaved her onto the muddy sand, Ebba managed to blink away the dots of white light from the blow and struggled to her feet.

"Speak when spoken to, mortal," one of the goat-men holding her upright hissed.

"Sod off," Ebba snarled.

His yellow eyes flared.

"Ye just spoke to me," she hurried to add.

The second beast looped one rope around her hands and another rope in a noose about her neck. They held one end each and she didn't need them to jerk the rope to gather she'd either keep up or be dragged.

The leader shouted a command, and she was forced in a run up the beach.

Ebba tried to limit her weaving, her face throbbing from the earlier blow. Her calves burned as she pushed through the dark, muddy sand. The clouds above were so thick it was like perpetual night here. As the sludgy sand gave way to dirt ground interspersed with wiry, thorny black vines, the heaviness in her stomach swelled.

She was the trap.

They'd gotten that half wrong, though. The Capricorn could've taken any member of the crew, and the rest would've done their darnedest to save the person. But how had the Capricorn known? Had they spied on the rowboat or *Felicity* without anyone realizing?

The goat-man she'd mouthed off to earlier yanked on the rope around her neck. Ebba stumbled forward, barely keeping her feet as she choked for air.

"Keep up," he barked.

Running on flat ground was easier than the beach though the occasional pebble and the presence of the thorns had her constantly scanning the island floor lest she step on one. Ebba picked up the pace, breath even and head clearing as she settled into a steady rhythm in tandem with the goat-men. How far would they take her? Ebba was fit, but she also hadn't had food or water in two days. Her wounds from entering Matey's mouth were largely healed, aside from the deepest one, but keeping this pace up for more than an hour would be a near-impossible task.

She'd have to worry about that later. Her task was to find out as much as she could about these things before her fathers arrived.

If they arrived.

The Capricorn had carted her here for two days and a night without stopping, their pace that of a ship at full speed. How would her fathers know where to find her? Or would they be helped to this spot since it was a trap? If Matey was still with them, they might be hot on her trail already. If they had to row themselves, the rescue party could be a week away, no match for the speed of the Capricorn.

She didn't even know if they'd all survived the attack.

Hopelessness threatened to overwhelm her, and Ebba did her best to force that back as she leaped over a wiry vine and ran down an incline after the creatures. It wasn't fair to have come so far and collected almost all the parts just to have their efforts thwarted. But she had to focus. There were five parts to secure. And every situation had a silver lining. Her fathers were coming to her, solving the problem of how she'd hold all five parts *and* how Ebba would find her crew again after escaping. There might even be a possibility the sixth part was on this island. A grim smile curved her lips. That had to be why these creatures wanted the other parts—the final piece of the weapon was here. Except the beasts were tainted, which she had to assume meant they wanted the weapon for the wrong reason.

The front of the herd slowed, and Ebba slowed with them.

Too soon, as she discovered.

Both beasts ripped on the ropes and sent her flying to the ground. Ebba yanked her arms up in front of her face, crying out as the ground tore at the skin on her forearms. She landed on the wound on the right side of her torso and screamed.

Gasping, she rolled onto her side, curling into a ball as pain licked her torso.

"Careful. Or it will be your head," snapped the leader. "The orders were clear. She must be intact."

His words permeated the fog of agony surrounding her skull. *Orders*.

Panting, she uncurled and rolled to her hands and knees, lifting an arm to cradle her side. They had orders. Which meant this wasn't the last stop. Where in Davy Jones' were they taking her?

Terror rooted her to the spot as something she'd missed clicked into place.

She gasped, but not from the pain. These creatures were *tainted*. Which meant they'd had contact with the six pillars' evil power. Her breath came fast. These beasts didn't want the weapon for themselves. They were taking her and the rest of her crew to the *pillars*. Along with the five parts, six if they had the remaining one in their possession.

Shite. This was bad. Really, really bad.

Ebba barely noticed as she was wrenched to her feet and the ropes removed.

The leader sneered at her, his goat face twisting. "She's filthy. Not fit to be seen."

She'd like to see him after the week she'd just had. Still, there might be an offer to be clean in his disgust, and she'd take it.

"What are ye?" she asked, tilting her chin.

"Satyr," he announced after peering down his nose at her. He drew himself to full height, puffing his chest out.

Satyr. That she'd never heard of them wasn't odd, but one of Plank's stories—or even his lifeless summary—would be appreciated right about now. They were clearly violent, and from what Ebba could tell, like the Capricorn, all of them were male. The Satyr leader seemed vain, but she didn't know if that was true of all Satyr. They were powerfully built, and without luck or the *dynami*, she wouldn't be winning any bouts against them.

The lead Satyr looked at the two who'd brought her there and then to another pair. "Take her to the females. Tell them to make her presentable. Her companions won't take long to arrive."

"How do ye know that?" she blurted. Warmth oozed out from her side. Blast it, the wound was open again.

She'd been wrong about the lack of female Satyr too. Were they kept somewhere else?

Ebba was shoved aside from the herd as the Satyr milled around the clearing.

The space they'd stopped in was a wide expanse bordered by black wiry vines, but the two Satyr led her north to a narrow ascending path also bordered with the thorned plants. The steep path wound up to the highest part of the island she'd seen so far—a small hill. The track to the top was only wide enough for the Satyr to trot shoulder-to-shoulder.

Ebba yelped as she stepped on a thorn.

"Move," the Satyr behind her snapped.

"Yeah, yeah," she muttered, hobbling now.

They reached the top of the small hill and began down the other side, moving in large circles around the outside of what appeared to be a circular canyon in the middle of the hill. It was like an apple with the core removed. The outer wall of the descending path was solid rock, but the inner edge opened into the canyon.

Ebba leaned to peer over the lip and gasped.

A blue lagoon glistened below.

The Satyr showed no signs of stopping before the bottom, and Ebba began to anticipate being clean in earnest. A change of clothes would be welcome, but she wouldn't hope for that much hospitality.

The ground gradually flattened, and the Satyr directed her to stand on a jutting rock.

She obeyed the immortals, but unease crept over her as they then turned to look at the water.

Why did she have to stand on this *exact* spot, right by the lagoon? For the first time, Ebba considered that something might be *living* in there.

One of the Satyr whistled, and Ebba reared back as something surged below the water. . . .

. . . Heading directly for her.

SEVENTEEN

"What's that?" Ebba shouted as the thing surged through the lagoon toward her.

A Satyr pushed her forward, and she toppled onto her hands and knees. She stared into the horizontal pupils of a goat and, mouth ajar, shifted her gaze to its tail and then back again. It was a Capricorn.

The creature rose out of the water, and she saw its bared chest. A *female* Capricorn. The Satyr weren't referring to the females of *their* kind.

"Clean and dress her," the Satyr ordered. "Geordian wants her presentable."

Ebba sat back, staring at the woman.

"I need food and water," Ebba said over her shoulder as her stomach rumbled. "Unless you want me to die afore you take me to the six pillars." She held her breath.

"Feed and water her," the Satyr ordered the female, who nodded frantically.

Sink her, should she take that as confirmation of the pillars' involvement?

The Capricorn held out her hand.

Ebba restrained the anger that wanted to lash out at the woman because of what had happened so far. Yet the female Capricorn were here, and subservient. And the male Capricorn had been afraid. As bitter as she was toward the creatures for turning over the parts to enemy hands, if her current theory was right, Ebba could understand why they'd done so.

"Wash yourself, mortal. And do not attempt to flee. This path is the only way out of the lagoon, and we will be standing guard in the clearing on the other side," the Satyr who had yet to speak said in a deep voice.

Ebba ignored them, and the Satyr left.

She looked into the female Capricorn's yellow eyes again before slipping down into the blue water fully clothed.

"I've had quite the day," Ebba told her. "I don't mean to be rude, but I'll kill ye with my bare hands if ye try anythin'."

The woman cast her a fearful glance.

The male Capricorn hadn't bothered to communicate with her though they'd understood pirate. The same seemed true of the females.

The immortal towed Ebba to the opposite side of the lagoon, to a bunch of rocks covered from overhead view with wiry shrubs. As they neared the rocks there, more female Capricorn popped out of the water. Dozens of them.

Most held back to the outer edges of the water, but the female carrying her bleated, and a handful of others swam over.

"Are all female Capricorn here then?" Ebba asked.

The creature lowered her head and nodded, directing Ebba to sit on a rock that was submerged in the water.

"I just saw yer menfolk, did ye know?"

The others circled her at this, their eyes wide. The woman who'd led her over clutched at her arm.

"Aye," she continued. "When they kidnapped me from my crew and handed me over to the Satyr."

Shame lit each of their gazes, and they bleated softly at one another before the woman clutching Ebba squeezed her arm gently.

The Capricorn held a hand over her heart and dragged a finger down her goat cheek.

They could understand her but couldn't speak the mortal tongue. Was that because they had goat heads? Or was their magic weaker? Matey said the ability to talk the mortal tongue had to do with how much power an immortal possessed.

Ebba blinked back a burning in her eyes. "It makes me right sad too."

She sat on the submerged rock as directed, the water at her waist, and watched as the female Capricorn pulled down various branches overhanging the water. They plucked in systematic order, and within minutes, a large leaf filled with berries and nuts was placed on the rock that jutted out behind her. A jug of water was deposited next to the leaf platter, and Ebba lunged for it first, gulping the contents before heeding the churning warning in her gut.

She selected some nuts that looked like almonds and popped them into her mouth. If the Satyr wanted to kill her, they'd had ample opportunity to do so. And she was too hungry to turn down the offer of food.

Ebba munched on the nuts, sipping more sedately at the water as the Capricorn approached with various brushes and roots. The women twisted the roots, and as they rubbed the split plant between their hands, bubbles frothed.

"Is that soap?"

A nod was her answer.

One of the women gestured for Ebba to remove her clothing, and she hesitated.

"Aye, but what if the Satyr come back?" she asked, peering around the lagoon.

The woman pointed to the overhanging vines. They didn't just conceal the spot from above but on each side.

Ebba drew off the stained tunic she'd worn for the last week and slid out of her sawn-off slops as well. They were whisked away, and she sat naked on the rock.

She glanced down at the open wound on her side. "Blast it. Still bleeding."

The Capricorn gasped, and within a minute, moss was pressed against the wound. Ebba applied pressure and peered up again as the women set to work washing her. It briefly occurred to her to take over, but in all honesty, she was surprised to still be relatively upright at this point.

"What be the deal then?" she asked them. "They keep ye here to blackmail yer men folk?"

Those within listening range dipped their heads.

"How long?" Ebba asked.

The closest creature held up five fingers.

"Five months?"

She shook her goat head.

"Years?" When that elicited the same reaction, Ebba said incredulously, "Fifty years?"

They confirmed her guess with a soft bleat, and Ebba felt physically sick. "And ye've just been in this lagoon that entire time?"

They were prisoners. And suffered the worst fate Ebba could imagine—they were separated from their loved ones. The men of their kind had to feel utterly hopeless; unable to attack the Satyr because they couldn't move on land, subject to carry out the Satyr's orders at sea to keep their women safe. Ebba wished she'd tried harder to talk to the men. Maybe they could have reached an agreement to save their women.

If only she'd been holding the *scio* at the time instead of the *dynami*.

"I'm sorry," she whispered to them. "That's right horrible."

The scrubbing stopped briefly as they squeezed and patted her.

"When my fathers free me, we'll take ye back to the sea," Ebba told them.

The Capricorn stopped, lowering the brushes and roots in their hands to stare at her. They didn't believe her.

"I ain't sayin' they'll get here," she added. "I was carried an awful long way. But if they do find me, we'll figure a way to get ye out."

They offered polite smiles and went back to work.

How many guests had been shoved at them to clean in the past? "Am I the first visitor ye've had in fifty years?"

A Capricorn ducked below the surface and reappeared with freshwater plants amassed in a wild array on her head.

Ebba snorted as the women made a stuttered bleating sound that she assumed was laughter.

"Ye've met a Jendu, I take. I met my first one only a few days ago. Ye're right. They have terrible hair."

The women laughed again.

They worked up her body, carefully cleaning her wound and placing fresh moss over it. She was encouraged farther into the water where they cleaned her dreads and face. Slowly, the grime that had accumulated since *Felicity*'s sinking was removed, and Ebba found new heart in that and having her hunger and thirst quenched.

They worked an oil over her skin that left her glistening and smelling of flowers.

Ebba sneezed. "What is that shite? It smells like brothel."

Her comment only caused confusion, and she waved the matter aside, popping another handful of berries into her mouth and gulping down more water.

"I thought ye'd eat fish, livin' in the water an' all. Ain't it hard to find berries and nuts in the sea?" she asked them. Was this their normal diet?

The closest immortal shook her head, pointing at the water.

She frowned. "There ain't any fish here?"

The Capricorn froze.

Ebba dropped her hand, freezing too. "Was that rude or sumpin'?"

Her words trickled away as music floated to them from above.

Soft, lilting music. If Ebba had to put a word to it, she'd say seductive, almost like Calypso was working his thrall with his voice alone. She knew the sound came from flutes. She'd seen the small instruments around the Satyrs' necks.

The Capricorn abandoned her, their faces dropping, and swam for the middle of the lagoon. All of them left the edges to join.

Ebba crossed her arms over her chest, scanning the area before her and above to check the Satyr couldn't see her. What was going on?

The Capricorn danced in the water, writhing, laying on their backs, chests bared. Ebba listened to the stamping coming from high above, the jeer and whistles, and bile rose up through her throat.

The Satyr had gathered to watch the female Capricorn dance, but the expression on the females' faces told her they were hating every minute of the show.

A burning anger filled her, ugly and dark. Lacking the outlet she wanted—to slaughter every single Satyr—the emotion swept to her welling eyes. Ebba turned away from the women's unwilling dance to the rocks behind her.

Her attention was drawn back as objects began to slap the water.

Fish.

The Satyr were throwing fish down.

"They only feed them if they dance," Ebba seethed, dashing at her wet face.

The Capricorn grabbed at the fish, collecting them. Her group returned, gazes dropped to the surface of the lagoon.

Ebba was going to free them if it was the last thing she did.

EIGHTEEN

The Capricorn's knowledge of land was understandably limited, so while Ebba was cleaner than she'd been in her life and smelling like a bloody bouquet, they'd dressed her and then dragged her through the water to await the Satyr. As a result, Ebba stood shivering in a dress that put Medusa's to shame. Was this her life now? Would the dresses only get smaller? Would she spend her life soaked through and shivering?

Where was the Caspian Sea when she needed its warmth and life? Take her away from this empty void filled with things meant to make her soul cry, she thought. Deliver her to what she'd known and what she loved.

Night had fallen.

She judged this by the drop in temperature and nothing else. Though the cold could be put down to her lack of clothing. The female Capricorn, courtesy of the Saytr no doubt, had brought several dress options that ranged from strategically placed plants to . . . *this.*

Ebba was covered from chest to mid-thigh by a royal blue shift. Overtop of the silk shift was a breezy full-length toga that left nothing beneath it to the imagination. Every curve was on show. If she bent over, Ebba trembled at the thought of what might be put on display to people she didn't know. Or did know. Over one shoulder, the gauzy material trailed down her back, floating in the breeze.

From what she could tell, nothing but magic held the dress up over her chest. If she ran, she was a goner; if she jumped, she was a goner. And after the show the female Capricorn were forced to put on, Ebba preferred not to battle the Satyr butt-naked.

But she would. Because she'd rather be naked and alive than dressed and dead.

"I be gettin' right sick 'o waitin'," she stuttered, arms around her body as shivers wracked her. She turned back to the Capricorn, who had gathered to keep her company. "I'm goin' to head up," Ebba told them.

They nodded back at her, and she noted the only hope present was in the eyes of the youngest creatures.

"I'll come back," she said firmly.

Hiking up her toga, Ebba stomped up the circling path, talking herself into a rage that would chase away her fear.

"Ye want a fight?" she hissed to herself. "I'll rip yer ugly horns off and shove 'em so far up yer goat parts, ye'll think ye're a horse."

Footsteps pounded down the path, and Ebba halted, pressing to the side of the path, away from the drop down into the lagoon. Her bravado fell away.

"I won't shove 'em anywhere," she whispered, yelping as thorns dug into her arm.

Two men appeared around the bend, and Ebba stared, skull buzzing for a full three seconds.

"Jagger?" she called.

The nearest of the men lifted his head, and Ebba's breath caught at the fury in his silver eyes. She looked past him.

"Caspian," she gasped.

He'd slowed behind Jagger, but he pushed past the pirate as she launched herself toward them. His arm wrapped around her, and she wrapped her arm around his middle, her other hand caught against his chest.

"What are ye doin' here?" she rushed to say. "There be goat-men about, Satyr—"

"We know," he said, his hand moving to the back of her head to press her closer. "We know."

"We've got to go," Jagger said in a low voice.

Caspian tipped her head back and brought his lips to hers. The kiss was fast, hard, life-affirming and left Ebba gaping at him. They'd never kissed in front of anyone before. Well actually, Jagger saw the first one. But they hadn't known that at the time.

It made her uncomfortable. But she had a feeling that her current discomfort wasn't over the publicity of the kiss but because the kiss was in front of Jagger specifically.

"We need to free the Capricorn down in the lagoon," she said, ignoring the sudden tension in the air.

Jagger hissed, "Capricorn."

"The males only brought me here because the Satyr imprisoned their females fifty years ago," she explained, moving past the prince to talk to Jagger.

That seemed to mollify him.

"I promised we'd get them out," Ebba said, turning to the prince for help.

His eyes were bloodshot, his face drawn as though he hadn't slept in days. But he nodded. "Okay, let's hurry."

"And how are ye proposin' we do that? Carry them back to the sea one at a time?" Jagger gripped Ebba's hand. "We can't save them. We need to leave."

She tried to break his hold. "Nay, you didn't see them, Jagger. They have to dance for the Satyr just for their food each day."

The stoniness of his gaze flickered at that. Then was gone.

"Ye're heartless," she said, trying to draw away from him again.

"Nay," he said tightly, stepping in so he was right before her.

"Never think that o' me, Viva. But gettin' ye away from here takes pr'ority. We can't win this round if we try to save them now."

She blinked at his nearness, and want swept through her with the force of a tidal wave. She yearned for his touch, his attention, in a way she'd never yearned for anything or anyone. Something had unlocked within her, and after recent events, she wasn't at a loss to understand the emotion.

Ebba was entirely attracted to Jagger. *Fiercely* attracted.

The heat Caspian inspired was pleasant. Safe. Secure. This entire time she'd waited to feel the deeper regard that he felt for her—her major concern being missing the arrival of it.

But, she realized, *this* is what regard felt like. A burning uncertainty that made her heart pound and her breath come short.

. . . And it wasn't for the prince.

Caspian rested a hand on her shoulder. "Ebba, maybe he's right. . . ."

She jumped. *What?*

"I am right," the pirate snapped. "Ye choose yer fathers or the Capricorn. Which is it?"

Ebba's chest rose and fell, and not for the reason it should. Focusing her thoughts on the present, she glanced down in the direction of the lagoon.

Jagger gripped her chin, dragging her gaze back to the sculpted lines of his face. She'd always recognized he was handsome. Why was she only just feeling this overwhelming inferno? Was it that the *veritas* had confirmed Ebba could trust Jagger? Or was the awakening of her body's urges entirely due to her meetings with Calypso?

Or was it both?

"Which is it?" he repeated angrily.

She jumped again, heart leaping into her mouth. "Huh?"

"Yer fathers or the Capricorn?"

Relief poured through her. She hadn't spoken aloud.

Ebba closed her eyes, dragging her thoughts back yet *again*. "My fathers, o' course."

"Exactly, forget the rest. Don't confuse yer priorities. There'll come a day when we might be able to save them, but not if we don't first save ourselves."

He was so cutting, so ruthless. To make a decision so forcefully shook her deep down. But if it came to her fathers or the Capricorn. . . . If she couldn't have both, as guilty as it made her feel, Ebba would choose her crew every time. She could respect his ruthlessness.

"Let's go," she said raggedly.

"It will all work out, Ebba," Caspian said in an undertone.

"Wait," Jagger said, pulling off his tunic. "Ye can't run in that. Though . . . I'd like to see ye try."

He would? Did he find her attractive? Did he feel what she felt?

Muffling a groan, Ebba realized her attraction to Jagger might not be entirely without its drawbacks. This angst had to be what Caspian felt for her; so uncertain and excited, so terrified and hopeful. She had to straighten out the expectations with the prince as soon as they got out of this mess. He deserved her complete honesty. This attraction she felt for the pirate was here to stay—for the time being, anyway. She had to tell the prince they couldn't be together because although Ebba trusted Caspian with her life, loved him as a friend, the mere thought of him didn't leave her breathless. She couldn't say if Jagger returned her regard, or if what she felt would become anything deeper, but she hoped the prince could come to understand her decision. That their friendship might soon be on the rocks made her wish she'd never agreed to explore things between them in the first place.

Sure, he'd known she might say no. But saying a simple no felt different than saying no because she'd developed a regard for someone else.

Sink her.

Ebba accepted Jagger's shirt without a word, shrugging it on and avoiding Caspian's sharp stare.

Once covered, she strode to the path's edge and called down, "I'll be back for ye, I swear it. Don't be losin' hope; ye have friends."

Feeling the weight of responsibility more than ever, Ebba set off after Caspian and the bare-chested Jagger up the path.

They reached the top of the small hill and started down the other side to the Satyr's clearing. They kept up their pace, and Ebba attempted to keep her footsteps as quiet as possible.

The prince sank to a crouch behind some of the wiry shrubs as they neared the bottom of the path. From their elevated position, she could see the clearing the Satyr had first led her to.

"Where are my fathers?" she said, clutching her side and panting.

"Ye're injured," Jagger whispered.

His intricate chest tattoo was on display, gleaming with a layer of perspiration. Ebba cleared her throat. "Nay, the wound just opened a tad. I ain't slept, drank or ate much in a few days. I'll be all right. Fill me in."

She wanted off this island with the five parts of the weapon, her crew, and ideally a ship. And the sixth part.

And the female Capricorn.

"Matey and the Jendu drew the Satyr's attention to the southern end of the island," Caspian said, eyes searching the darkness.

"The Jendu are helpin'?" she asked.

"You saved the niece of someone important, from what I gather. They forgave us for drawing the Capricorn with the bloody bandages and even came here to help us. Either that or the *amare* has a lingering effect, but I don't think that's the case."

"Ye'd know," muttered Jagger to the prince.

The prince quietened.

"What?" Ebba glanced between them. "What about the *amare*?"

Caspian shook his head. "Not important."

Jagger looked like he had something to say about that, but at a sharp look from the prince, he smirked instead of replying.

Right. "What do ye both know about the Satyr?"

Jagger said darkly, "Enough to drive us all insane the last three days. We didn't think we'd find ye in one piece. As ye were."

Ebba didn't pretend to misunderstand his meaning. "Aye, I was worried about that myself when I saw what they did to the women in the lagoon." She shivered but forced away those somber thoughts. "They weren't to harm me, though. They—"

She said in alarm, "It's a trap. They were tryin' to lure all o' ye here to deliver us to someone else. The pillars, I think. They're collectin' the parts. That's why they cleaned me up. To make me pr'sentable for their boss."

Caspian sighed. "You should have told us immediately. We have to warn the crew."

His disappointment stung. Yet she thought jealousy might be at work under his words too. "I'm sorry; it hasn't been that long. We have to alert my fathers that the pillars could be on their way."

"It wouldn't have changed a thing until now," Jagger said in a calm voice. "Worryin' about the pillars will only distract from what needs to be done. We'll handle that when it needs handlin'."

She threw a grateful smile at him, but he didn't see, scanning the area ahead.

Her eyes dropped to his chest tattoos, and her mouth dried.

Seriously? Right now? This attraction stuff was not to be underestimated.

"I ain't sure I can forget about the pillars," Ebba admitted, her eyes tracing the inked tip of a spear that ran in line with his collarbone. "I swore I'd never go through what happened on *Malice* again. I ain't sure I could handle it a second time."

Jagger glanced at Caspian and then at her.

She tore her eyes from his body, horror flooding through her.

"If the kraken lost their attention, yer fathers were to make a ruckus on the eastern beach," Jagger said, arching a brow, but thankfully not commenting on her staring.

But he'd noticed.

Cheeks flaming, Ebba rose in a stooped crouch. "Let's go to them."

"No, we need to get the parts back," Caspian said.

"Aye," Jagger agreed.

Frustration needled her. "Well, where are the parts?"

Both turned to her and Ebba shrugged. "I have no idea. They carried them in nets, but I was parted from the Satyr hours ago. They could be anywhere."

"*Get down,*" Jagger suddenly hissed.

Ebba lowered and shrank into a small ball, her head raised just high enough above the wiry shrubs to watch as flaming torches moved in a procession toward the clearing below.

She could hear the clop of the Satyr's hooves. A lot of them. And another sound.

"My fathers are on the eastern beach, ye say?" she said in the quietest voice possible.

Neither male answered.

Wherever they'd been, her fathers weren't there anymore.

They were being dragged, hands and necks trussed up as hers had been, into a ring of stomping Satyr.

NINETEEN

"Get the female mortal."

Ebba froze at the Satyr's order, wedged between the warm bodies of Caspian and Jagger.

"*I'm* the female mortal," she frantically whispered to them. "They'll come up the path to find *me*."

To her astonishment, Jagger looked ready to laugh at her exclamation.

"Ye've got one twisted sense o' humor. It ain't funny," she snapped. "We've got to move."

"Have I ever said I like it when ye get mad, Viva?" Jagger answered, eyes fixed on her. "It's like watchin' a tropical storm from afar."

She stared at him, her stomach erupting into flutters—as though a hundred drunken Sallys flew within. That comment could be taken as an insult, but instead it made her feel giddy.

"Where to?" Caspian said forcefully. "We'll get torn to shreds if we head into those vines. And even then, I doubt they'll miss us."

Ebba shook off the flustered heat Jagger's comment had caused. They needed somewhere to hide.

"Is there anywhere else to escape from the lagoon?" Jagger asked, the amusement gone from his eyes as hooves pounded toward them.

There was nowhere. Nothing but a lagoon. They could hold their breath underwater, perhaps. But for how long? And if Ebba wasn't found, how would the female Capricorn be punished by the Satyr?

Something occurred to her.

"Stay here," she said.

The galloping thunder swelled, and Ebba launched herself upright and sprinted down the path toward the Satyr, who had no idea Jagger and Caspian were there. If the pair were smart, they'd stay put and figure out a way to save her and the rest of the crew.

Rounding the corner, Ebba shrieked as four Satyr bowled up the path toward her. She lifted an arm to protect her face, curling her body to protect her injured side and waited to be trampled to death.

The air whooshed from her as she was swept up with the delicacy of a stone wall.

At least they'd connected with her left side, not her wounded side. She still gasped for air, trying to orient herself with the violent cantering of the Satyr holding her.

She didn't miss the sharp turn of her escort. They were galloping downhill toward the clearing. Ebba schooled her features, hoping not a speck of elation showed on her face.

Caspian and Jagger were still free.

"Ebba! Get yer hands off her, ye horned bastard," Peg-leg howled.

The Satyr dropped her before their leader, but Ebba was up as soon as she landed, clutching her side as she raced to her fathers.

Locks sank to his knees, emerald eye blazing. "Ebba, love. Are ye okay?"

Plank wrapped her in his arms wordlessly, and she hugged him tightly before going to Locks and Peg-leg, and then Barrels and Stubby.

"Lass, please don't ever sacrifice yerself for a Jendu again," Stubby whispered. "I don't care who dies if it means ye live."

Ebba didn't share that same cold-blooded streak as her fathers, but she understood he meant every word. Her fathers *would* kill others to save her—the Satyr, Jagger, Caspian, and even each other. It repelled her as surely as it wound her closer to them. For no one could love her as much as they did, and despite the brutality that lay buried under so many layers, her soul knew theirs, needed theirs.

"They had the parts. I had to. Where's Grubby?" she asked, peering over Stubby's shoulder.

"Hey, Ebba!" He waved, smiling a toothy grin.

She sucked in a breath.

Stubby nodded subtly. "Aye, he's back."

Ebba released him to inspect Grubby as the Satyr pressed in behind their group. "The knock left his . . . skull empty o' rum again?"

"As far as we can tell, lass," Stubby answered. "And we don't have the *purgium* to heal him." This comment was accompanied by a sigh of hearty relief.

Ebba looked pointedly at him, denying the twin twinges of relief within her. If they didn't have the *purgium*, Grubby could stay his usual happy self. Ebba had to admit that she wasn't eager to see the arrogant selkie version of him anytime soon—no matter how smart that version was.

"How many?" the leader yelled behind her.

Her fathers closed around her, but Ebba wasn't having any of that. She squeezed between Barrels and Plank, staring out at the Satyr.

One of the goat-men trotted down the line. "Seven."

The leader shoved the larger Satyr aside and glared at their crew. "Two are missing."

She trained her eyes on his horned head so as not to give Jagger and Caspian's location away. Where in Davy Jones' were they getting their information? How could this Satyr possibly know anything about the workings of their ship and its crew?

Peg-leg shrugged as the Satyr glared down at him. "Don't look at me, matey. I can't count."

"—Aye, I can't remember past five *seconds* ago—"

"—It's our age—"

"—But don't ask us how old. I lost count at twenty—"

"My last memory be my . . . my twelfth birthday—"

"I can't think," Grubby said happily.

"Enough," the Satyr roared. "There were two young male mortals in your company. Where are they?"

"Was one of them bald as the day he was born?" Ebba asked, screwing up her face.

The Satyr's fury dropped like an unfurled sail as he neared Ebba and lowered his horned head. He inhaled deeply.

"It's flower stuff," she supplied. "Do ye like it?"

"Male," he hissed.

Ebba frowned. That was pretty accurate on a day-to-day basis, but she knew for a fact she smelled of one million pungent blossoms right now.

She glanced down. At Jagger's tunic. "Why're yer sails in a wad? I was cold and put my tunic back on."

He inhaled again, and her fathers crowded on either side.

"No," the leader said with a cruel smile. "The scent is fresh. A strong male."

He turned so quickly that Ebba threw herself back from his kicking legs.

"Check the lagoon path for the others," the Satyr boomed.

Eight of the beasts peeled away from the back of the group and cantered up the hill toward the start of the descending lagoon path.

She exchanged a loaded look with Plank.

"The parts, little nymph. Where are they?"

Ebba dropped her voice. "I lost sight o' them a while back. But this was always a trap. They want us gathered so they can take us to their boss. I'm thinkin' it be the pillars. The Satyr are filled with taint. I saw it when I held the sword." Her voice shook. Sink her, her crew couldn't be tainted any more. She couldn't be tainted again. They had to get out of here.

"Silence," one of the beasts bellowed.

Clothes were thrown at her fathers' feet.

"Change into these. You will be presentable."

The Satyr clearly had some serious hang-ups about presentation. And why did Ebba have a strong suspicion these clothes had belonged to people who were now dead?

"I'm pr'sentable," Peg-leg countered.

"You smell of an animal." The Satyr knocked her father back with his spear.

He hooked a doublet, eyeing the garment. "That's rich comin' from ye, goat-man."

The butt of the spear was driven into Peg-leg's stomach, and Ebba gritted her teeth, glaring at the Satyr until he stepped back.

"Satyr have a complex about bein' half-animal," Plank whispered to their group.

That explained the vanity thing. "And their flutes?"

"Used to . . . seduce. And to talk with each other at long distance, from what we can tell."

Sure enough, a trilling sound echoed from the direction of the lagoon. The leader smirked at Ebba, and her hands curled into fists.

They'd found Jagger and Caspian. Bugger it.

"Don't all look at once, but," Stubby said, jerking his head, "behind ye."

The entire crew looked.

Stubby hissed at them. "I said don't all look at once, ye eejits."

All of them glanced away.

Her father muttered about fools to himself. "*One at a time.*"

Ebba stole a peek first.

There, around fifteen feet behind them and hung on pegs in a row against a small shelter, housing all manners of rope, sat five mesh nets.

The root parts.

She faced forward again and waited as the others took their turns to look.

"We take the leader hostage," Barrels whispered, shrugging on one of the new tunics with ruffled cuffs.

Ebba shook her head. "They be violent. I ain't sure that'll cut it. But," she said, lifting her eyes to Plank's, "they be tainted inside. We can heal them. And use the *dynami* to hold 'em off."

Peg-leg pulled on the purple doublet coat. "The sword be handy just as a weapon too. And I'm thinkin' that rope will be best o' all around their legs. They don't bend like ours; it'll be hard for them to get free."

"Quiet," the leader snarled.

The crew of *Felicity* spread out in a line, and Ebba concealed her smirk. They had a plan. They'd wait for Stubby's call.

They could still get out of this.

Both Caspian and Jagger were bleeding when the Satyr returned, throwing them to the ground before the rest of their group.

Ebba scowled at the Satyr leader and watched as Barrels and Peg-leg leaned down to help the younger men. She watched as their mouths moved, no doubt whispering the plan to the pair.

"I thought ye said ye needed us all in one piece," she said to the leader loudly. "I hope yer boss won't punish ye for mishandlin' the goods."

The Satyr regarded her and dismissed her.

"Geordian," another beast hushed in his ear. "The pass will soon open. If you want to deliver them this night, we must leave now."

"Shake a leg," roared Stubby, bursting into action.

She sprinted alongside Grubby and Plank for the ropes. Her hands closed around them and she tossed three coils back overhead to the others before lunging for mesh nets. She hurriedly ran down the line, ignoring the shouting turmoil at her back. *Scio, amare, dynami*.

Ebba grabbed the third and whirled. "Jagger," she yelled.

He turned, and she lobbed the *dynami* to him, not waiting to see if he'd caught it.

She jumped as Caspian ran up beside her. He ripped open the

net holding the sword and drew *veritas* out, leaving her to join the battle behind them.

The *purgium.* Grinning grimly, Ebba fumbled with the net and managed to draw the silver tube out.

"Drop it," snarled a beast.

She ducked, and her eyes widened as a fist crashed into the wooden wall where her head had been. Ebba spun in her crouch and pressed the *purgium* against the Satyr's leg.

The beast dropped like a sack of shite.

"Ha! *Purgium* worked," she called to Barrels.

More of the creatures broke through, and Ebba widened her stance as they rushed her.

A boulder smashed into the one on the far right, and everyone stilled to watch as the line of Satyr charging her were knocked over like dominoes. Not by a boulder. A *man.*

Jagger, bare-chested and looking every bit the tribesperson, rolled to his feet, recovering from his tackling assault. *Dynami* in hand, the pirate plucked the closest spear from the ground and plunged it into one of the fallen Satyr.

Caspian sank the *veritas* into another. They worked down the line together, and Ebba looked past them to where her fathers had successfully tangled the ropes around other Satyr's legs. Some roamed free but they circled the anarchy warily, waiting for their moment.

Ebba reached back. The *scio.* She gripped it in her other hand.

"I need someone else to hold the last part," she called, watching as some of the Satyr worked around the edges of the clearing toward her.

She held two. She wasn't about to test if holding three was possible.

The rest of her fathers clutched the ends of the ropes to restrain the tangled beasts.

"Jagger," puffed Plank. "Swap with me."

The leader of the Satyr glowered at Ebba, slowly stalking toward her. "Come and get it then," she shouted at him, holding the *purgium* aloft. "Ye'll end up dead just like yer goat friends."

Ebba didn't know if the creature she'd dropped before was actually dead, but the leader couldn't know either.

Jagger sprinted to switch with Plank. He took the rope, and her father jogged to her.

The Satyr leader launched himself at Ebba, bearing down on her with a flurry of lethal hooves and coiled muscle. He spun his spear before him effortlessly. Her gut warned her there was no getting the *purgium* past that weapon in such skilled hands.

But he couldn't get the parts. The *pillars* couldn't get the parts. They couldn't get her or her crew. She had to keep the Satyr away from the root.

Breath coming fast, Ebba turned and reached for the bag with the *amare* inside. Her fingers gripped the mesh.

White light exploded, and a scream ripped from her throat as a surge of undiluted power slammed through her like a tidal wave, picking her up and throwing her.

Her mind and body numbed. She landed. Hard. And rolled amidst a tangle of limbs.

She could feel her eyes were open but could only see white. A ringing filled her skull, drowning out all sound, and as she attempted to sit, Ebba wavered on the spot and fell back down. Hands dragged her up.

She leaned heavily against the body of one of her fathers. Black punctured the white light in her head. Shadows formed, and outlines appeared. Ebba blinked to help her vision, but all that remained was blurriness and fuzziness.

"The leader has Plank," Peg-leg whispered in her ear.

She could barely discern his words through the high-pitched whine in her ears.

Ebba came to realize she still held the *purgium* and the *scio,* as though they'd melded to her hands during her stunned flight. Where the *amare* was, Ebba had no idea. The three pieces had exploded when she tried to hold them. What had they done to her?

"Is Plank okay?" she croaked.

There was movement behind her, and Ebba turned, still blinking on repeat. The Satyr in the ropes were recovering. Peg-leg sighed and took the *scio* from her belt, throwing it at the ground before them.

Surrender?

They were surrendering?

Her heart beat fast. This was her fault. She should have obeyed the warning in her gut and not touched the third piece. "Is Plank all right?" she asked again.

"Aye, he'll be fine, lass," he answered. "They're comin' for the *purgium*. Drop it in the bag."

That couldn't be it. They'd so nearly gained the upper hand.

"Nay," she said.

"They have a blade to his throat. We'll live to fight another day. Ye do as I've said."

Her harsh inhale echoed in her ears, in time to the deep thud in her chest. She'd ruined their chances of getting away, but she wouldn't be responsible for Plank's death. That would be too much to bear.

As the Satyr approached, Ebba felt for the mesh bag and dropped the *purgium* inside.

That was it. The fight was over.

TWENTY

Stubby and Plank all but carried her the first half of the walk, even restrained as they all were with ropes around their necks. She'd regained her sight after thirty minutes or so, but for a blurriness at the very edges. They'd found blood dripping from her ears, too. That was now dried and scrubbed away at the forceful insistence of the Satyr.

As they were shoved north at a fast clip, Ebba replayed the obliterating moment she'd held the three parts of the weapon at once. The force that tore through her was five times stronger than when she'd been thrown from holding only two parts.

But that wasn't important right now.

Ahead, the island tapered to a point. Ebba peered at the rocky outcrop, which extended into the distance farther than she could see. It was almost like a stone jetty leading away from the island, wide enough for only one person.

Though flat on top, large jutting stones bordered the outcrop on each side, disappearing down into the eddying sea.

Where did the jetty go?

They were stopped and forced to their knees in a small space at the entrance of the rock jetty. Only a few Satyr could fit there with them while the rest crowded the way they'd come, blocking their escape.

To her astonishment, the leader dragged her upright and planted her at the start of the never-ending jetty. He placed the mesh net holding the *purgium* in her hand.

Was he serious?

"Walk," he snarled, rearing back out of reach. The Satyr jerked his head to where one of his herd held the tip of a spear to Grubby's throat.

Walk *where*? She couldn't see the other side. Or did the path just lead into the middle of the Dynami? If so, why give them the weapon parts when they'd gone to so much trouble to collect them?

. . . With a sinking heart, Ebba realized the jetty must lead to the Satyr's boss.

She placed one bare foot on the outcrop to placate the leader then asked, "Are my crew comin' with me?"

"You will all go," the Satyr announced. "But hurry," he said with a hard smile. "Once the path is cleared, there is only enough time to reach the other side before the tide closes in again."

Seemed a shaky security for their safe delivery to the big boss.

What was to stop her crew from jumping off and swimming? Ebba glanced either side of the path. From here, she could count six small whirlpools. She'd wager a guess the eddies grew far more powerful the farther out the jetty went. Not water they wanted to swim in.

The urge to refuse hovered on the tip of her tongue. Yet how could she with the spear to Grubby's throat?

They weren't getting out of this. She shrugged, feeling the loose strands of her dress slip across her back. "Okay."

Turning, Ebba walked out on the pathway that split the Dynami Sea, the net containing the *purgium* in her hand. Once a fair distance away, she carefully rotated back to the Satyr. They were already forcing Jagger on after her.

They shoved a mesh net at him. The *amare.*

The pirate worked his way toward her, displaying the grace she knew came from his childhood in the rainforest. She watched as the Satyr did the same with Caspian and the *veritas*. Then Grubby and the *dynami*, Plank and the *scio*, followed by the remainder of the crew.

"They said we be havin' just enough time to reach the other side," Jagger said in an urgent undertone.

She wasn't leaving without all of her fathers.

"Don't let me fall in," she told him. Ebba leaned out and peered back at the island. The Satyr had gathered around the start of the jetty now, their spears extended out to block escape.

She sighed, exhaustion stabbing at her temples. "We're all on the path. The Satyr be blockin' the way off. We ain't gettin' out that way. Oi," she shouted. "We pushin' onward?"

"They're jabbing spears in my back," Barrels yelled.

That was that, then.

Ebba swallowed and turned, eyeing the endless jetty that led to a place she was certain none of them wished to be.

"We need to get goin', Viva."

She moved her lips. "I don't think we should. I have a bad feelin'." That they were walking toward the pillars.

There was a shuffling behind her. "Don't mind me freezin' me nipples off without a tunic," Jagger said.

Ebba coughed and shook her head. "Do ye need yer tunic?" she called back.

"Nay," he answered. "Keep it until ye get other clothes."

"Thanks," she said.

"But yer dress will get in the way, methinks. Ye need yer legs free."

Right enough. Ebba leaned down and lifted the long, breezy ends and tied them up above the side of one knee. "Better," she declared.

She started forward at a pace Peg-leg and Barrels could manage.

Ebba raised her voice so Caspian would hear. "Thanks to both of ye for findin' me. I was right terrified alone with the Satyr."

Jagger snorted, close behind her. "Ye looked like ye were ready to do battle. Yer green eyes blazin' fire. Yer lips pressed together like they do when yer ravin' mad. I was afraid ye'd do me in."

"I still will if ye're not careful," she said, studying the path.

"Perhaps I should be more reckless then."

Jagger was teasing her. *Flirting* with her.

Suddenly, every place on her back that Jagger might be looking at was alight with awareness. Her skin there prickled, and she straightened, her easy lop growing awkward and irregular.

His words thrilled her, exhilarated her like nothing else ever had. And yet she wished he wouldn't say such things in the prince's hearing. Caspian was right behind Jagger. Until she spoke to him, she didn't want to exacerbate his jealousy.

"Did the Satyr hurt you, Ebba?" Caspian called.

Ebba sighed, focusing on the ground ahead. "Nay, not really. Just frightened me, I s'pose. I was hurt more by holdin' the three parts than anythin' else."

"We were all thrown to the ground," the prince replied, his voice drifting forward over the sound of slapping waves and the low howl of the wind. "I wonder why you can hold two pieces of the root and not three."

"No notion."

"Maybe ye need practice," Jagger said.

Ebba hummed. "Nay, my gut warned me not to touch the third part, but I didn't listen. And it doesn't matter, does it? We'll just avoid that in the future."

The quiet after her words was the pregnant kind. Like when her fathers had whispered secrets to each other before Pleo.

Jagger and Caspian were keeping something from her. "Out with it," she demanded, wiping away the spray from her eyes.

She had no idea how far they'd walked so far, but the other side wasn't in sight. Was the water rising already? The heavy darkness made it hard to tell.

"We had a few days with the kraken while catchin' up with ye," Jagger said.

"He recalled more about the three watchers?"

"Aye. Some."

What she wanted to do was stop and listen, but she forced her body to continue walking at a steady pace. She blinked as the scene before her changed. What could be a sliver of land at the end of the path appeared on the horizon. Either that or her eyes were playing tricks.

"And?" she said impatiently.

"One of us is the bearer," Caspian said. "Whatever that means. Matey needs to check his grandfather's journals to clarify. Which I guess means that he has no idea."

Ebba smiled sadly at the mention of the kraken and glanced around the ocean. If luck was with them, Matey would miraculously appear, but they couldn't count on that.

"*The bearer*," she repeated. "One o' us bears sumpin', then. Holds the weapon, mayhaps?"

"Beats me," the prince answered.

Jagger replied, "Let's hope if it be Caspian's job, ye don't need two arms for it."

Ebba's eyes rounded, and a scalding insult balanced on the tip of her tongue.

Except Caspian choked on a laugh. A *laugh*. At a joke about only having one arm.

She bit her tongue hard, pressing back her protective instincts.

"That would be a cruel trick," the prince joked back.

She couldn't detect any bitterness or anger in his tone. The last she'd checked, Jagger had merely tolerated Caspian's presence. Now the pair were bantering?

Unable to help herself, Ebba glanced back at Jagger. He quirked a brow, and she faced forward again.

"Don't ye want to know what the third watcher be named?" Jagger asked her.

Yes. And no. Ebba couldn't decide. She could probably carry something, if she was the bearer. Could she choose?

"Are ye scared, Viva?" he teased her.

Utterly. "I think I can see the end o' the path ahead. The jetty connects us to another island," she said, almost certain the shadowed mass in front of them was real. If they could reach the island before the tide changed, they might live . . . to meet the Satyr's boss.

"Changin' the subject. Aye, ye're *scared*, methinks," the pirate whispered.

Ebba swallowed. "What if I can't do what needs doin'? I can handle failin' the realm, but I can't handle failin' my friends and family. What if I don't just do what I'm meant to, like ye, Jagger? Ye just stand there and yer immunity works without effort. But what if I'm meant to *do* sumpin', learn a skill, not just stand there."

Jagger snorted. "Thanks."

Despite herself, she choked on a laugh. "S'cuse me. That was rude."

"And accurate," Caspian added.

Jagger snickered with him.

More banter. . . . What exactly had happened in the last four days?

Ebba picked up her pace. She heard her fathers grumble, but the water was definitely higher. They had to hurry.

"Go on then." She scowled. "Tell me."

"Ye're the cleaner," Jagger answered.

The . . . cleaner. She didn't want to be *the cleaner*. "What? Ye're sure? How do ye know it ain't Caspian?"

Both sniggered.

"Jagger, are ye touchin' Caspian with the *amare*?" she asked. "Ye're both bein' weird."

Ebba picked up her pace again. The shadows and black night made it hard, but she could make out the island's full outline now. There were cliffs there. The crew could take refuge on top until the tide shifted again.

"We're just jokin'," Jagger said. "There ain't no cleaner. No need to sulk."

She shot over her shoulder. "I ain't sulkin', I be survivin'. Unlike the pair 'o ye."

"One of us is the bearer. And then one of us is the assembler," Caspian said.

"The assembler?" she asked despite herself. Or were they still teasing her?

"Aye," Jagger grumbled.

Her stomach plummeted. "That's a right fierce name." Better then 'the cleaner'.

Had the wind picked up? She hadn't noticed the increasing pitch of her voice. Her throat was sore. Ebba had been shouting at the others without realizing.

"What can ye see, lass?" The yell came from the back. Peg-leg or Stubby.

"There be another island at the end o' the jetty," she answered. "Hard to tell how far."

They didn't answer, and she said to the men directly behind her, "The *assembler*. I'll take the other one, the bearer."

Jagger snorted. "I ain't sure ye get to choose."

Ebba peered back. "Are ye ashamed ye ain't called the bearer or assembler, then? Ye just get the measly immune."

"I knew ye'd be annoyin' about it," the pirate groaned.

She grinned. "Ye ain't immune to envy, I see."

Caspian laughed and warmth spread through her chest. *That's* how things were meant to be. She and Caspian against Jagger. None of this lad's club shite. The prince was her best friend. Though . . . people could have more than one friend. There had been Sally, after all.

Ebba's mouth dried. Sally!

"Caspian." She rushed, turning her head to speak back over her shoulder. "How do ye think the wind works to take messages to Sal? She said to just use the wind, didn't she?"

He blurted, "I have no idea. There's ample wind here, though. If that's the only thing required, the wind sprites might hear us."

"It be worth a try," Jagger said.

Ebba cupped her hands around her mouth. "Oi, Sal! Uh—" She broke off. "What's her queen name again?"

"Saliha," the prince supplied.

"Oi, Queen Saliha," she roared. "We're in the Dynami. *Felicity* be sunk."

"Tell her to send the Daedalion," Jagger cut in.

"So send the Daedalion. They owe us. The Satyr, evil buggers that they are, have us marchin' across a rocky path to some island belongin' to their boss who we think might be the—" She lowered her hands, aghast as she recalled.

"We're marchin' toward the pillars," she croaked. "We can't go forward."

Ebba whirled, and the others cried out as they drew up short, arms circling for balance as they shouted in alarm.

"The pillars be that way," she said, panic closing over her.

"And the tide be nigh. The time to lose yer head ain't here," Jagger countered.

"Jagger, but the taint. . . ." Ebba trailed off, seeing the tightness around the pirate's eyes for the first time.

Beyond him, Caspian looked much the same. They'd realized this entire time and had. . . .

"Ye distracted me on purpose," she said flatly. "Ye bloody cons."

Jagger crossed his arms. "Told ye it were too forced. We'd have done better to be at each other's throats."

Ebba glared at the pair of them, oddly touched by their ploy to keep her from worrying. She spun back around and hurried down the path again. "I thought ye were friends at last."

The pirate. The *arrogant* pirate answered, "Be honest, ye didn't like that we might be friends. Ye want Caspian all to yerself."

"Ye think ye know everythin', Jagger," she sneered. He was right. Caspian was her friend.

Ebba scanned the shadows with a terror as cold as the spray hitting her face. They'd assumed the six pillars would take up their seat in Exosia, in Caspian's rightful place. Yet hadn't Medusa called them forth when she believed the crew of *Felicity* was caught in her grasp only weeks before?

When they hadn't found the pirates at Medusa's Lair, had they widened their net, knowing *Felicity* was somewhere in the Dynami Sea?

Were her crew walking to their doom?

"Jagger," she said aloud as memories of the taint pitched and heaved like bile burning her gut.

"Viva."

She took a breath. "I'm thinkin' it be better to get in the water and swim than to go farther. None o' us but ye stand a chance against them now they have their bodies."

Ebba stumbled and Jagger's hands shot out to grip her sides. "Viva," he said again.

Something hot burst through her at his touch. Passion. Fire. Endless. *Consuming*.

Ebba clutched her chest as the wild, untampered longing surged and burned through her with breathtaking ferocity.

She whirled around, hardly knowing she moved, and her gaze dropped to the *amare* in Jagger's hand.

He'd just touched her while holding the tube.

Stupefied, Ebba lifted her chin to look at the frozen pirate. Silver eyes bore down into hers. She couldn't decide if she wished to break the crackling tension between them or never let it end. Ebba couldn't think of a single thing to say anyway. Nothing could explain what she'd just felt when the *amare* touched her.

She dropped her gaze to her hands, completely stunned, completely at a loss. When the *amare* was touched to another, it drew out their real emotion.

Ebba had already discovered her attraction for Jagger. But that just now? That wasn't attraction. Attraction looked like a weak, withered nothingness beside what just surged through her.

It had stolen away the very urge to survive.

"Do ye think I'd let harm befall ye?" Jagger said hoarsely.

Right. As the person holding the tube, he wouldn't have felt a thing. And she was staring at him like a flaming idiot. She latched onto his question, attempting to push at the dumbstruck wonder coating her mind.

"N-nay?" she said with difficulty. Ebba could trust him with her life. But what had they been talking of?

"I'll keep all o' ye safe usin' my immunity *if* things come to that. But we don't know what be ahead. To jump in the ocean is certain death without the kraken's help. Grubby can't keep us all afloat."

Ebba focused on steadying her breath and uncoiling her braced frame.

"I hear ye," she said, recovering from her sharp shock. "I'll wait to drown myself."

She wouldn't dream of jumping in there now. Not after what she'd just felt.

Jagger chuckled. As she turned to keep walking, Ebba wondered at the deep sound.

"The bearer will fight another day," she announced shakily, claiming the title.

. . . *If* they got through whatever happened next. Which seemed a large 'if' as water broke over the path.

"Speedin' up," she muttered, increasing her walk until it rested just below a jog.

If Matey or Sally or the Daedalions were coming, this was the time to miraculously appear. Ebba kept fast to the current speed, knowing Barrels and Peg-leg would find this pace far harder than she did.

The shadows loomed ahead as the water began to edge on top, narrowing the path farther, and she forced away mounting fear.

They were close. So very close.

Jagger was right. No matter what waited on that island, they had to get there before making the next decision.

When the water lapped at her feet, Ebba broke into a light jog that sent water flying everywhere. She listened to the splashes behind as the others followed suit.

Ebba ran, studying the slick black rocks ahead.

"Will we have to climb the cliffs?" Jagger yelled.

"I'd say so," she replied, running faster. Peg-leg wouldn't be able to keep up with this pace. Neither would Barrels. Which meant they'd soon need help.

The path was only wide enough for one person, and she was at the front of the line. She had to get to the wider area at the exit so the others could get out of the way. She'd go back for her fathers with Grubby.

Ebba pumped her arms, the mesh net with the *purgium* thumping against her thigh, her eyes torn between the ground at her feet and the cliffs ahead.

"Nearly there." Her legs burned.

As she ran, droplets of water burst upward with each of her pounding steps. Only a sliver of the jetty remained.

Her breath was harsh to her ears. Her heart galloped. She traversed the remaining section of the path. Three hundred feet. One-fifty. Seventy. Thirty. Fifteen.

Her eyes widened as the cliffs became fully visible.

The path just stopped! The jetty ended in a slippery, sheer cliff with no ledge or space to access the rest of the island and no visible handholds.

No means of escaping the water.

Ebba was moving too fast to pull up. She lifted both arms as she crashed into the wall.

Except. . .*she didn't.*

She fell to the ground, rolling.

She curled into a ball as an invisible sludge poured through her insides right down into her feet. The heavy thickness filled her limbs, her heart, her mind. It left her face slack, her body wavering, her senses out of calibration.

As though sand bags filled her frame, she heaved onto her back.

Why couldn't she see the others? There was only a black wall. No way. She couldn't have run through that.

Her mouth dropped open as Jagger burst through it behind her. *Through solid rock.*

His face slackened, and she watched panic fill the silver eyes that always showed control and competence.

Caspian entered through the wall, tripping over Jagger. Plank, Grubby, Locks, and Stubby were close behind and did the same, forming a heap on top of the pirate.

Barrels and Peg-leg.

The thought waded to her as though weighted with an iron and chain, and even then, she had to think extra hard to recall why that mattered.

"The others," she slurred to Grubby. He could swim. He had to come.

Ebba staggered back to the solid wall and placed her hands upon it, relieved when they sank through.

She took another step, sighing in bliss as the heaviness was peeled from her like shedding ten layers of clothes on a scorching day. Her mind cleared; her heart soared; her very soul rejoiced.

"Ebba!"

She caught sight of Barrels and Peg-leg making their way down the path, about twelve feet out. The path was submerged, and the black water continued to swiftly rise, already to her fathers' knees as they inched their way toward her.

They were feeling for the path.

Rope. Ebba needed rope; some way to tether them to her. Futilely, she searched, patting her frame. There was only the mesh net containing the *purgium*. And her dress.

Her dress.

Careful not to drop the tube, she yanked off Jagger's tunic and then the full length of the gauzy top layer of the dress.

The wait as her fathers shuffled within reach was torture, but Ebba stayed fixed on them. When near enough, she tossed out one end of the dress, the knot she'd tied earlier in one side adding weight to her throw. With the loose strands that had trailed down her back, the garment extended the better part of six feet.

Peg-leg swooped to latch on to the material.

Behind him, Barrels grabbed hold of the cook's belt, and Ebba sagged in relief, holding tight to her end. She had a link to them.

They inched inward to where she stood shivering in the royal blue shift. Black water swilled high around her bare thighs.

"Where be the others?" Peg-leg rushed as they reached her.

Ebba didn't waste time explaining, just grabbed hold of their arms and yanked them backward through the wall.

Though braced for the sickening heaviness on the other side of the stone wall, it still left her a slackened mess with ragged breath. Ebba got ahold of herself faster than the others, just in time to see Plank drop his hands.

"Don't come in," he finished lamely.

"What?" she asked, tongue heavy from the feeling of treacle filling her.

He reached out a hand to the wall. When he reached the black rock, his hand stopped.

"I just went out, though," she said in a stupor.

Ebba placed her hand on the wall and her arm sank through to the other side without resistance. "Why can't ye get out?"

Dread filled her as she took in her surroundings for the first time.

They stood in a crevice between two towering cliffs. In the immediate space around her, there was enough room to fit a rowboat, but the crevice narrowed as it disappeared farther between the sheer cliffs.

The ground underfoot was dry black sand. The whipping wind and sound of hissing water had disappeared as though switched off.

Though the rising sea existed on the other side of the wall, the inside of the cliff wasn't slimy with moisture but . . . dry.

. . . It was as if this hidden area existed in an entirely different place to the one three steps to her right.

"What's goin' on, Plank? Do ye know?" Stubby's voice was slurred too.

Each of them sagged, faces expressionless. The mere effort of smiling was beyond her. What was this place?

Cruel laughter echoed down at them from above, ricocheting between the cliff faces down over their heads.

"To me, lads," Stubby hissed.

They slowly converged in a tighter group, each of them moving sluggishly.

Ebba peered into the shadows of the black crevasse.

"Who goes there?" Jagger asked, the words almost incoherent with the slur. "Show yerself."

The laughter changed directions, blasting through the passage and blowing her hanging dreads back. Her stomach twisted as she listened to the crunch of sand ahead.

Not one person. More than two, but beyond that she couldn't tell.

Shadows masked the front person's face as they stopped just out of range.

"Arrived at last," the voice called. "I told the beasts everythin' I knew, and they still took weeks. Stupid mules."

The harsh voice rooted her to the spot. After witnessing impossible things for months, *this* was what finally destroyed the fabric of what could and could not be. Panic pushed up her throat as the person stepped forward from the shadows.

Mercer Pockmark, the dead captain of *Malice,* straightened before them.

Swindles appeared on his right.

Riot on his left.

"Ye have no idea how I've looked forward to seein' ye all again." A merciless smirk split Pockmark's face, and he spat at their feet.

Ebba stared at him. "But ye're *dead*."

Yet was he? The castle stairway had collapsed, but she hadn't seen his lifeless body.

"Aye," Pockmark said, eyes flaring to crazed proportions. "I am."

What was he saying? That wasn't possible.

"How?" Jagger asked hoarsely.

Swindles and Riot sniggered, and Pockmark shot them the exact gloating look he'd had in life. This *was* real, not an illusion of some kind.

Or the pirates were lying about being dead and were somehow still alive.

"I've looked forward to seein' fish lips," the *Malice* captain said. "But I might be most excited to see ye, Jagger."

The pirate spat on the black sand again, glaring at Jagger with murder in his eyes.

Plank croaked. "Where are we, then?"

Ebba glanced at her father, watching as he peered back to the wall he hadn't been able to exit.

He jerked suddenly, and his eyes filled with fear.

"Where are we?" Plank pressed, stepping forward.

Pockmark removed his tricorn hat and bowed mockingly as Swindles and Riot snickered. "It be my pleasure to welcome the lot o' ye to Davy Jones' Locker."

Her ears rang high.

"My grandfather be eager to meet ye all again," the captain said smugly.

Her knees threatened to buckle.

This wasn't happening. It couldn't be happening.

"Grandfather?" she whispered, unable to help the tremble in her voice.

His cruel grin widened as he replaced his hat.

"Aye, my *grandfather*." He ran his eyes over her fathers and laughed harshly. "Mutinous Cannon."

ACKNOWLEDGMENTS

I may write the books, but the final product is a team effort—not just from my manuscript team, but beta readers, and my support network of family, friends, and readers.

When I get to this part, it never gets easier to put my gratitude for the people around me into words. It means so much that I can pursue this dream and passion. Thank you, *thank you*, from the bottom of my heart.

My swashbuckling manuscript team:

Editor One
Melissa Scott

Editor Two
Robin Schroffel

Proofreaders
Patti Geesey and Dawn Yacovetta

Map Illustrator

Laura Diehl

Cover Designer & Illustrator
Amalia Chitulescu

Happy Reading,
Kelly

ABOUT KELLY ST. CLARE

When Kelly is not reading or writing, she is lost in her latest reverie. Books have always been magical and mysterious to her. One day she decided to unravel this mystery and began writing.

The Tainted Accords was her debut series. Her other works include *The After Trilogy*, *The Darkest Drae*, and *Pirates of Felicity*.

A New Zealander in origin and in heart, Kelly currently resides in Australia with her ginger-haired husband, a great group of friends, and some huntsman spiders who love to come inside when it rains. Their love is not returned.

ALSO BY KELLY ST. CLARE

The Tainted Accords:

Fantasy of Frost

Fantasy of Flight

Fantasy of Fire

Fantasy of Freedom

The Tainted Accords Novellas:

Sin

Olandon

Rhone

Shard

The After Trilogy:

The Retreat

The Return

The Reprisal

The Darkest Drae (Trilogy) Co-written with Raye Wagner

Blood Oath

Shadow Wings

Black Crown

Pirates of Felicity:

Immortal Plunder

Stolen Princess

Pillars of Six

Dynami's Wrath

Veritas

Eternal Gambit

www.ingramcontent.com/pod-product-compliance
Lightning Source LLC
Chambersburg PA
CBHW020934310726
48980CB00007B/763/J

* 9 7 8 0 6 4 8 3 3 4 4 3 9 *